The King of Camelot

by

John Stone

This book is a work of fiction. Places, events, and situations in this story are purely fictional. Any resemblance to actual persons, living or dead, is coincidental.

ISBN: 1-4033-9858-5 (e-book)
ISBN: 1-4033-9859-3 (Paperback)

Library of Congress Control Number: 2004091909

This book is printed on acid free paper.

Printed in the United States of America
Bloomington, IN

1stBooks - rev. 04/02/04

For anyone that has ever dared to dream a dream

Acknowledgements

A special thanks to Carla and Mary for helping to make this book possible
and to Tom, for his skillful creation of an incredible cover

Arthur's Dream

"How do we know he will come?" Vortigern asked, his breathing heavily labored. As if waiting for a sign—permission that his time in the earth was now complete—his weakened body held onto life.

Seated by the fire, Merlin glanced toward the bedridden King, his eyes adjusting to the dark chamber. Clearly seeing Vortigern's resistance in leaving our world, "He will come."

"I have no time for your games," the King demanded, the frustration straining his body as his wheezing cough revealed the depth of his illness.

"He will come. Would your God leave you with no king to rule your lands?"

Resting his head deeply into his pillow, Vortigern tried to find comfort, "He will be cursed if he seeks your counsel."

"Have I not often helped you?"

"*Cursed,*" Vortigern replied.

Merlin, quietly amused, "You needn't worry about our future now."

"It is no matter, this body, very soon, will no longer allow my influence here," wrestling the aches of fever, his voice creaked just above a whisper.

"You have done your job," Merlin consoled.

"And I pray that he may do his," he whispered.

Looking back toward the King, "He has a greater interest in this world than you know."

Vortigern, his consciousness already beginning to slip, waited for Merlin to continue.

"He has brought peace to our lands during many ages."

Closing his eyes, Merlin leaned backward—waiting for the moment Vortigern might depart this life.

Silently, Vortigern drifted away.

* * *

In the highest dimensions of the spirit world, it began—a powerful dream born to instill into the earth's consciousness, the belief in love and truth. Descending from the highest realms, it reached the world with our greatest aspirations. We never doubted what effect it would have on the planet. God's hope was with us.

This is a story from a time when love was power, and magic still ruled the people's lives. It is also the story of a broken dream. My name then, was Arthur.

The millennium was approaching and a cycle of darkness had been completed. With light flooding the earth, many powerful beings had incarnated to be a part of the God-energy arising here. Such an event would require many beings that could see a higher vision and hold a higher vibration than Briton had ever before known. With the help of many great beings, we would aspire to live truths that had been long forgotten from this world. It was now time, once again, for the people of Europe to live a great, great dream.

Still in the spirit world, and many years before my birth, I would often descend into the lower dimensions and closer to earth, where the separation from God becomes more apparent. After a being is born into this world, the conscious loss of God's love often creates great conflict as many resist their newfound individuality. Where this dream was created, love was communication. But in this lower realm, a place where God can be forgotten, it would be necessary to speak words. And it would be here, while visiting Merlin in a dream, that I would speak to him about this life to come.

"Hello, Merlin," I told him, upon entering his dimension.

"Hello, David," he answered, affectionately calling me by his favorite name from my past.

A deep blue firelight, refracting through the clear crystal fireplace, washed the walls and ceiling of his home. Leaning against the mantle, Merlin faced me, adorned in a robe of purple and blue. Feeling the energy from the earth's overseers, he had already received a vision .

"We have a powerful lifetime ahead," I told him.

"I've seen the visions," he replied. "I do hope that you will allow me to guide you."

"That could be quite torturous."

"If you would only listen," he insisted, as if to taunt me of my failures in the earth.

Always prepared to share his gift with me, Merlin's job was to make me aware of my doubt and to force me to grow in self-trust.

"Your day will come. You're just impatient," I said. "You must be able to hold a high vision before God can use you as you desire."

Rolling his eyes, "And what about Bathsheba?"

"We all make mistakes."

"If you would only let me help."

"Merlin, you always do your job," I assured him.

"And I'll do it again—be your stepping stone to freedom in the earth," he complained.

"And you do not wish this?"

"I only wish to be of greater assistance."

"You do not have to have all of the answers to be of value."

Merlin sighed in frustration.

"Can you find no peace?" I asked.

"No," he insisted.

With my body of light beginning to shift dimensions, I told him, "I must go."

"Don't think I will allow you to do as you please," he countered.

"I would expect no less," I said, as my body left his dimension.

After being born into the earth, I was subject to the same forgetfulness that everyone experiences here. Loved ones remaining in the spirit world would speak with me during the awake and sleep states, trying to help me find comfort in the chaotic world in which I would be born. Although their influence was beyond my awareness, their guidance was crucial to my growth.

The challenges that I would face as a child would purify my body in a way to allow me to consciously become aware of the spirit world's dimension. After the purification, I would receive psychic gifts that would enable to expand beyond the earth and directly interact with my friends in spirit when I sought comfort.

Although I would initially live a very harsh life, it would be these challenges in the earth that would eventually set me free. Every situation that allowed me to face and release fear would move me closer to God and the ability to transcend earth's heavy dimension.

* * *

After recently being orphaned as a young boy, James Lott's inheritance had turned him into a wealthy landowner and with the help of the neighboring townspeople, had commissioned the construction of a great castle. With Lott agreeing to provide the funding and the townspeople providing the labor for its construction, Lott received a second castle at a fraction of its value. On September 20, 941 AD, construction began.

A well, a garden, stables for horses, a place to raise livestock and grounds to train men were all located within its walls allowing the castle to be self-sufficient for lengthy periods of time. Secret passages and chambers inside provided greater safety for its inhabitants. In a few years, Lott's men could live in a small portion of the castle while construction continued, but a total of twenty years would pass before its completion.

Slowly its massive white stone walls began to peer out above the trees on the hill as the men continued to labor, constructing this great castle. Crowning the thick and lush forest, it could be seen for miles. Built in a well-protected area with only one road permitting reasonable access, any enemy was easily seen approaching. It became a symbol of hope for the people that brought with it, the possibility that peace in the land could exist.

But even though the castle's creation brought hope to people of Lott's kingdom, petty wars within Briton, between the neighboring kings persisted throughout its construction.

After the loss of his wife during a Saxon invasion, Jasper Neely became deeply devoted to making the land within Lott's domain as safe as possible. Well known in Cornwall and in many other kingdoms, most any king would have granted him the honors of knighthood, but he refused to swear his loyalty to anyone other than himself. Instead, he had hired on with Lott as a protector of the land. There, he was his own man and free to go at any time.

Jasper's daughter Igraine had been about seven at the time of the attack that took the life of her mother. She and her two sisters remained with their aunt initially, but Igraine was maturing quickly and her destiny, rapidly approaching.

Igraine sat by the brook behind her aunt's home as she watched her friends from the next dimension scurry around her. A faery buzzed above her head as the gnomes in front of her gathered food from vines that hung from the trees alongside the water. Sweet fragrance of honeysuckle filled the air. Igraine had yet to realize that not everyone could see these sights. In her innocence, she had never questioned their existence, or her ability to perceive them. But she did wonder how others could just walk by without acknowledging their love and appreciation for the magic and hope that they so delicately held.

She lifted her arm, hand palm up toward the faery above her.

"Hello," she said.

The faery, held within its blue sphere and twice the size of her small hand, flew closer until touching her palm.

"Ahh," she chirped, jerking her hand away as she laughed, feeling the tingle of its energy.

Becoming excited and thankful for being acknowledged, the faery began to fly in circles above her. Igraine ran with it as the playful laughter poured from deep within her being.

"Igraine!" her aunt called. "Time for dinner!"

"Coming!" she answered, as she prepared to leave, gathering her things as she spoke to her friends.

"I have to go now, but I'll be back soon," she assured them. Feeling their response of adoration for her, she knew that she was loved.

"Bye. Bye," she waved.

Igraine's vision was special. Touched by the sweetness of a soul tempered from many lifetimes in the earth, she had the ability to see things even more important than her friends in spirit. Igraine could see into the soul of the world.

*

Francois Gorlois (Gohr-lah) succeeded the recently killed Duke of Cornwall in the spring of 943. He then took the former Duke's home Tintagel, Cornwall's most prestigious castle, built upon the mystical and powerful cliffs that stood towering above the sea.

An inspiring sight, Tintagel's creation and existence had brought a sense of calm to the land and made their enemies surprise, and often crippling attacks on the land, no longer possible. Although Tintagel itself remained vulnerable to an enemy, and was a place destined to know the desperation of war, never again could the Saxon's find refuge in Cornwall before messengers were sent to every kingdom in the land.

Even though Igraine was still young, barely twelve years old, she had already come to the attention of Gorlois. An acquaintance of Jasper's, Gorlois found her gentle and loving nature to be very attractive, but never understood her beauty's true source, the uninhibited expression that emanated from deep within. She lived in a state of love and was destined to grow in love. And someone determined to live in such a deep state of trust could never be compatible with a man as shallow as Gorlois. He was just not yet ready to see.

Gorlois, having had little success with women, believed that he must find a young girl who could be trained to be his mate. Realizing the great burden placed upon the children's aunt, Gorlois asked Jasper to betroth Igraine to him. Although reluctant at first, Jasper eventually agreed. The three children were too much work for their aunt, who had her own family to raise.

Under the agreement, Igraine would live and be schooled at Tintagel. She would be well cared for and have several maidens to watch over her, and when she reached sixteen years of age, would marry Gorlois.

When Jasper finally accepted, Igraine was given no choice but to leave for Tintagel immediately.

Inside the castle, a few days after her arrival, Gorlois closely eyed Igraine. His severe look frightened her and she kept her distance from him. Gorlois, determined to influence her growth, became troubled by her behavior after watching her play. Alone in the nursery, he leaned down in front of her, placing one hand upon his knee, the other arm reaching toward her, forefinger angrily pointing, "Who is it that you are speaking to? There is no one else in these quarters."

"I have many friends here," she replied, continuing with her play.

"Friends, here? Now?" he asked, his right eye slightly twitching.

"Yes," she innocently replied. "I have many friends."

Uneasily leaning up, he crossed his thin and bony arms over his chest, "There is no one here!"

Her soft eyes grew wide as she looked around the room, her lip almost turning upward as she glanced toward the window, a faery dancing upon the edge of the streaming morning light. Her words stopped before they reached her lips.

"You are alone here," he insisted, the pressure from his heartless demands bearing down upon her.

"But I am never alone," she insisted, as tears began to well up in her eyes.

"You are alone now!" he demanded, his anger reaching the surface. "And you will not be talking to people that don't exist!"

With her tears now flowing, Igraine immediately ran from the room, seeking her maiden.

"Damn it, Igraine! Get back in here!" he yelled, following her into Helen's chamber. "I'm not through with you!"

"But she's just a baby," Helen pleaded, holding Igraine tightly against her stomach as she sobbed.

Gorlois began to shake his head, trying to find the words to control the situation, his lip slightly quivering.

"A witch! I've gone and brought a witch into my castle!" he cursed, placing the palm of his hand against the side of his head. Turning to walk away, he continued mumbling, "A damn witch."

After a few years, Igraine adjusted to her new surroundings and learned to enjoy her new life. But she never stopped missing her father and sisters. Her maiden Helen had grown dear to her and was loved by her in return. Still, the years passed slowly.

Igraine's relationship with Gorlois had now turned torturous at best, and she found his company, quite revolting. With no patience for him, she did her best to avoid interacting with him altogether.

When Igraine's eldest sister Kathleen married a prosperous farmer, Igraine's heart pined for a visit. Gorlois, relieved by the opportunity to be rid of her for a time, had her taken by coach to her sister's farm.

Igraine's heart soared upon first seeing Kathleen, reaching for her, then holding her in an unrelenting embrace. The tears poured down both of their cheeks. Already in Igraine's mind—she was home—she had found her home.

Kathleen lived in a large stone house built on a sizeable parcel of land nestled among standing oaks at the foot of their property and not far from Lott's new castle. In Kathleen, her blood relation, Igraine found warmth that she did not have at Tintagel and now living with her sister, she quickly became a part of the family and community.

*

Light continued to flood the earth, and our dream was beginning to take form. While many loving ones had found their place here, more were prepared to come. It was a time for a tremendous expansion of light as well as the expansion of its balancing force, darkness. And a powerful feminine energy, still in the spirit world was preparing to come and to hold that place. Her mysterious entrance into the earth would alert no one of her identity for many years.

The Abbey, not far from Kathleen's farm was the home that would receive this female. Early one morning, a basket was placed upon its front step. Within it, a baby and a piece of paper—a little girl only a few weeks old. Written on the paper was the name—Vivianne.

This child of mystery was destined to spend the first years of her life at the Abbey, to establish her existence in the earth. She would be better cared for there, than at the home where her destiny lay. But now, she *had* found her place in the earth.

*

A year had passed since Igraine had left Tintagel, and her time with Kathleen had brought to her, a greater sense of calm. Fifteen years old now, her long sandy blonde locks set off sparkling blue eyes that were certain to attract another open and loving heart. And they did. A man who frequented the farm to purchase horses had already grown dear to her.

Content with his place in life, Uthur Pendragon was different than most in that age and with no greater ambitions than to live a passionate and love filled life, he could see deep into Igraine's heart. Kindred spirits, their love and commitment to each other could only grow.

Igraine had mischievously sent Tintagel's coach, ordered by Gorlois to retrieve her, back to the castle on two different occasions empty. The driver had been instructed not to return without her, but what could he do? She would remain hidden, leaving him little choice but to return to Tintagel. Igraine was now pretending that Gorlois did not even exist.

Gorlois had never expected her to be gone for more than a few weeks, a month at most and now she was refusing to return at all. Infuriated, he sent word to Jasper, reminding him of their agreement. Jasper soon left for Kathleen's.

He stood beneath the stone archway spanning the front porch, just in front of the entry doors to her home, his face becoming somber as he prepared to confront her. Igraine still sat at that table from which they had just shared lunch. Jasper's eyes, for a moment, had been held by the magnificent view of the countryside. Then he turned to her.

"Why are you hiding here?"

"I am not hiding," she answered, beginning to feel uneasy as she fidgeted with the cloth napkin beside her plate.

"You know this is not your home."

"Well, I feel at home here," she smiled.

"Your place is at Tintagel and it will soon be time for you to marry," he told her, his brow tensing as he took a step toward her, taking a seat at the table.

"I cannot marry Gorlois."

"You know this must be," he said.

She slowly shook her head from side to side, "No, I cannot do that."

"But you must. He helped us when we were in need," he reasoned.

"How could you ask this of me?" she said, her eyes filling with tears as she pulled the napkin into her lap.

"He has done much for us and for you. He has paid for your education," he insisted.

"It sounds like I've been sold to him," she turned her head to the side.

"Igraine, you have not been sold. But you must return to Tintagel and marry him. I've given my word," he insisted.

"I cannot, father. I cannot," she said. "If I marry him, I will die."

"You need not give him your heart. It is just a marriage," Jasper replied.

"Do not ask this of me," she said, wrenching the napkin in her hands.

"Take a few days if you like. Enjoy your time here with Kathleen. But in two weeks time, you will be at Tintagel," he demanded.

"I have no intentions of returning."

"You most certainly will!"

"I will never marry that man. I would rather die!" she plainly told him, then stood up and left the table.

In her own chamber, she sat on her bed and stared at her reflection in the small piece of polished sheet copper that hung on the wall. She picked up her favorite rock, a magnetic lodestone that she had found long ago while playing behind her aunts home and rolled it in her hand.

"Can I do this? Marry Gorlois?" she thought. Wondering how her father could ask this of her, not believing she could survive as Gorlois' wife. She was miserable at the thought and remained alone in her chamber for the remainder of the evening.

Jasper left Kathleen's the following morning and Igraine, refusing to acknowledge him, was terribly distressed. Her father's love was important to her, but he asked for too much.

For Gorlois, this entire affair had turned into a personal embarrassment. To him, she was merely property, and when she hadn't arrived in two weeks time as Jasper had promised, he set out on his own to find her. It didn't take him long to arrive at Kathleen's, and to realize just how far his authority went.

Gorlois' coach stopped at the base of the hill, before Kathleen's home, to prevent Igraine from noticing his arrival. He stepped out of the coach and looked up the hill.

"The house is just ahead, my Lord," the driver told him.

Nodding, Gorlois began to sneak his way up a tree line leading to the cottage, followed closely by a squire. Keeping his eye out for Igraine, he stumbled over an unseen rock and cursed, "Damn it."

Looking back over his shoulder, he could see that the two pages remaining at the coach were laughing. "Shut your mouths," he yelled to them.

Proceeding up the hill, he was soon stopped by a short stone privacy fence that limited the range of the grazing goats. Looking for an entrance, he realized that he would have to climb it here, or risk being seen entering through a gate directly in front of the house. Lifting his leg up, he placed one foot on top of the fence, and with his hand beside it, swung the other foot into the air. Trying to clear the fence and hop down to the ground, his boot caught the top edge and sent him tumbling.

Standing up and dusting himself off, he looked up through an open kitchen door to see Igraine sitting at a table knitting. He quietly snuck his way closer.

"Get your things Igraine. We're leaving," he demanded, from just outside the door.

Bolting out of her chair in surprise, she turned toward him, "I am going nowhere."

Already beginning to feel weak, Gorlois quickly started to walk toward her, as if going to take her by force. Igraine turned toward the breezeway door, looking for an escape as Gorlois stopped.

"You have been betrothed to me, Igraine. This was not a choice of your own," he called out to her.

Turning back to face him, "You took advantage of my father. That is the only reason he would do this to me."

"You make marrying me sound horrible. Many women would desire to marry a Duke."

"And I have no quarrel with any of them. Let one of those women be your wife," she told him.

"Your father will see to it that we are wed. He has given me his word," he replied, his voice now revealing his weakness.

In an instant, Igraine could finally see that she had, up until now, refused to consider that this situation would not be resolved on her own terms. In her frustration, she threw her arms down to her side, as if trying to break free.

"I do not love you," she insisted. "I don't want to be your wife."

"What is wrong with me?" Gorlois asked.

"Nothing, I just don't love you," Igraine told him, shaking her head. Placing her hands on the table where she had been sitting, she looked down to the floor.

"This is an arrangement. It's not about love," he shrugged.

Igraine looked up, "Arrangement?" she asked.

"Yes."

"What is it then that you want from me?" she asked, trying to find acceptance for her fate.

"Your job is to take care of the domestic duties in the castle."

Stepping back from the table, she slid her chair back into its place, "That is all?"

"Yes, what else could there be?" he replied, as if to pretend he had no genuine interest in her.

"Are you telling me that do we do not have to be intimately involved?" she asked, still holding onto the chair.

"That is correct," he answered uneasily.

Sensing Gorlois weaken, she felt her power trickling back to her, "Can I have a lover of my own?"

"Igraine, you are to be my wife," he said, walking closer, his eyes revealing that she had asked for too much.

"Can I take a lover?" she insisted.

Clearly shaken and at a loss for words, he replied, "I do not care what you do on your own time."

Taking a long moment before responding, she felt the uneasiness in the pit of her stomach, but she was tired of running and tired of hiding. A part of her said no, yet she still felt the burden of the decision upon her, believing that no rest could come to her without her acceptance.

Finally, she answered, "I agree to your arrangement," she told him, and reluctantly returned to Tintagel.

Igraine's life at Tintagel became much more bearable now, but as Gorlois' wife, she could feel him desiring her interest and believed that he had recently had a change of heart. Certain that he would prevent any suitor from reaching her, her resulting loss of hope fueled her resolve.

Igraine leaned against the carved stone railing on the upper deck of the castle as she looked out to the sea. Turning her head to the north, the strong winds of the sea whisked the unrestrained locks of her hair across her face. Running a fingernail across her forehead, she pulled them from her eyes.

Finding solace in its tides, sounds and smells, the ocean brought peace to her, making her feel protected and safe. She was grateful for the prevailing sense of stability it provided. Running her fingers down the railing, she cast her eyes down to the distant shore below while holding thoughts of Uthur. She asked herself, "Does he still think of me?"

Having been separated from him for months now, she could no longer bear it. Abruptly, she turned around and walked back into the castle. Finding a piece of paper, she wrote her feelings down of misery, suffering and of her deep longing for him. Leaving with the next courier, Igraine's note would soon be in the hands of her beloved. And a few weeks later, Uthur was on his way to Tintagel.

During the final night of his trip, Uthur received a powerful dream. In it, he saw himself riding toward the castle the following evening, just before dusk as they prepared to close the gates when he noticed that his perception had changed. Although the world around him seemed no different, the awareness of the ones around him had changed. They could not see him. And when he arrived at the gate, he rode his horse right in without question. No one even looked in his direction.

Upon awaking the following morning, he could still feel the power of the dream and believed that the vision he had seen, was actually foretelling his future. When he found himself, later that evening riding up to the castle's gate as he had seen in the dream, he was confident that the events would transpire as within his vision. He simply proceeded through the gate and into the castle in pursuit of his love. No one looked up.

Igraine was surprised and delighted when she found Uthur wandering through Tintagel's corridors in search of her and grabbing him quickly, led him into a vacant passage in its far reaches.

"How did you get past the guard?" she whispered in delight, holding tightly to his sleeve.

"I just rode right in," he answered.

"Without a word?"

"No one noticed."

"Gorlois would have a fit if he knew. But now you're *my* guest. And I will keep you all to myself," she said, eyes twinkling as she took his hand, leading him deeper into the dark recesses of the castle.

"I've dreamed of this day for so long. I was afraid you wouldn't come," she whispered back to him.

"Well, I am here now," he replied.

The light had grown so dim that he could barely see, but Igraine knew the castle well, and she had a sense of belonging here that could not be taken away from her. Her heart had brought Uthur here, and there was no one who could deny him from her now.

Suddenly stopping, Uthur supposed they had reached quarters where they might be alone. Instead, she pushed him against the wall and gently pressed her lips against his, the sound of voices approaching interrupting them. Igraine began to giggle. Reaching across his chest, she pushed hard against the thick and heavy oak door and when it opened, pulled him inside with her. Now they were safe, in her private and secret sanctuary.

Uthur remained hidden in the castle for three days. And during his stay, for the first time, they would share their love physically. Realizing the fullness of their sentiment for each other, they made a pact on the final night of his stay.

Together they lay upon a heavily cushioned window seat behind two tall stone archways, overlooking the moonlit night sea. Igraine's mood turning serious, she was realizing her time with Uthur was almost over. Tracing her fingernail across his shoulder and down his arm, she leaned backward to look into his eyes.

"I won't be able to stay here without you, Uthur," she told him.

Returning her interest, Uthur sighed. "I will be lost too," he agreed. Igraine leaned forward again and her eyes returned to the ocean.

"Why does our God ask so much of us?" she asked.

"Too much," he replied.

Igraine turned to him, "Too much?"

"We should be allowed to be together," he answered.

Holding their silence, with their bodies lying entangled, they listened to the sounds of the waves crashing below. An occasional seagull cried, and their restless hearts had yet to find resolve.

"What shall we do?" she finally asked.

"I don't know," Uthur answered. Pulling her closer, he breathed her scent into his body and brought his lips closer, touching them to her neck, tasting her skin.

"Our world is so cruel," Igraine told him, softly moaning.

"We can't know what tomorrow will bring," he said, dragging his lips across her skin. "I can't believe you will be forced into this arrangement forever."

Looking down, Igraine reached for Uthur's hand, clasped it and held tightly. The sea breeze pulled against her hair.

"We will find a way to be together," Uthur promised. "I will wait for you."

"You will wait? I can't ask that of you," she told him. "It is not your destiny to be restrained, as it is mine."

Pulling her closer, he buried his face in her hair as he kissed her neck and whispered, "Do you believe in me? In my words and in my feelings?"

Leaning back, she looked at him for a moment, feeling his heart, "Yes, I do."

"I will wait," he assured her.

Finding freedom she sought, she gave her body to his as she contentedly wove her arm into an unending embrace. And upon this starry night, as witnessed only by the moon and the transient waters of the ocean, I was conceived, Arthur, the future King of all Briton.

* * *

In a small abandoned fortress near Lott's recently completed castle, many women lived together in a home that was known by some, as Avalon. There were others that called it the witch house.

Although they had enough land to raise livestock and to keep a small garden, the women of Avalon made their living by sewing. With many rumors circling the community about the mystery within their home, some gravely feared Avalon. But known as seers, their guidance and counsel was often sought during times of turmoil in the land.

One night, a woman living at Avalon received an important dream. In it, she saw a little girl searching for their home. The woman could tell that the child's name was Vivianne, and in the distance, saw the Abbey. Upon waking, she became convinced that the girl must be living there, and quickly made arrangements to visit.

The woman, together with a man from an all male home similar to Avalon, went to the Abbey in search of her. After meeting several children, a maidservant finally brought Vivianne out.

The girl, seven or eight years old, floated through the room as if hovering above the stone floor. Her almond eyes, wide and round, peaked from beneath her brown bangs as she scanned the room's walls, finally focusing upon her seeker. There was no mistaking the power in this girl's still innocent eyes.

"She is of the earth," the woman of Avalon whispered. "But lives in the ethereal worlds."

The woman watched Vivianne closely for a moment, as she allowed the memory of her dream to return. Then she smiled.

"She is absolutely enchanting," she told the Abbess as she reached for the girl's hand, squeezing it in delight. "I just adore her."

"There is something very special about her," the Abbess agreed, placing her hands upon the little girl's shoulders from behind.

Vivianne remained quiet, observing and silently agreeing to play her role.

"I'm surprised no one has already taken her," the woman added.

"Well, times are hard," the Abbess explained. "We've placed so few children in recent years. But Vivianne would make anyone a wonderful daughter. She works very hard."

"I am sure she does," the woman answered, her eyes sparkling brightly.

"And never complains. A model child," the Abbess added.

Vivianne, her face expressionless but calm and powerful, was still uncertain of her future.

"May I take her with me today?" the woman asked, unconsciously placing her hand over her heart. Only then did Vivianne react, her head quickly turning toward the Abbess as her eyes widened further.

"These are wonderful people Vivianne," the Abbess assured her. "And they are looking for a daughter just like you."

Turning back toward the couple, the Abbess added, "She can be ready to leave in just a few minutes. And I know that you will have no regrets."

"Wonderful," the women answered, her eyes twinkling. "We'll wait for her to get ready."

And Vivianne moved one step closer to her destiny.

*

My eyes first opened within the walls of Castle Tintagel on September 20, 960, A.D., as I was born to this world, Arthur Gorlois. A great destiny waited. In the years prior to my birth, a magical sword had been left upon an altar, within a sanctuary that the earth had now reclaimed. Its only entrance, a small opening in an earthen wall, gave it the appearance of a cave. It was not a secret that this place existed. For years there had been a rumor of a sword that lay hidden somewhere nearby in the forest. Left by its owner during an earlier age, a great king from the past had placed it inside of this special sanctuary, knowing that he would one day return to the earth to claim it. The people knew this legend and believed the king would one day return to fulfill his promise, reclaiming the sword and becoming the next king of all Briton.

*

Growing up at Tintagel, I was treated as if I were the son of Gorlois, even though many of Igraine's closest confidants at the castle knew that I was not—that it was not even a possibility. Gorlois, remaining distant, was even considering accepting me as his own, until one day when I was about four years old. As he was watched me in the nursery, he thought he saw a familiar resemblance in my face, the face of a man that he had seen in the busy castle, and a face that he had recently grown to hate.

"Igraine!" he yelled. Leaving the nursery, he began walking the corridors of the castle in search of her.

"Igraine!" he yelled again, moments before finding her in her chambers.

"Who is that boy's father?" he demanded.

"You do not know him," she assured him, standing up from her seat across from the mirror.

"How do you know?" he insisted, his voice reeking with the need to control. "Who is he?"

"You could not possibly have met," she promised.

"That bastard Pendragon! That's whom he belongs to. A damned Pendragon baby," he yelled.

"You are making no sense."

"Oh yes I am," he said, and began to walk quickly toward the nursery. Igraine followed closely behind.

"What are you going to do?" she asked.

"That little bastard boy's not going to live here," he told her, as he entered the nursery.

Picking me up, he put me under one arm, while using the other to push her away.

"Stay back!" he angrily yelled. "I should have never allowed this bastard in."

"Please no, Francois. I'll do anything you want!" she pleaded, deeply sobbing.

"It's too late for that!" he told her, moving with resolve through the corridor.

Reaching the courtyard, Gorlois saddled his horse while Igraine, hysterical, violently beat two squires who were instructed to hold her. I cried.

It only took Gorlois moments to finish preparing for the journey and after mounting his horse and placing me behind him, we abruptly left the castle. In no time had ridden far beyond the castle walls, although the ride would take hours. I eventually calmed down, but remained in a state of shock. Disoriented, I had little choice but to await my fate.

Finally stopping at a home near the edge of the forest, just a few feet off the horse trail, we had reached our destination. An ugly and mean looking man stood in front of the house with his arms crossed. One of Gorlois' knights, he angrily glared at us as we approached.

"Ector!" Gorlois yelled. "I want you to take this boy."

"I will not!" he answered.

Gorlois put me down and then stepped from his horse. His expression threatening, he walked toward Ector.

"You damned sure will! You don't have to keep him," Gorlois told him. "Give him away. I don't care. But he's not making the trip back with me."

"He's your problem, not mine!" Ector argued.

"Not anymore!" Gorlois said as he stepped back on his horse and rode away.

Ector and his wife were furious about my arrival. Barely able to handle their own son, Kay, I could be nothing but a burden for them.

"That damned Gorlois," Ector cursed.

After having been loved so deeply by Igraine, I was now being exposed to its opposite emotion, hatred. And it felt horrible. I immediately began to feel ill and to withdraw.

*

Igraine dragged herself back to her chambers and collapsed on her bed as she tried to gather her thoughts. Being a very intuitive woman, she could not believe what she had allowed to occur. There was nothing that could have grieved her more than the loss of her child and she hated herself for her part in it. Another struggle presenting itself, she searched for resolve, but what she did not yet understand was that she had in fact followed her intuition. This was meant to be. Her intuition gave her no warning because this was an event that had to come to pass. It was essential for her growth, and for mine.

It would take days for her head to clear as she waited for Gorlois to release her. Initially, she was not allowed out of the castle, as Gorlois believed he could hold her prisoner there. But Igraine's loving nature had all but disappeared for him. It was anything but! In fact, she had become so intolerable that within a few days, Gorlois had her thrown out. Then, with help of Kathleen and Uthur, she began to scour the countryside.

Obviously traumatized, I was in need of a friend. The spirit world was already prepared for the opportunity. A great being that watches over our world with his powerful love, was about to visit. Already within the plan for my life, Jesus, known then as Joshua, reentered our dimension.

Standing in Ector's front yard, the day after my arrival, a handsome man approached. Wearing the usual dress for the day, he appeared as though he might be a farmer or tradesmen, perhaps even a blacksmith.

"Hello!" he called out.

Silently watching him, I waited for him to approach. When he was just a few feet away, he said, "My name is Joshua."

Having unusually soft and understanding eyes, much like my mother's, he seemed particularly interested in me. My silence didn't seem to bother him.

"I have a nephew your age," he said. "He's very special."

"What's your name?" he asked.

Still unable to speak, I hoped that he could somehow understand what had happened to me.

"This is a very beautiful place you live. I bet you have fun playing in the forest."

Joshua lifted his eyes above my head and to the house behind me. With his right hand, he pushed his long brown hair out of his face, tucking it behind an ear and asked, "Is your mother home?"

"My mother doesn't know where I . . . "

And I broke down into a dreadful cry. Joshua, immediately kneeling down beside me, began touching my arms and shoulders as if straightening my shirt.

"Your mother is looking for you right now," he whispered. "You will not be here forever, I promise this. Just for a time. She's going to find you."

Joshua's reassurance and deep trust quickly calmed my heart, as I believed his words to be true. As if my mother was just moments away, I knew that I could wait for her to find me.

Stopping by the house every day for the next few weeks, Joshua helped me to adjust to my new life. When Ector became convinced that he posed no serious threat to me he left us alone, even once suggesting that he take me with him. But Joshua had to decline, forcing Ector to continue looking for another home.

Eventually my days had become bearable, and Joshua's job, at least in this dimension, was almost complete. The challenges in my life had to be faced alone as it was necessary for me to maintain my vision of God without his help.

"Arthur, it's time for me to return home," Joshua told me, after we returned from a walk in the forest.

"Where do you live?" I asked, my stomach becoming uneasy. I stood beside him, looking up into his eyes.

"It is a place that is far from here," he answered, nodding toward the road, the same road that I had traveled on with Gorlois only weeks before.

"My mother lives there," I told him. "Can you take me to her?"

"This road goes in many directions, Arthur. It will not be easy to find her," he said. "But I will do what I can to help you. That, I promise. This will not be the last time we see each other."

With his deep sense of trust soothing my fear, I knew that we would once again meet.

"When?" I asked.

"It will be a while. But not too long," he told me, lifting me up into the air. Sitting me in his arms so that our faces were just inches apart, he added, "Now I want you to make me a promise. Will you do that?"

I watched his eyes.

"I want you to keep thinking about your mother, and about me too," he said. "Keep dreaming about her finding you. Don't ever give that dream up. Yes?"

I nodded.

"Dreams always come true. It is the nature of a dream. But you can't give up. This is very important Arthur. You must remember this," he told me. "You must be true to your dreams."

"Now, I must go," he said, squeezing my body to his, then placing me back down on the ground.

"And what are you going to do?" he asked.

"Dream," I told him.

"That's right, Arthur. Never stop," he said. "I will be back as soon as I can."

As I had done many times before, I watched him leave, my eyes following him until he reached the bend in the road that cut through the forest. As he disappeared into the trees, I reluctantly wandered closer to Ector's home and back into the new life that awaited me.

Within a few days of Joshua's absence, the stresses of my new life had overwhelmed me. My body, refusing to survive, caused me to fall ill with pneumonia. Drifting in and out of consciousness, I seldom got out of bed. Ector's wife, infuriated by my illness, demanded that I get up and work for my keep.

"Get in here, Arthur!" she yelled from the other room.

Too sick to move, my head rested deeply in my pillow. But after a few moments, when I hadn't joined her, she became enraged. Entering the room I shared with Kay, she yelled, "Get out of bed!"

Bolting up and out of bed, I reached for my pants as I felt a stick strike the backside of my leg.

"If you're going to live here, you'll work for your food," she demanded.

Instantly throwing up, a blackness enveloped me as my body slumped to the floor. Waking up hours later, my stomach was still wrenching and my head ached—I could only think of how desperately I needed my mother. I looked down to see my shirt covered in dried vomit. Too dizzy to stand, I crawled back into bed, and quickly drifted back to sleep.

*

It had been three weeks since I had seen Joshua and I was barely able to endure as a part of Ector's family. I did not like where I was and my mistrust of Ector grated upon his nerves.

"Arthur," he called from the kitchen. "I've found you a new home, boy."

Sitting quietly in Kay's room, I tried to disappear.

"Come in here, boy," he called again.

Walking into the kitchen, I watched him stoke the fire as he placed a log beneath the pot of stew that would soon be our evening meal.

"Don't just stand there, go outside and bring some wood in. Help Kay," he demanded.

Walking out the door, unable to find Kay, I grabbed a log and carried it inside.

"Did you hear me earlier? I've found you a home," he said, half out of breath, his face still red from blowing on the coals.

I nodded.

"You'll be much happier with these people," he told me. "They need a boy like you."

Ector was agitated, fretting over the fire as he tried to get the new log to catch. He turned sharply to look at me.

"I'll take you there in the morning," he told me.

I nodded.

"Go on now, get out of here," he told me, motioning me out of the room.

The following morning, as promised, I was dropped off at a neighbor's home and received a similar welcome to the one Ector had given me upon my arrival. These people didn't want me either. But for the next several weeks, I made my home with them. Then, once again, I'd be sent on my way.

These events traumatized me into near silence. But the life that lay ahead of me called for a humble and thankful heart. My power could not come to me otherwise, and it was necessary that I face these challenges in preparation. As Joshua had promised, I would not be experiencing these horrible situations forever. But I would first need to become open to receive, before I could allow my destiny to come. Then, much later, healing could begin.

*

Lott's second castle had only been completed for a few years but had already become a dark and lonely place—inhabited mostly by men that frequently engaged in war. Not really a place for a child, but at the age of six, my final foster family dropped me off there. Telling me to go inside, they promised that I would be cared for.

Walking through the castle's massive gates, eyes wide, it was difficult for me to stay out of the way of the many knights, horses, and mules that were passing in front of me. Pulling my sandy blonde hair from my eyes, hair that had now grown too long, my head leaned backward as I stopped to marvel at the grandeur of the castle.

Surrounded by stone walls, sixty feet tall, the training yard was relatively small in comparison to the rest of the castle. Still, it could easily hold fifty men and their warhorses, with room left over. To my left was the entrance to the stable, where a boy, a few years my senior, waved to me.

"Bring me that bucket!" he yelled. Carrying a large flake of hay, his hands were already full.

Walking over to the bucket, I tried to pick it up, but filled to the rim with water, it was much too heavy. Seeing that I could not lift it, he put down the hay and walked toward me.

"Here," he angrily told me, handing me the lead to a goat. "Follow me."

Lifting the bucket, he walked across the yard as I followed. A man dressed mostly in black rode in beside us. Guessing that he was a knight, I decided that he was very mean. When we reached the stable, we were just a few feet from him.

"Whom do you belong to?" he asked, seemingly preoccupied with removing the leather gloves from his hands. I shrugged, finding his abrupt manner unsettling.

"Good. Follow me," he told me, throwing a saddlebag, along with a blanket onto the ground. Picking up the dusty bag and the sweat soaked blanket, I followed him into the den, a place where the men ate and gathered to talk.

Inside the dark cave-like chamber, my eyes had difficulty adjusting to the lack of light. Its stone walls and ceiling were partially covered with soot from the large fireplace that heated the room. A thin cloud of smoke hung in the air.

"Drop my things over there and wait for me," he said. Then walking over to another angry looking man, he began to talk. With my eyes burning from the smoke, I sat down on the large bag he had carried in before me and looked around the room. The quarters was full of men, some laughing, others arguing. A man sitting across from me noticed my arrival.

"What's your name, lad?" he asked.

Unable to reply, he smiled an understanding smile. Shortly, the knight returned.

"Let's go!"

"The boy stays with me!"

The words, piercing the air, caused me to hesitate.

"I said, let's go!" the knight repeated, refusing to acknowledge the challenge.

"I said – the boy stays with me!"

The once busy and violently loud room fell quiet in an instant—all eyes turning to the challenger, the man who had just asked me for my name.

"He's mine, Jasper! I've already claimed him!" the knight demanded, beginning to walk toward me.

The challenger, pulling his sword, violently swung it through the air deeply burying its blade into the table that separated us. Several men jumped up to gather around us, others watched from a distance.

"He stays with me," the challenger told him, powerfully holding onto his sword's hilt.

"You'll have to fight for him!" the knight yelled.

"As you wish," he calmly replied.

"I'll meet you in the morning!" the dark knight replied, walking away in defeat.

Then his challenger turned to me. Seeing the terror in my face, all traces of fierceness were replaced with compassion.

"You have nothing to be frightened of, lad. You're quite safe now," he assured me.

Immediately feeling the innocent trust of a child, I knew that I was safe. Finally—I knew I was safe.

"I bet you're hungry," he added.

I nodded.

Pointing to the back of the den, he said, "Go back there and ask for a plate."

Following his advice, I waited in line for my turn at the window. Soon, a woman sliced a piece of meat from a large quarter and dropped it on a plate. Adding a few small potatoes, she handed it to me.

"You made quite a scene tonight," she told me.

Taking the plate without expression, I walked over to a table and sat down to eat. The disturbance had upset many of the people in the castle and my protector had to talk to them before they could calm down. Then he returned to my side.

"Where are you from, Lad?" he asked.

I shrugged.

Momentarily troubled, he added, "You're not the first boy to end up here with no family. There are many others just like you, yes. I think you will like it here. Many nice people live here as well as lots of little boys who need playmates," he said. "Did you get enough to eat?"

Nodding, my eyes were already beginning to droop.

"Well, it's been a big day for you. Would you like to get some sleep?"

Nodding again, the sun had long since set and I was very sleepy. Jasper then ushered me down the long and dark stone corridor that led toward his chamber. Passing a candle sconce that hung from the wall, my face was illuminated as I looked up to him and spoke for the first time.

"I'm Arthur," I said.

"I see that," he replied with a smile, patting me on the head.

*

Jasper was a man who believed in destiny and that purpose existed behind every life situation, even though great suffering might have to be endured. He was very confused about what to make of this event that he had been presented with. What was he supposed to do with me? Troubled, later that night, a dream brought further clarity to him.

Sitting upon his horse at the peak of a rolling meadow, he was dressed in a half suit of armor as he waited, watching the forest's edge in the distance. After a moment, a knight similarly dressed appeared, and slowly walked his horse toward him, finally stopping just a few feet away. There was no doubt in his mind—it was me, several years into the future.

When he awoke the next morning, he felt sure that I was now where I belonged, with him, and that there was a greater destiny awaiting me than he could comprehend. God had brought us together—he could only comply.

Opening my eyes after a restful sleep, I first noticed the heavy rough sawn timbers that formed the ceiling above me, then listened to the sounds coming from the chamber at our side. Realizing I was alone, I jumped out of bed, put my clothes on, and ran out into the courtyard. Jasper was standing near the entrance to the den speaking to another man, and as my pace slowed, he noticed me.

"What's the hurry, lad?" he asked. "Someone bothering you?"

I shook my head no, in reply.

"Well, run into the den before they stop serving breakfast. They'll begin preparing for the pass meal soon," he motioned. "I'll wait for you here."

Sitting alone, I ate my breakfast, a small slab of meat with a hardboiled egg. Realizing the mug the server handed me contained apple cider, I quickly gulped down two swallows, enjoying its sweet taste.

Looking across the room, I noticed the smoke had cleared from the night before and that several of the men were watching me, some occasionally pointing in my direction. It was apparent that I had at least temporarily become the center of attention. I listened in on a conversation, two men speaking about a fight that had occurred earlier. Jasper had already fought the challenging knight—the knight had died from his wounds.

It was such a strange turn of events for me. For the past two years, hardly a soul had shown any care for me at all. And now, a man that I did not even know had killed another in my defense. I could not help but be deeply affected, and from that moment on, I became convinced that Jasper was the greatest man alive.

"Did you get enough to eat?" Jasper asked, as I approached him in the courtyard.

I nodded.

"I don't know what your life has been like Arthur, but you will be treated well here. Do you understand?"

I nodded again.

"Good. I will find you some more clothes, but for now I want you to stay out of the cold. All right?"

With my head bobbing replies to him, he continued to reassure me. And when he was confidant that I had gained a sense of security, he gave me a job.

"There are many fireplaces scattered throughout the castle. And I need you to find every one of them. That is your job, and it's a very important one. You'll be stocking them with wood later. But for now, I just want you to find them. All right?"

Continuing to impress his concern for my well-being, he added, "No one will bother you. Now go on. It's a big castle."

*

A few days later, Alden watched me from the distance as I carried a few logs to a fireplace. Having never seen him in the castle before, I wasn't sure what to make of him, until he approached.

"What are you doing?" he asked, the outline of his thin frame becoming narrower as he pushed his hands deeper into his pockets.

"Taking wood to the fireplaces. It's my job," I answered.

"Can I help?" he asked.

"I guess so," I replied.

Perhaps a year older than me, he was much taller. His long and narrow face held gentle eyes that had already come to understand sadness, but his smile revealed a slightly mischievous nature.

"What do we do?" he asked.

"Carry wood—all day long," I smiled.

Taking one of my logs, he walked by my side.

Alden often visited the castle for lengthy periods, as he was sometimes too much for his mother to handle. His father, a knight, made his residence at the castle.

It was not that Alden was a bad child. He was just curious about our world and it was difficult to keep him occupied when at home. He was one who could venture off in search of some new discovery with no regards as to where it might lead him. Like the time he once followed a rainbow after an abrupt morning downpour. Making it into the next county before its moisture evaporated and its colors disappeared, it took him two days to find his way back home.

I guess Alden thought I had a good job. I certainly did. Everyone was always glad to see me, especially when their fires began to grow cold. We worked hard to gain their respect.

But Alden, an ancient friend of my distant past was destined to find me, and he took our work together—as did I—very seriously. Through our efforts, we grew confidence within and between us. It made us feel important while introducing us to everyone in the castle. And as a result, I got to know it like few others. But perhaps more importantly, I got to know the people who lived there.

*

Within a couple of months, I had earned the nicknames "Little Jasper" and "Shadow," had found a place as a fire keeper, and had grown quite fond of Jasper. But there were a couple of men who seemed to dislike our relationship, or me in particular, and teased me about my affection for him. I asked Jasper why.

"They are frightened of friendship," he explained.

"They don't seem frightened. They fight all of the time," I replied.

"And that is what men do who are afraid," he said. "They truly desire to be closer to each other."

"Why aren't they?" I asked.

"It is not an easy thing for everyone. They come as close as they can. You'll see."

I trusted that one day I would.

Although I had to work hard each day to keep the fireplaces burning, I still had time to play. And I was even known to get in trouble from time to time, as Alden seemed to draw out the mischievous part of me. There were a few individuals who occasionally became the target of our pranks.

"Damn it, Jasper! If that little bastard boy pulls one more stunt like that I'll kill him myself!" the potter told him.

"I promise it won't happen again," Jasper assured him.

Having an immense dislike for the potter, we had rigged some of the shelving in his shop to fall. It was just that we expected it to happen in a few days, not moments after we walked out of his door. We had to run for our lives and were fortunate to know the castle so well. Finding a hiding place in a seldom-used chamber, we remained there for hours, trusting we would be safe until he cooled down.

"Arthur, you best avoid the potter for a few days," Jasper told me, entering our quarters late that evening after finally coming out of hiding. "He's very angry with you."

I hesitated.

"He told me all about it. I pleaded mercy for you but I don't believe he'll be so easily appeased next time," he added, trying to prevent his lips from curling into a smile.

"Thanks," I answered.

Although he was very much a father to me, his grandfatherly energy could not be overlooked. He wanted me to be happy and to find a wide range of expression, even if it meant occasionally getting into trouble.

I loved the people of the castle, many of them, but I received my greatest comfort in the forest. There, I found my sanctuary and church. Within minutes, I could walk through the castle's gates and be lost among the age-old oaks, moonflowers and lichen-covered stones. It was there, in the silence of the forest that I learned about life, and of the reasons for the problems my friends faced in their day-to-day lives. And it was there that I was the closest to the spirit world and most able to receive its wisdom.

Carved by nature into a perfect seat, a very large, almost flat piece of granite had become a favorite resting place for me. Just a few feet above the forest's floor, its concave surface made it comfortable to sit in and I often spent time there in contemplation. Surrounded by tall pines and oaks, I had a clear view of the landscape to my front, while my back was completely obscure, vines and hanging moss concealing my location from anyone approaching. Further down to my right was a meadow, often partially concealed by the early morning fog. And to my left, were miles of dense forest. It made me feel very powerful to observe nature there in my seat of stone.

Small spheres of color, visible only to ones that can still see into our ethereal world, followed me as I walked through the forest on my way home. Occasionally, I would glance up, feeling the energy of the faery inside, as their vibration of pureness and truth pulled me into their world.

With my arms stretched out to my sides, almost in dance, I fully acknowledged their presence as I walked. Slowly waving my hands up and down, I gently released my awareness of the physical earth, while moving closer to their world. Gnomes were scattering about on the forest's floor below.

Abruptly stopping, I found myself standing just a few feet away from an unusual looking, but familiar man. I hesitated, studying his expression. His long gray hair was clasped behind his head and his imposing brow made him look threatening. Pronounced, thick gray eyebrows accented his dark eyes.

"Hello!" he said, beaming to me.

"Hi," I responded, still surprised by his unexpected appearance.

"I guess you didn't see me approaching. I was just taking a short walk before returning to the castle. I didn't mean to frighten you."

Recognizing him as a friend of Jasper's, I didn't feel the need to respond.

"I've noticed you come to the forest often," he said.

"Yes, I do."

"You must love it here," he replied, replacing his natural expression with a less severe one.

"I like it a lot," I answered, still feeling a little uncomfortable in his presence.

"I like the forest too. I visit here often," his eyes scanning the lush greenery surrounding us before focusing on a large standing oak at the edge of the castle's meadow.

"I've got to get back now," I told him. "I've been here for awhile and they will be needing more wood soon."

"Oh yes, I understand," he assured me. "Perhaps we will meet here again, someday."

"I'm here everyday," I replied.

"We then, we surely will," he said, his eyes intently focused upon me.

"I'm Arthur," I told him, introducing myself.

"And I'm Merlin," he replied, a small flash of light escaping his right eye.

Nodding to me, "I will look forward to it," and he proceeded on his way.

*

After building our evening fire, we stopped for the first moment after a long ride through the forest. Miles from home, Jasper had taken me on a journey to teach me the ways of the land. Taking a seat on the soft earth, he reached his hands toward the fire, warming his calloused fingers. Seated across from me, the flames danced between us.

"Fire is magic, Arthur. It does many things. Some things that I do not even understand," Jasper told me. "But if you are ever riding across the country, and chilled to the bone, stop and build a fire. It will restore your hope like nothing else."

Jasper becoming quiet for a moment, I thought back to an experience earlier in the day, when stalking a deer. He had told me, "Deer are very sensitive animals. If we were to come here, anxious to kill, it is unlikely that we would see one at all. If we are uneasy, they will be uneasy. But if we trust, they will give themselves to us. It is their wish that we survive."

After fashioning a bow from a tree limb that he cut moments earlier, he nocked an arrow and pulled the string back, as if preparing to shoot, stopping when the string reached his mouth.

"Let the string touch your lips each time, locking your thumb beneath your chin. You'll have greater accuracy by positioning yourself in the same way with each arrow."

Now resting our bodies, Jasper leaned back and reached for another log. Placing it on the fire, hundreds of sparks flew into the air. I leaned away until they floated high above me.

"Arthur, I am an old man," he told me. "We can't always explain why things happen as they do, but regardless, we must accept them. You don't have the fortune of having a father of your own, one that you could expect to be with you for a long time. Instead, you have me. Not such good luck, huh?"

He paused, smiling at his own humor and added a small twig to the fire.

"I will do what I can, teach you all that I know, as quickly as I can. Make no mistake, I plan to be around a while. But you will one day be on your own, and it is important that you learn quickly. Our world does not allow for many errors. You will need all of your resources to survive."

Sensing his focus upon me, I looked up from the fire and toward him. Appearing very different this evening, the flickering shadows from the firelight accentuated his features.

"You are a good boy, Arthur," he told me. "Don't ever let anyone take that from you."

Reaching for a blanket, he covered his body as he lay down, resting himself against the earth.

"Sleep well," he said. "We have much to do tomorrow."

* * *

My father had taken his mother's name because of his illegitimate birth, but his true lineage, had been of royalty. Uthur was the son and only heir to the powerful King Midean. Although Uthur never challenged his right to ascend to the throne, royal blood flowed in his veins, and that blood had been passed on to me. This is how my place in the earth was held.

Midean, having never liked the idea of Lott's new castle being so close to his own land, had secretly decided long ago that at the right time, he was going to capture it and make it his own. I was about seven, only about a year after my arrival, when he attacked.

He came with such force that we were unable to defend ourselves and in a matter of hours, they had forced entry and were in control of our castle. Lott's men were given the choice of either swearing loyalty to Midean, or die. Forced to agree, Jasper had his own plan. A few days after our capture, he sent word to Lott, assuring him that if he would attack, we would open our gates and join forces with him. Midean would have little hope of winning under such circumstances.

Although Lott would wait several months before making his challenge, he was constantly preparing for the attack. Having set up watch over the castle, he waited for the moment in which Midean was most vulnerable. It finally arrived.

With several of Midean's knights on a trip far from the castle, Lott was now ready and within a few hours, his men were in full force and approaching its gate. It must have been a horrible shock for Midean, watching Lott's former knights open the gates to the castle. He surely knew that it was all over for him. And it was. Midean and all of his men were killed, leaving Lott with his entire kingdom.

With holdings near the size of two kingdoms, Lott became the stabilizing force of the country. And he was not even royalty. But this event changed the way Lott perceived himself, and finally realizing his own power, proclaimed himself a king.

*

Merlin caught up with me one afternoon as I approached the forest's edge.

"Hello!" he yelled, hurrying toward me. "May I come along?"

"Sure," I answered and we began our walk together.

Cutting into the tree line, we entered the silence of the forest—the trees creating a ceiling, hiding our passage from the world above. Sharing an appreciation for the land, we allowed ourselves to be taken in by all of the life it contained. With both of us able to see the spirits of the forest, we were very conscious of their presence as they joined us on our journey. After reaching a clearing, we stopped to watch a deer grazing on the far side of the meadow as Merlin spoke to me for the first time since we began. Gnomes, the small spirit beings of the forest, were at our heels.

"You are much at ease here," he said. "Do you ever worry about getting lost?"

"I don't think much about it, but I've been lost a couple times," I answered, removing a briar that had clung to my pants.

"What did you do?" he asked.

"Just kept walking. Tried to reach a peak so that I could see better," I answered.

"That was very smart," he replied, his eyes returning to deer, still feeding in the meadow.

After a moment, I asked him, "You been here before?"

"No, I haven't."

"I could show you around some," I told him.

"I would like that," he agreed.

By now the deer had seen us and began to snort, as if demanding that we leave. But we stood still. Swishing her tail, first down, then up, she ran into the woods and we continued walking.

I immediately headed for one of my favorite places, the fish pool, a favorite of the gnomes too. Walking through the meadow and crossing a small creek before arriving, we had time to get to know each other better on the way. I found out that he liked Jasper very much and that he was known, as a seer into other worlds. He explained that in these "other" worlds, he often could catch glimpses of the future. I became very excited when I heard this and asked if he could see *my* future.

"Well Arthur, a very exciting future awaits you. That, I can assure you."

Not satisfied with his answer, I still wanted to know more.

"I want to become a knight. Do you see that?" I asked, inquisitively.

"Arthur, there may be greater things in your future. Do not hold to any one vision," he told me.

"Greater than being a knight? What else could there be?" I inquired.

"You will learn many things as you grow older. But the gift of vision does not come to all," he said as he turned to look me squarely in the eyes. "You have that vision. And it is up to you to cultivate it."

"What does that mean?"

"Your ability to live in both worlds. Very few remain aware of the spirit world while in the physical earth. But this ability is your gift. You must cherish and protect it."

"Become a witch?" I asked.

"No, I am just saying stay open to all possibilities."

Already knowing that I wanted to live a life like Jasper's, I began to lose interest in our conversation.

"I want to be like Jasper," I told him.

Merlin, abruptly stopping, gained my full attention, "You needn't worry about your future, Arthur. *It*, will choose you."

Pushing through the low cedar boughs, I revealed the clear, shallow water of the pool to Merlin.

"This is beautiful. It must be one of your favorite places," he whispered.

"It is."

A large fish hovered just inches below the water and several perch swam nearby. The pool was a part of a creek that expanded beneath a canopy of oaks, leaving most of the water shaded from direct sunlight. Long drapes of moss hung from the large oak next to me and a squirrel sat on a limb, watching us while eating an acorn.

"I come here often. No one else knows about it," I added.

Glancing upward through a hole in the trees, I could see a hawk flying above us and felt its power pulling on my body.

I pointed to the sky.

"Yes, the hawk. A very powerful bird," he told me.

"Powerful? What kind of power does it have?"

"In addition to his earthly duties, he fulfills a spiritual purpose. Each animal holds a vibration that collectively reminds us of God. Each one has something to tell us."

"What does the hawk say?" I asked.

"He doesn't speak with words, he brings us his vision. It's difficult for ones mind to understand. But someone who observes nature as the hawk does, sees things from a higher perspective," he told me.

Thinking about his words, I began to imagine the hawk within my mind, trying to understand his purpose, while feeling his energy affect my body.

"Yes, Arthur. This is what I'm talking about. I didn't even have to show you how. You have the vision, and this hawk and all of these animals that you know as friends, will be your allies," he smiled. "They can take you to great heights."

"Do you know about the blue-jay?" I asked.

"Oh now that is a torturous one, with his horrendous squawking. I'm afraid I know very little about him," he confessed.

I nodded.

"We've been walking quite a while, Arthur. I believe Jasper will be wondering where you are," Merlin added.

"Oh, no. He knows where I am," I assured him.

"Well, I must be getting back soon," he said.

"We can go," I agreed.

Taking a short cut, we soon found ourselves approaching the meadow that surrounded the castle. And bidding each other good day, we promised to meet again soon.

We were perhaps an odd couple, but our friendship had begun long before this life. And its rocky and demanding existence has often caused me to search for the highest levels of truth within myself. But like many spiritual teachers, Merlin believed he was *All* knowing, and that he had the answer for every situation that might arise. He believed that I must agree with him if I were to succeed and to survive.

But Merlin's only true job was to position me for the kingship, as it would be by his blessing that the people would accept me. From that point forward, it was up to me to find qualities of leadership within myself.

The challenge was again before me. Release more fear so that my heart could remain strong, and I could continue to inspire the ones around me and lead them in the purest vision. This would one day be my job.

But today was a new day, a new opportunity to learn from the past, and again I had found myself next to Merlin. He would inspire me, hate me, occasionally love me, cause me untold internal anguish, and demand that I somehow grow. The slate was clean, we would begin again, and somehow, God's dream for the earth was a little closer to becoming reality.

*

Growing quickly, I was characteristically anxious to learn. It was often hard for me to keep myself from reaching beyond my ability, requiring Jasper to watch over me carefully.

A young colt in the paddock had caught my eye and I had been waiting for the last few months for him to mature. Wanting to be the first person to ride him, I was anxiously waiting for the opportunity.

"You can ride him," Alden told me, as we admired him through the fence. The colt was in the round pen, standing alone in a corner, his sleepy eyes half closed.

"I know," I answered.

Both Alden and myself were quite experienced with horses, for our age, often taking rides into the forest. But neither of us had ever been on a fresh colt that had never felt the pressure of a rider on his back.

"Just hop up on him," he said.

"I've got to have a bridle," I replied, casting a look of uncertainty upon him. "Why would I ride him without a bridle?"

Glancing over to the tack room, we could see its rickety, weathered door had been left wide-open, "Well?" he said.

"Take a bridle? We would be thrashed to no end!" I told him.

"No one will know. We'll put it back as soon as we're finished," he assured me.

Hesitating, Alden could see that I wanted to ride the colt and walked into the tack room. Moments later, he appeared, a bridle draped across his shoulder. I bent down, sliding my small body through the timber fence and met Alden inside the pen.

The gentle colt had already received some handling and accepted the bit without protest. But his demeanor changed after Alden legged me up and onto his back. Jumping forward, he half skipped in a circle around the pen, very unsure of my presence looking down at him from above. He didn't like me on his back and was pulling hard against the bit, trying to run. Jasper immediately spotted me and ran across the courtyard.

"Lean into him!" he yelled. "He doesn't understand what you're asking of him!"

The colt was fretting and briskly carrying me around the pen in circles.

"Take him to the wall," he said. "Face him to the wall so that he must stop, then pet his shoulder. And talk to him, Arthur, he's frightened. He wants to be certain of himself, and he's confused."

Trying to hold him at the wall, he was too afraid to slow down and pulled hard against the reins.

"Let him walk it out," Jasper called to me. "But keep turning him into the wall until he calms down. Let him wear himself down a bit."

Allowing him to carry me in circles, I occasionally turned him into the wall of the barn at back end of the pen. After a few minutes he let out a deep breath telling me that trust was growing between us.

"Good job, Arthur. He's yours now. But don't forget he's young. If he gets confused, slow him down and let him collect himself. He just wants to know he's doing right," he added.

Turning to Alden, "You put him up to this, didn't you?" Jasper told him, his eyes edging toward anger.

Innocently shaking his head from side to side, Alden refused responsibility.

"I know you did and I ought to take those reins to your ass when Arthur is finished," Jasper threatened.

With his arms and legs draped through the timber pen, Alden remained seated on the second rung. He was surely hoping that I did not get hurt.

But rather than reprimand me for making such a foolish choice, Jasper handled me as I had handled the colt, helping me to master the situation. Knowing that it would be difficult to stop me, he encouraged me to a place where I might find a sense of accomplishment. And this was no easy task. It took a large part of his focus to ensure my safety.

Although I still had no true knowledge of my abilities, Jasper's job was to prepare me to meet the demands of the physical world. At the same time, Merlin continuously tuned my spiritual awareness. They were both masters in their area of expertise, but alone neither could have prepared me for what I would soon have to face.

*

Since arriving at the castle, Jasper had reintroduced a sense of trust to me. And in the several years that had passed, he had taught me a great deal, but we had never directly touched upon the more serious matters of war. Now he believed it to be the appropriate time.

Entering the round pen, I could feel it was a special moment as he carefully explained himself, ensuring that I absorbed every word he said. He pulled his sword from its scabbard and pointed it into the air as he positioned himself directly across from me.

"Always know where your sword is Arthur. It is not necessary to look at it, but *feel* it," he told me, walking to the pen's edge to pick up a different sword that he had laid down upon entering. Walking over to me, he placed it in my hands. It was the first time I had held a real one of this caliber. Gazing into my eyes, he continued.

"The sword, better than any man, knows the difference between truth and falsehood. A sword wielded in darkness will always yield to one held by greater truth. The outcome of any challenge is decided before the fight begins," he insisted. "Before you agree to any challenge, you must first know where you're heart lies. No good can come from an unnecessary fight."

Walking slowly around the pen, he gently waved his sword from side to side. The power of his action was unmistakable.

"Do you understand?" he asked.

I nodded.

"Hold your sword into the air," he told me.

Lifting the heavy sword into the air, Jasper could see that it was still too much for me.

"It's quite a responsibility, isn't it," he said, putting the tip of his sword into the ground, it sliding a couple of inches below the sand's surface. I followed his example.

"Arthur, let *no* man be your guide," he said, looking around the castle and nodding toward several men standing at the opposite end of the courtyard. "Many of the men here have no concern for themselves and no concern for life. It's not their fault. They do the best they can. But you must never be drawn into their world of desperation. We have to stay above them, and bring them into *our* world."

With his feet spread apart, he rested his muscular arms on the hilt of his sword, its tip still dug into the sand.

"This is a very important day. What I have already told you is truly all that you need to know," he added. "We will talk more about this another day."

"Can we play with them?" I asked, hoping that we could spar for a moment.

"I need you to do something for me."

I nodded.

"I want you to spend time thinking about what I've told you today."

"All right," I answered.

"This is very important, Arthur. And we will have plenty of time to practice sword fighting, but on another day. I want you to think over what I've said."

And with that, the lesson seemed over. I had barely lifted my sword's blade from the ground. But Jasper was—in my belief—the greatest teacher alive. I was not disappointed.

"Watch me," Jasper told me as he put his sword down, while walking around the pen, slowly moving his arms up and down, perhaps pretending to be a swan.

"Where does your heart take you?" he asked.

Leaning my sword against the fence, I turned around and ran toward him with long, reaching strides. Jumping, I firmly landed with both feet together, spraying sand into the air and stopping a few feet short of him. Raising my arms, I playfully joined him in the dance.

"I see you know how to do this."

As if his shadow, I walked behind him, mimicking his actions as we made our way around the circle. Then he grabbed me and swung me into the air.

"Ha!" he laughed, squeezing my arms together.

"Ahh, no," I whined, as he swung me back down, placing me back on the sand, my feet digging down into the sand.

"All right, playtime's over. I have things to do," he told me.

"It will be time for the pass meal soon, so don't go running off into the forest."

"I won't," I assured him, and ran off in search of Alden.

* * *

By the time I reached the age of twelve, and perhaps ushered in by the strength of our castle, a sense of peace became a part of our land. It was then that I began a tradition with Jasper that would continue for the remainder of his days in earth. Each night near dusk, we would stop what we were doing and walk into the forest. Seeing Jasper's interest in the land peaked my own, fueling my curiosity to discover and visit every area of land in our kingdom.

"Come here, Arthur!" Merlin called from across the courtyard.

Hurrying over to him, I was anxious to understand his concern.

"Hurry, now. Let me see what you have," he insisted, already reaching for the sword that I held in my arms.

"It's a sword," I answered, holding it up to him.

"Yes it is," he said, captivated by its magnificence. "Where did you find it?"

"In a cave," I explained. "We were playing near the base of the castle, when we found a cave in the side of a mound. We think it's a faery mound."

A serious look crossed his face.

"Do you know to whom this sword belongs?" he asked.

"No, Can I have it?" I asked.

"Come here, Arthur," he told me, as he shuffled over to the stone stairway that led up to the crow's nest overlooking the front gate. In this vacant corner of the courtyard, it was much quieter. Merlin sat down on a step and pointed toward the blacksmith's stool, "Take a seat, please."

"Arthur, this is a very special sword," he began. "Do you know anything about it?"

"No, just that I found it with Alden, when we were playing," I answered.

Remaining solemn, his very mind was busy thinking, searching for the correct words, and wondering if it was indeed time to speak of the sword's meaning. Looking up, he hesitated, then continued,

"This is the sword that belongs to the next king of Briton."

"I can't keep it?" I replied.

"Arthur, it is not that easy," he said, slowly shaking his head as he ran his feeble fingers down the length of its blade.

"Arthur!" the cook yelled, from the den. "We need wood!"

"Coming!" I yelled back to her.

"Sorry Merlin, I need to go," I told him.

"It's all right, go ahead. And take your sword with you. Do not let it out of your sight."

Thinking alone, Merlin sat on the steps of the stairway while considering the possibilities for the immediate future, a future that I had just changed by finding and accepting the sword. Slowly getting up, he walked across the courtyard in search of Jasper.

Entering the den and seeing the empty chairs, he expected Jasper might be training, but unsure, he walked down the corridor to Jasper's chamber—he was not there. Returning to the den, he took a seat at a small oak table in the corner of the room. Late in the afternoon, the smoke from the fireplace had already begun to thicken in the air. Minutes later, Jasper entered through the door and Merlin motioned toward him.

"Jasper, I must speak with you."

Jasper walked closer, "Merlin, I'm very busy, perhaps later?"

"He has found the sword," Merlin told him. "The Lost Sword."

"Who has found the sword?"

"Your Arthur."

Jasper silently looked around the room and pulling a chair from beneath Merlin's table, sat down, "How can this be?"

"I have seen it. It is the sword. Playing in the forest, he stumbled upon it in the cave."

"I can't believe it. He's just a boy," Jasper told him.

"He is a king, always has been," Merlin answered.

"This is not what we need at the moment," Jasper added.

"Would there ever be a good time?"

"What do you think we should do?" Jasper asked, almost to himself. Placing his elbows on the table, he clasped his hands together, making a rest for his chin.

"It will not be an easy thing, to make this come about," Merlin told him.

"What do you know about the myth?" Jasper asked.

Merlin leaned back for a moment and stretched his arms. Glancing to his side to be certain that no one could hear, he leaned forward to whisper.

"It is no myth. Arthur has reclaimed his sword, the same sword that he once left in the Highlands."

With Jasper's interest peaking, he asked, "Could it be? My Arthur, the next king of Briton?"

"He is the one. But it will be up to us to make it happen," Merlin replied.

Leaning backward in his chair, Jasper seemed lost in thought, "We would have to take the castle. It would be the only way to see that he is crowned."

Merlin nodded.

"Have you told Arthur?" Jasper asked.

"I've not yet told him, but he found the sword. He has made the choice."

Merlin's attention suddenly shifted toward the den's door.

"There he is," Merlin told Jasper, nodding in my direction. "He just walked in."

Turning around, Jasper waved to me. Waiting for my eyes to adjust to the den's dark interior, I walked over to their table.

"Can you join us?" Jasper asked.

"Sure," I said, dragging a chair across the stone floor from another table before sitting down.

"Arthur, we want to talk to you about the sword you've found," Merlin began. "It is very important."

Still carrying it with me, I glanced down to it. Stunningly crafted of silver, its hilt was still too big for my hand and thickened iron blade weighed much too much for a boy my age.

"Have you heard of the lost sword?" Jasper asked me.

"Yes."

Jasper's eyes moved toward Merlin. Then Merlin looked at me.

"Arthur, this *is* the lost sword. You have found the lost sword."

Unsure of his meaning, I waited for him to continue. Hesitating, Merlin rolled in his hand a medallion that was chained to his neck.

"Quite simply. The legend states, that the one whom recovers this sword shall become the king over every kingdom in Briton," Merlin explained. "You have recovered the sword, and it is you that shall be king."

"I am the king?"

"Unless you refuse to accept it," Merlin answered.

"Of course, it is also up to the people. It will be their job to accept or reject you," Jasper added.

"What do you think about this?" Merlin asked.

I shrugged. Merlin chuckled to himself.

"Would you like to be the king?" Merlin asked.

"I suppose so," I answered. "Can we live here?"

"I think that you will have to, but there are many responsibilities that come with a kingship," he replied, looking to Jasper. Sharing a moment of silence, Merlin considered the possibility that I might be too young for the job.

"Well, Arthur. You can go now. But do not tell anyone what we have just talked about. Agreed?" Merlin said.

"Sure," I answered.

Turning to Jasper, I asked, "Will you keep this for me?" referring to the heavy sword that I had been carrying around all morning. "I have so much wood to haul this morning."

"Sure, I'll take it to our chamber," he answered as I returned to my work of stocking the fireplaces with wood.

"He's too young," Merlin stated. "It will be up to us to govern the land, until he grows older."

"Perhaps. But he's already wiser than any king in the land," Jasper replied.

Merlin nodded.

After hours of negotiation, Merlin and Jasper still could not agree upon a course of action. Needing a break, they walked across the courtyard, surprised by how much attention they received. Several of the castle laborers watched them closely from a distance.

An old man tugged on Merlin's robe from behind, his aged voice asking, "Merlin, is it true?"

"Is what true?" Merlin replied, turning around to face him.

"The boy, has a boy found the sword? We've heard the lost sword has been found," the old man answered. His tattered clothes gave him a desperate look, desperate for any change that might make his life easier.

"And where, may I ask, did you hear this?"

"Everyone in the castle has heard, and probably all the townspeople by now. It's no secret. Do we have a new king?" he pressed.

"Everyone in the castle?" Merlin inquired. "My God, has everyone heard this rumor?"

"Is it only a rumor?" the man asked.

"We are uncertain, Sir," Merlin replied, "I cannot tell you anymore than that."

"When will you know?" he persisted.

"I cannot answer that," Merlin told him.

"We have a king!" the old man yelled—loud enough for everyone in the courtyard to hear. *"A boy has found the lost sword!"*

Instantly surrounded, Jasper and Merlin were pressed up against each other. Knights and laborers alike were demanding answers.

"Who found it!" a woman called, while drying her hands upon a kitchen towel. "The boy? Young Arthur? Is he the new king?"

"Jasper, Your Arthur? Is he the king?" another man questioned.

Pushing his way through the crowd, Jasper put his arm around Merlin. Pulling him toward the den, he whispered, "It's out of our hands now. We must take the castle."

Merlin nodded in agreement.

The men of the castle converged upon Merlin and Jasper in the den, demanding their questions be answered and talk continued into the early morning hours. Throughout the night, our numbers began to increase as men from all over the country arrived to pledge their support. By morning, our castle held the greatest force in the land.

After a long and intense night of discussion, Jasper walked outside, out into the brisk morning air. With several of the men following, he turned to face them as the sun crested the horizon just behind him, "We will take this castle for the people of Briton."

"It's the will of the land, Jasper," a man said.

"Then so be it."

* * *

Jasper took me to the king's quarters later in the afternoon. Its massive entrance door overwhelmed me as I stood before it, my eyes carefully admiring the craftsmanship used to create it. Hung from large black wrought iron hinges, dowels were mortised through the double layers of oak for strength, and a large timber bolt inside prevented the entrance of an intruder.

Inside the chamber were many doors, one that led out onto a verandah overlooking the front grounds, another opening to a spiraling staircase leading down to the ground floor. At the far end of the chamber was a room, larger than our previous quarters, to hold a king's armaments.

"I think it best that you move up here," he told me.

"By myself?" I asked

Being very comfortable living with Jasper in our small room, it seemed ridiculous that one person should take up so much space.

"It is the king's chamber," he said.

"Can we both live here?"

With uncertainty, he nodded, "For now."

Carrying our few belongings up the stairs, we made our home in the new quarters. It was a sudden change for us, but very small compared to the other changes that lay ahead.

Feeling threatened, many of the kings still refused to accept me as the King of Briton, or even to acknowledge my presence in the land. But their people would not allow for this and demanded their leadership listen to me. Believing in the sword, the people trusted that it could bring peace to their lands and continued to put pressure upon their own kings, until negotiations began.

When it was seen that I only wished to put an end to our wars, and that I had an ability and willingness to negotiate for peace, hope for a united kingdom became a reality—and each kingdom eventually became a part of the alliance.

More often now, I found myself drawn to the forest. As the pressures in my outer world continued to grow, I was compelled to seek refuge, to sort out my uncertainties. Constant negotiations were required to keep the peace and the demands were pulling me deeply into the illusion of the physical world. Unwilling to forget the world of spirit, I worked very hard to stay aware of the natural world.

Crossing through the knee-high grass of the meadow, I glanced upward after sensing movement high above me. Seeing the hawk soar, I felt him tugging on my spirit. My openness allowing me to feel his feelings, I began to see our world from his perspective, from high above the earth.

Taking a seat beneath a tall and peaceful pine tree, I leaned back against its trunk, feeling its ridged bark lightly pressing into my back. Looking back up to the hawk, I wondered, and once again allowed its vibration to pull me higher. Allowing myself to feel the portion of the God energy that the hawk held, my vision began to clear.

Feeling much more grounded and centered now, my thoughts returned to some of the problems I faced as King. The fighting that had gripped the land for so long, no longer seemed necessary. I could see that by bringing the kings together, and allowing them to express their uniquely different opinions, they would learn to understand each other, and in time, move toward peace.

Standing up, I released the hawk and continued upon my walk, pressing through the cedars that surrounded me on my way back to the fish pool. Reaching the waters edge, I took a seat on a gnarled and bent willow that stretched out over the water, just a few feet above its surface. I sat quietly watching a small perch below me search for food beneath an algae covered rock. Feeling at peace now, I was able to hear the words being spoken to me by my guide in the spirit world.

"Each animal holds a specific vibration. For instance, when you could not see beyond a troubling situation, the hawk's vibration restored you to balance. When you became the hawk, felt his feelings, you could see that fear was not real. This is the purpose of the animals. Your own vibration will draw the animal to you that would restore you to balance or take you to greater heights."

Watching the perch swim away, I looked up to notice for the first time that the seasons had begun to change. Already early fall, more of the sun was able to reach through the trees now and its light flickered across the top of the water. Focusing upon one fish, a small bass, I soon began to feel its energy pull upon me. Feeling as though I might drown, my consciousness was being sucked into dark quarters, deeper into the earth and into my emotions.

The fish had its own gift for me, a very challenging one, and I began to consider its vibration. Could I experience his life of physical limitations, and remain at peace? In his small world, he had no possibility of escape *and* must live in close proximity to his predators.

Returning my awareness to my own body, I felt deeply grounded in the earth, then returned my awareness to the water, again watching the fish while noticing a sick feeling in my stomach. The fish had brought me closer to myself, saturating me in my own emotions, but had left me feeling uneasy. My spirit guide spoke to me on the internal plane.

"The fish's vibration does not allow for the manipulation of one's environment. It is only about peace. If he fears, he will lose his presence and be devoured by another.

Seeing the fish's vulnerability had frightened me. The challenges had begun to intensify and I was beginning to get a sense that perhaps I was not pure enough to succeed, that my fear might actually stop me.

Being open enough to feel the fish's energy had brought me this warning. But the question remained, could I do anything about it. Would I remain open and continue to release fear, finding greater protection, or would I close to the world and have what I loved taken from me.

*

Lancelot, a boy of fifteen, had often frequented the castle seeking the company of men, in particular, a mentor that would train him into knighthood. Since being orphaned during a Saxon invasion, he had made his home at Avalon and with each visit to the castle, had tried very hard to impress us. Although I initially resisted him, I felt an unexplainable connection to him, the karmic bonds from prior lifetimes uncontrollably pulling us toward one another. Even though I could feel reservations about him from our past, I could see that his place was with us. Unable to accept as much power as he truly desired, he had, in all of our lives together, lusted after things that belonged to me. And it was now my job to teach him to believe in his own power.

As I began to grow up and mature, more often than not, Merlin seemed to disapprove of my thoughts and actions. Standing beside a stream, after stopping for a rest during a typical walk through the forest, Merlin seemed particularly annoyed.

"Arthur, I have a name for you. A special name," he teased. "A power name."

Looking toward him, I was surprised and intrigued by his thoughtfulness, "A power name?"

"Yes, a name that is a map of sorts, to remind you how to find your power—if you find yourself lost," he added.

"Please tell me."

"It is very important. I'm afraid that you will not take it serious enough," he prodded.

"I will try."

"Alright," Merlin paused, "Wart."

"*Wart!*" I repeated back to him, confidently assuring him, "It does not make me feel powerful."

"What does it make you think of?" he asked.

A Blue Jay landed on the limb of a nearby tree, "*Rock, Rock, Rock,*" it called. Looking at the Jay for a moment, I turned back to Merlin and feeling a little betrayed, I answered, "Well I suppose it reminds me of a frog."

"Precisely! And that is why it is your power name. It is the frog that holds your power," he said.

"Can I have another name?"

"Arthur, listen to me. I'm giving you this name because I wish for you to understand the vibration of the frog."

"I think you're giving it to me to be mean," I insisted.

"The frog is very important," Merlin insisted, very entertained by his own genius.

"And what would his gift be?" I asked.

"Purification," he said. "You must purify your soul if you are to survive this life."

"I understand," I replied, turning away, my patience for Merlin's antics at an extreme low.

"It's only your first name, there will be others when you have made peace with the him."

Making no attempt to conceal my disappointment, I could not help but to become more interested in the frog.

Walking near a creek bed that afternoon, alone, I spotted a baby frog hopping by what used to be the shoreline. Leaping toward it, I followed it as it bounced away, and after a few more hops, captured it in my hand. Holding it tightly as it tried to squirm free, I waited to feel its energy and listened on the internal plane.

"The frog is an energy of purity. To sit for lengthy periods of time and to continue to vibrate with the God energy requires great internal peace. He must trust that he will be provided for. Even his food comes to him."

Barely able feel it's vibration, I lacked the trust necessary to find oneness with him, but I was beginning to understand. War was not to be my power in this life. It was peace—and I could only allow that to exist if my heart remained still. My power was in the purification of my body, in facing and releasing as much fear as I could.

Continuing my walk, I passed the fish pool when a very chaotic energy, the squirrel, joined me. Easily vibrating in oneness with him, I watched him run about as he gathered food for himself. His activities almost dizzying, I had much in common with him. Then I listened.

"His greatest drive is to gather. He pulls to himself what he needs to survive and stores it for future sustenance."

He was much like myself. Intuitively pulling others to me, I realized that I could do nothing alone and had little difficulty feeling this vibration. My challenge, which I had yet to understand, would be about discretion. To learn whom could I trust, and perhaps more importantly, who would betray me.

*

Often appearing wise, Merlin's true nature of a trickster was seldom noticed. Because he couldn't live the wisdom of higher truths, he was magnetized to ones that could, and since he couldn't inspire ones to grow in heart, he was forced into convincing others that he was needed. It was his confidence that made him powerful in our world. But as I grew in confidence, I realized that I didn't need his help—and he slowly shifted into the role of my adversary, trying to control every move I made.

"Arthur, it would not be wise to take money from the church," he told me, after hearing that I had plans to repeal our tax law, lowering the church's revenue.

"They receive more than they need," I insisted.

"And they'll become an enemy you do *not* need!" he began to demand.

"They may just have to get used to it," I answered.

"You are very young and do not realize how desperate these people can be. If you anger them, you'll never find peace," he told me.

Feeling some of my power slip away, my ancient fear of the church surfaced as I felt myself giving into his belief.

"The people want to be free from this burden," I argued.

"The people do not know what they want. They need the church," he demanded.

"I don't agree."

"God damn it, Arthur, it will be a mistake of grave consequences!" he insisted.

Remaining quiet, Merlin could feel my attention slipping away from him.

"God damn you, Arthur! You listen to me and do as I say! You would not even be known without me!" he yelled. "You'd have no say on this matter at all!"

Feeling my resolve continue to weaken, I excused myself, but his words had already begun to influence my thoughts.

Wavering on my decision regarding the tax, I could find no support to repeal the law and I reluctantly allowed it to stand. My karmic fear of the church, my unconscious memory of their actions during past lives, along with Merlin's doubt caused me to freeze on the matter. And my hands were full with many other important issues to consider.

In addition to running my own kingdom, I had the responsibility of settling all of the disputes between any of the kings within the alliance. I also organized all of the defensive efforts during the Saxon invasions. And, I was still in training with Jasper at arms, as at my age I would normally not yet even have reached knighthood. With all these pressing matters, the tax law seemed a low priority.

All of these things took an enormous amount of focus and I continued to heavily rely upon the forest. Sitting in my chair of stone, in the forest after a particularly stressful morning, my eyes focused upon a woodpecker, clinging to the side of an oak while tapping its beak against its trunk, "*Knock, Knock, Knock.*" With my ears listening to earth sounds, my spirit drifted to the ethereal plane. My guide spoke through.

"By forgetting your inner world, you can escape the pain of ancient wounds you still hold inside. The solace you find here in the forest will help you to work this energy up to the surface where it can be released."

Returning my focus into the earth, I watched the woodpecker continue his search for food. He never doubted his work, just persisted, believing he would find all that he needed to survive.

Contemplating my guide's words, I saw the importance of time alone with my own thoughts, without the pressures of others near me. I could see that my choices needed to be made using my own intuition and not another's rationalization. There were many near me that would gain satisfaction from the use of my power, and I decided in that moment, that all of my most important decisions must be made in the forest—*alone.*

*

With my body still growing, I had already reached beyond the height of most men, and at the age of sixteen, stood an even six-feet tall, weighing one hundred and ninety pounds. Having the physical advantage over most any challenger, I still retained the innocence held by my mother. My long tresses of sandy blonde hair and blue eyes resembled Igraine's, but my face clearly marked me as the son of Uthur.

With my kingship secured, we felt it was time to honor the men who served me. Having yet to take a knight, I chose to do so in an official ceremony, where five of my most trusted men would receive honors, Jasper being elevated to the level of a knight. McCoy, Galahad, Heath, and Lancelot all were receiving the rank of major.

People began to arrive from all across the land and we soon realized that we could not possibly provide accommodations for everyone within the castle, forcing us to create a tent city just outside the walls. My initial plan, to have the commencement in the Great Hall, would also have to be changed. Instead, we chose to use a peak of one of the rolling hills on the castle grounds.

For me, this idea had come as an innocent gesture of my appreciation. But as the event neared, its profound importance became more obvious. And when the ceremony began, my understanding of what I was doing changed. The words I had planned to use now seemed unimportant as I looked out into the crowd. Our guests had come to bear witness because of the difference we might make in their world. Realizing this left me feeling very humble.

Jasper and the men stood upon on a platform, built upon the peak of the hill.

"We didn't realize that so many people would wish to witness this day," I began, looking out over the large crowd that stood before us, "We're honored."

Feeling a little uncomfortable, I glanced toward Jasper. He nodded to me.

"You gave us a castle when we had only a dream. It was your belief that created us," I continued, as a few in the crowd cheered.

As the quiet returned, a light breeze washed over us as a woodpecker called out, momentarily drawing my thoughts back to my home in the forest. I turned to Jasper and pulled my sword. He walked over to me.

"Are you sure about this?" I said and began to laugh quietly.

"Of course," he said with a wry smile that implied his sense of humor.

"I accept you, Jasper, as my first knight," I told him, lifting my sword, touching each of his shoulders with its blade. "You may regret this."

Jasper winked.

Some of the people in the crowd laughed. I turned to the remaining men.

"We have others to honor today," I continued, pointing to each one as I introduced them. "McCoy, Galahad, Heath and Lancelot, have each earned the rank of major."

As the ceremony proceeded, Vivianne, watching from a distance, was not impressed.

"Arrogant boy," she whispered to her maiden, Jennifer. "He stands up there in his pretty make-believe world, turning his back on his people. This will not be an easy kingship for him."

"What do you mean?" Jennifer asked with a sparked interest.

"We are paying for this ceremony. The people cannot afford this ridiculous tax," with her hand, Vivianne brushed back her long dark hair, now streaked by the sun, while feeling the weight of the several silver bracelets that adorned her wrist.

"What choice do we have?" she asked.

"Someone must stand up to him," Vivianne answered, drifting off into thought. "Arthur has made the choice. He could have repealed the law."

"Are you going to confront him?" Jennifer uneasily asked, squeezing her crossed arms tightly against her frail body.

Vivianne eyes sparkled, "He believes that Avalon has no power over his choices. We will show him otherwise."

Placing her hand upon Jennifer's back, Vivianne delicately caressed the soft skin of her neck, "Do not worry. We will be safe. Arthur will never know," she smiled.

Jennifer's eyes returned to the ceremony, "I trust you have a plan?"

"Oh, yes," Vivianne confidently replied. "One that will shake him to his core."

*

Upon returning from the forest, I was informed that King Pellenore had arrived hours earlier. Bringing with him an entourage of thirty courtiers, we would have to move swiftly to make accommodations. But having never met, I was delighted by the news. He was very leery of leaving his kingdom and it had taken me months to coax him into a visit.

Pelly stood about six foot two and weighed near two hundred and fifty pounds. A very solid man, he preferred to remain at least partially dressed in armor, often wearing chain mail that covered his head and neck, always prepared for an attack.

I understood Pelly to have an appreciation for the forest and was eager to show him my own holdings. After spending the first day touring the grounds, we had become great friends. On the second, I challenged him to a contest.

I stood forty yards from the target as I pulled the back string of the long bow, my arm stopping as the strands grazed my lips.

"I'm not a bad shot, Pelly," I told him, the string partially inhibiting the movement of my lips.

"Arthur, we shall let the arrow decide that," he insisted.

Releasing, it penetrated the air, swiftly striking the target, *"Thump,"* one ring from the bull's eye.

Pelly nodded, then nocked his arrow, raised his bow and pulled the string back, "We shall see."

Releasing the arrow, he placed it directly in the center of the bull's eye.

"You have seen a bow," I smiled.

"I have seen many things," he replied, his tone noticeably changing.

"I don't doubt that," I smiled.

"Arthur, may we speak?"

"Certainly." Already prepared to shoot again, I let go of the bowstring, placing my next arrow just inside the bull's eye.

"Please do not take offence," he began, while pulling back his bowstring and taking aim. "But I am uneasy."

"How so?" I asked.

Releasing his next shot, his arrow struck lower this time, but still within the second circle, "I am worried—You trust so easily. Do you never worry about your enemies?"

"I don't know," I paused. "I believe I am careful."

"You must know this, Arthur," he lowered his bow, turning toward me. "You do have enemies. Do not think everyone is your friend."

Standing still for a moment, I reached for another arrow, "I suppose we all have enemies."

"But *you* have many," he insisted, turning around while reaching down for another arrow.

"I must give everyone the opportunity to be trustworthy," I answered.

"No, Arthur," he insisted, raising his bow, taking aim and again placing the arrow at the edge of the center circle. "You have enemies that *will* betray you, given the chance. They are just waiting for you to make a mistake. Many of Briton's kings became part of the alliance because they were forced. Their people demanded it."

I paused as he nocked another arrow.

"I will be careful."

"Good. You have stumbled into this place as king rather quickly and there are many dangers you have yet to discover."

"I will be careful," I assured him, feeling a little uneasy.

"I like you or I would have said nothing," he smiled.

Grateful for his interest, his words remained with me, my mind momentarily searching for potential adversaries.

After archery, he challenged me in knife throwing, our challenges continuing late into the evening. After winning one contest, I always allowed him to win the next. Perhaps he did the same for me.

On the fourth day of Pelly's stay, he informed me that although he was greatly enjoying himself, he would soon have to depart. Giving him no resistance, I suggested he wait until the following morning. He agreed. After the feast, I made a toast in his honor.

"Let us drink to our new and dear friend, Pelly. May you always remain strong. I will be disappointed when you leave and will look forward to your return."

Raising our glasses to him, I then sat down to speak more intimately to my companion.

"When you return, we will have to spend several days hunting," I told him.

"I will enjoy that," he answered. "You have been most hospitable Arthur, and I wish to leave you with a gift."

"It isn't necessary," I assured him.

"It was quite a labor getting it here. Will you make me take it with me when I return?"

"Of course, as you wish."

Turning around, Pelly called out to his squire, "Bring Arthur's gift."

"Here, my King? Inside the castle?" the squire asked.

"I think so," Pelly smiled.

Noticing my confusion, Pelly leaned toward me, "You will like this."

Moments later, we heard a familiar sound, the clip, clop of a horse's hooves striking against a stone floor. Looking toward Pelly, "You've brought a horse into our castle?"

Pelly laughed, "Not just any horse. It is a daughter of my greatest warhorse."

Walking through the doorway, his squire led an unbroken, and slightly fractious dark bay filly into the great hall and toward our table.

"She is beautiful," I told him, as my mouth dropped open. A tall horse, she already stood sixteen hands and her broad nose and dappled body revealed an excellent bloodline. I stood up and walked over to her, placing my hand on her withers. She jerked her head slightly and pulled against the shank that lay across her nose.

"She's yours," Pelly told me.

"I don't know what to say," I replied, touched by his sentiment as I ran my hand across and down the length of her back. She watched me closely.

"Its all right," I told her.

"She will make a fine horse for you, Arthur. I almost kept her for myself," he added, walking over to the opposite side, putting his hand upon her neck. "She's still growing. Her father's chest was narrower at this age."

"I like her, Pelly. Very much," I told him, understanding a great warhorse could mean the difference in life and death, "I'm sorry, I just don't know what to say. An invaluable gift."

"You needn't say anything," he smiled.

"You are genuine, my friend. I can easily see. I must find a way to repay you."

"If you wish to repay me, do not allow yourself to be deceived by your enemy," he said sharply.

Smiling, I walked back to the table and reached for my glass. Lifting it into the air, "To my new and dear friend King Pellenore. May our friendship grow. May your Kingship prosper. And may you be gifted, as you so generously give," I told him, gratefully bowing.

Touched by his thoughtfulness, I promised, upon his request, that within the month, I would be a guest at his castle.

* * *

The beginning of each growing season was marked during this age, with a special celebration to bless the earth and to thank God for providing our future sustenance. Known as Beltane, it was celebrated on the night before May 1. Caretakers of the lands stoked bonfires in their fields and created ceremonies to help them express their thankfulness. Light from the fires glowed across the horizon, from county to county, throughout the land deep into the night. This focus of making a special moment to be with God, to carefully consider the blessings that we received, made us more aware of our purpose in earth and of the higher power that existed to help us with our lives.

This time of year was particularly sacred to a local indigenous group of people that still lived very close to the earth. During the spring of my sixteenth year, I received an invitation from them, asking that I visit during Beltane so that I might receive their blessing. Accepting their request, I left for their encampment, a few days prior to the date with McCoy and Galahad.

Still a day's ride from our destination, we had made our camp for the night and were seated at the fire when McCoy began to question me. Galahad, stretched out on the ground, was preparing for sleep.

"So Merlin told you that these people want to take your clothes off and dress you like a stag? Is that right?" he said, pretending seriousness.

I reluctantly answered, "Yes, McCoy."

"Then you'll walk into the forest, at night, to be with real deer?" he continued, nudging a fallen ember back into the fire with his boot.

I nodded.

"Well, you wouldn't catch me running around like that," he stated as he leaned back against the trunk of a fallen tree. Galahad laughed to himself.

"I'm really glad to know that," I said as McCoy joined Galahads laughter. "You will totally embarrass me in front of the natives."

"We'd never do that," McCoy promised.

"I am truly comforted," I told them. "I just hope they can overlook you. But I'm sure they will see you to be less gifted than the average person and have sympathy for you."

Bringing more laughter, I shook my head as though pretending to be disgusted. I was guaranteed to be entertained when in their presence.

Reaching the native's encampment, the following morning, we were warmly greeted and after initial introductions and a gracious meal, they allowed us to experience their way of life first hand. I immediately noticed there seemed to be a predominate sense that each individual was to some degree equal, that no one person regardless of their position, held absolute authority. And because each individual was honored for his or her uniqueness, they all found a depth of expression that freed them from the need to fight amongst themselves, since each member was encouraged to speak his or her mind. Hostilities were seldom withheld and they existed very peacefully with each other. Inspired by what I saw, I was determined to make this a part of our own kingdom.

As the sun dipped below the horizon, the natives began to make their way up the hill to an area that we had not yet visited. In pairs and small groups, they quietly proceeded along a path, carrying drums, stag horns, skins and other ceremonial items. Without instruction, we followed.

Reaching the peak, a cleared plateau of a small, forested mesa, I admired their sacred circle, how they had co-existed with nature to create this powerful site. Large limbs, from oaks and junipers lined the circle, stretching out to conceal much of the sky, while fragrant smoke from burning sacred herbs, hung in the air.

Gathering in the center, we faced a stone altar, at the base of two large trees. After many years of growth, the oaks having partially engulfed the stone, they clearly held it securely in place. As the drums silenced, their leader, standing behind the altar, prepared to speak.

"We have prayed for a king who could bring peace to the land," he told us. "And now, we believe that our prayer has been answered."

He began a prayer to their Celtic God.

"We see hope in this young man that has many challenges to face in his earth life. Help us to instill greater memories of his purpose to him. Protect him and make him strong," he paused. "We honor the courage of this one that has accepted the challenge of the stag, and tonight his tests will begin." Turning to me, "Your bold heart will bring you back to us at dawn."

I lowered my head.

With several of the females at my side, my clothing was removed and I stood naked before everyone. A woman, taking all of my belongings toward the fire, dropped them upon the burning embers causing the flames to leap higher. Then a female covered my body with a large deerskin, while two others affixed stag horns to my head, just above my brow.

"You are now the stag, Arthur," their leader continued. "And the spirit of the deer controls your destiny. Should you return to us, at the end of a dark night of challenge alive, your first test will be complete. We shall know if you are the chosen one when the sun next crests the horizon."

Feeling comfortably in control, I exited their circle and walked a great distance into the dark forest, becoming aware of an unusual sensation. Sensing a change in my physical body, I could feel the sounds of chirping crickets sending vibrations through me, reminding me of the power in this night. Every tree, even the ground below me seemed to be alive, seemingly as if I had walked into the ethers, having left the earth dimension behind.

Several hours into the night, an owl swooped down from a tree and silently hovered above my head. After disappearing into the trees, a voice called out to me from the darkness.

"What are you doing in my forest?"

"This forest belongs to no one man," I answered, my eyes searching the darkness for the outline of a man.

"You must leave," the voice told me.

"I will not."

"Then you will be forced."

"Do as you must, but I will remain here till dawn," I replied, awaiting the challenge.

After a few minutes, a large stag rushed through dense brush charging me head on. With his head down, prepared to fight, I reached for my own antlers and we locked horns. With his body a solid fifty pounds above my own weight, I believed I had no chance of besting him and he began to push me backward, but a thought entered my mind—he had come to me. He had found me in a place where I believed I belonged.

Feeling a sharp pain in my left leg, his antler sliced through the skins. Seemingly determined to injure me, his horns were dangerously prodding close to my face. I only had time to protect myself and when I refused to become aggressive, strangely enough, he turned and walked away.

Despite a few bruises and scrapes across my arm and the cut on my left leg, I was not severely injured and remained alone in peace for the remainder of the night. Leaning against the trunk of an old oak, my eyes diffused into the darkness as my spirit reached upward, seeking wisdom.

Thinking to myself, "Would my enemies react similarly? Are they only seeking ones that are willing to fight?" Knowing the mirror of earth to be embedded with many metaphors of simple truths, I considered the possibilities.

Contemplating the challenge through the night, splinters of light finally began to peer through the forest's heavy vegetation and I stood up, realizing the test complete. Having left the ceremonial fire from the south, I was now in a position to return from the east.

With no trees standing between the sun, barely peering over the horizon, and the circle, I walked up the hill, my shadow arriving before me. Stopping just short of the circle's center, my body prevented the light behind me from casting itself upon the fire and I looked to faces of my friends. Sensing their surprise, I glanced at my body for the first time, seeing crusted blood upon my leg and arms. A female reached for my hand and led me to their altar where she lay me down as another retrieved a large bowl of water.

After attending my wounds, the Natives honored me with many gifts including a bow presented to me by their leader.

With so few in the earth that walked with a great awareness of God, I felt blessed to have had the opportunity to connect with these people. This meeting brought me closer to myself and their challenge had instilled greater consciousness into my body. I left them grounded, confidant and with greater hope for the future than what I had known.

We next began what mostly would be an uneventful trip home, with one exception. A bloodied stag jumped out in front of our horses within an hour of our departure. As it darted into the woods, I glanced over to McCoy and Galahad. Their sleepy eyes perked up for a moment as we shared the silent acknowledgment.

* * *

Saxon ships had been spotted by Tintagel's lookout, and their castle would soon be under siege. The year was 977.

A meeting of the alliance was called, and men were dispatched in the attempt to defend three locations where the Saxons based their operations. Greatly tested now, every choice I made was important. The spirit world offered their assistance.

Walking alone in the forest, I saw in the distance a man seemingly a few years beyond my age. And as our paths almost crossed, I saw in his eyes, an almost unhumanly sparkle. Innocent, yet deep, they seemed to know me, and I could not help but notice the sense of compassion that he carried. His long brown hair and thin beard gave him a similar look to other men of the age.

"Hello," I said, my feet still moving me in his direction.

"Good day," he answered.

Pleased by our meeting, I paused adding, "You seem familiar, yet I cannot place your face."

"We have in fact met," he smiled.

"Then you know my name is Arthur."

"Yes, I do. And I'm Joshua," he warmly replied, nodding. "It was quite a long time ago, when you were just a small boy—that was the last time we were together. You lived in the forest, not far from here."

"I don't remember much about my childhood."

"You were quite small."

"That is very interesting. I would like to know more, if you do not mind," I answered, trying to engage him in conversation.

"Well, you told me that you had lost your mother," he paused, his face expressing the grief of my loss. "And I promised you that you would one day find her."

Eliciting an unexpected response in my emotions, "Well, that day has not yet come, I am sorry to say."

"But it will," he assured me.

Being in his presence caused my focus to dramatically change, and soon found myself once again drawn in by the land.

"Do you know Merlin?"

"Yes I do," he smiled, turning his head toward a doe that just stepped from the cover of the forest, into the meadow.

Looking toward the deer, I withheld my words for a moment, watching the deer's breath escape her lungs as fog into the crisp morning air. Turning back to Joshua, who was now sitting on a large stone half buried into the earth, I noticed the courage that marked his unearthly face. Slowly, the awareness of his power seeped into my conscious mind.

"You are from the other world," I said.

Joshua nodded.

Feeling my body become ungrounded, a sense of knowing enveloped me as I recognized him, the master Jesus.

"Are we doing well?" I asked.

"Yes, very well, Arthur," he smiled.

"It is good to hear."

I looked back toward the deer, now grazing on the sweet grass of the meadow. A light mist hung in the air, sometimes becoming dense enough to limit our vision to the immediate area.

"I don't like to make mistakes," I paused. "There are ones here that believe I will bring doom to the country, like Merlin—curses every move I make."

"He believes the world rests upon his shoulders, that it's up to him to save it," he said. "But it is up to no one man. Just remember to only do your part. Leave the rest for someone else."

After briefly looking away, I returned my glance toward Joshua and even though I had heard no sounds of his departure, I found that he had disappeared. Looking in all directions for him believing perhaps he had moved, he had clearly left this dimension, no longer remaining in the physical earth. But our simple conversation had raised my awareness, stilled my heart and reminded me of God's greater purpose for our world.

*

Although the war persisted for many years, the country remained hopeful throughout the challenge, allowing for the veil near the castle between earth and spirit, to become very thin. Many people were finding themselves drawn to us wishing to be closer to the source of the changes in the land. Some chose to visit. Even the trip, they told me, was an inspiring adventure.

The road to the castle weaved its way through miles of dense forest. Tall trees forming a canopy over the road, obscured most of the sky. The sweet air and sense of magic changed the vibration of all who entered *our* forest. Beyond the awareness of most travelers, gnomes, faery folk and other earth spirits ushered each individual on their journey. About a half hour before arrival and while still surrounded by the thick growth of trees and vines, the castle would come into view, framed inside a hollow tunnel through the forest. It was a powerful sight—one certain to lift your spirit.

When I reached nineteen years of age, my mother, like many others, felt herself being drawn to us. Proud of her father's contribution to the country's changes, she wished to visit and soon made her own preparations for a trip. After her arrival and a lengthy chat with her father in her guest chamber, the subject finally turned toward the new King.

"Have you ever met King Arthur?" Jasper asked, his voice growing with unease.

"No," she replied, carefully unpacking one of her bags.

"He's very special to me. I found him here when he was just a small boy. I took care of him, and we lived together in a small room off the courtyard. Did you know that?" he asked, almost uneasily.

"No, I didn't," she replied with growing interest, turning around to face him and taking a seat upon the bed.

"He's very handsome and quite a gentleman," he added.

"It is wonderful that you care so much about him. I'm sure he feels the same about you."

Pausing briefly, he searched for more words, sitting with his elbows and arms at rest upon an aged wooden table.

"I've taken very good care of him and have seen to it that his needs were met," he continued.

Looking at him, she tried to hear words that he had not yet spoken.

"I saw something in him the first time I laid eyes upon him. I probably would have done this for any child so badly in need, but he is different."

The tears were already starting to well up in Igraine's eyes, her face draining of its color.

"I'm sorry, my dear. I'm so sorry," he paused as he began to sob. "I don't know how else to say this. He *is* Arthur—your Arthur. He's *our* Arthur."

Immediately standing up, her ashen face shocked as age-old tears began to pour from her eyes. Her pained, broken heart was bleeding.

"Where is he?" she asked, already walking in search of me.

"He's probably in the den," he answered. "Wait for me, I'll show you."

Unable to hear him, she hastily made her way through the corridors while Jasper followed close behind. Momentarily lost in a dark corridor, she stopped and leaned her back against the cold stone, her eyes closing, lost in emotion. Hearing Jasper's footsteps, she forced open her eyes and looked to her father.

"Left there," he pointed.

Resuming her search, she turned two corners and hearing men's voices, stopped short of an entrance. Looking into the room from several feet away, she saw me sitting at a table alone and turned to Jasper.

"Is that him?" she asked.

"Yes."

"Wait here for a moment and I'll go talk to him. We will wait for you," he told her.

After walking in, Jasper sat down across from me, not far from the table where we had first met and began to talk about the events of the day. In time, he changed the subject.

"I have a guest I'd like you to meet."

"Who would that be?" I asked.

"My daughter," he replied.

"Oh, I didn't know she was here."

"Yes, she arrived only moments ago. I've wanted you to meet her for some time. Perhaps it would have been best years ago, I don't know," he said.

Igraine was already approaching our table, her cheeks stained from her tears. A familiar radiance glowed from her.

"Hello Arthur," she eloquently stated. With a soulful smile, her head tilted slightly forward.

Standing to greet her, I warmly replied, "Hello."

"Come sit with us, dear," Jasper told her.

Pulling a chair from beneath our table, she took a seat next to me and my attention to returned to Jasper. Responding with a moment of silence, he finally began, "I have a confession to make."

Feeling uncomfortable, I waited for him to continue.

"Years ago, a terrible event had to come to pass. A young boy was taken from his mother, from my daughter," he said, his hand motioning to Igraine. Leaning forward while repositioning himself in his chair, he gathered his thoughts. Igraine openly sobbed.

"My daughter Igraine here, lost her child."

"I am very sorry, I didn't know," I told her, my mind racing.

"There is always hope beyond pain. What I am trying to say is that you play a part in this story," he paused. "I don't know how else to say this. But I'm very sorry that this had to occur, for it is in part my fault. Much of the responsibility belongs to me. It was I that put Igraine into this horrible situation."

"You didn't know this would happen," Igraine told Jasper, reaching for his hand.

"No, I didn't. But it did, and a great tragedy has resulted," he paused. "I'm sure you're quite confused, Arthur, but we are telling you this for a reason."

With her free hand, Igraine reached over to touch my hand, openly lying upon the table.

"It was *you*. You were the child who was taken from her. Igraine is your mother," he again paused. "And I am your grandfather."

Unable to speak, I could not help but to join Igraine in her tears as Jasper began recounting all of the details to me as the sadness continued to overwhelm us. He began with the death of his wife and the unjust pressure that was forced upon Igraine. And continued to include the story of Igraine's life with her aunt and later at Tintagel. He told me everything that he knew.

"I was heartbroken," Igraine told me. "I searched and searched for you – for years. I thought your loss would kill me."

"I'm sorry," I said.

"No—it is not you who should be sorry. It is me. I did not protect you," she insisted.

Jasper then told me about his dream, seeing me in the future and of his troubling decision to keep me from my mother. The evidence was clear—it was the appropriate thing to do. I was now King, a destiny that could not have come to me any other way. But a part of me did not understand.

We spent much of the afternoon and a part of the evening trying to reconcile our injuries, but now it was up to God and time.

After staying for a week, it was time for Igraine to leave, although she promised to return soon for a lengthier visit. Having already told her goodbye, I had turned away from her carriage when I felt her hands touch my body. Yet unable to leave, she had stepped down and from behind me, reached her arms beneath my own, wrapping them tightly around my chest. With her face pressing against my the side of my cheek, she whispered, "I've never left you Arthur—not for a day, not for an hour, not for a moment."

Placing my hands upon hers, "I know," I answered. "I know."

* * *

For the time, the war still remained a primary focus of my life, and it was necessary for me to meet with several of the kings to discuss strategy. Lionel, Lodegrance and Lott traveled to our castle, to spend the days negotiating difficult treaties for the warring kings within our alliance. Focusing intently upon the country each day, but each evening without exception, they demanded to be entertained long into the night. They would never leave me alone until deeply saturated with large amounts of my finest ale.

King Lodegrance was a temperamental man and loved the excitement of castle life, of the feasts, contests of skill and in particular, the playful wit of a beautiful maiden. He believed it to be very important for a king to be well loved. Perhaps wishing to gain favor, one evening he pulled me aside.

"I like you Arthur!" he stammered, reaching for my shoulder with his left arm. Having just stood up from the feasting table, he led me a few steps to a corner in the great hall.

"I'm very glad, I like you too," I told him.

"Don't patronize me!" he demanded, softly patting my chest. His head seemed to weave from side to side, "I'm trying to help you."

Becoming docile, he pulled me closer as if to tell me a secret, "I have something for you," he teased. "You will be pleased."

"You don't need to give me anything. It really is not necessary," I answered.

"Arthur, you're being much too difficult! You are in need, and I am just trying to help," he paused, his demeanor softening. "You have no queen."

"I appreciate your . . ."

"Stop! You've not even met her. There is no obligation," he softly toyed. "You will see. She's quite beautiful—blonde hair—green eyes. When I get back to my castle, I will prepare her to visit."

"I really have my hands full . . ."

"I promise," he interrupted. "You won't be disappointed. She's my niece, Gwenevere," he said with a wink.

Determined to send her to me, he would not allow me to argue with him and he promised that there was no obligation. I thought to myself, "What problem could there be?"

"Thank you very much, I will expect her arrival," I agreed.

After her arrival, I realized that Lodegrance had indeed told me the truth. Gwenevere was beautiful—stunning. When she walked into a room, she commanded its attention. But not because of love that emanated from her; it was the edgy sense of danger contained in her aura.

At least for a time, she would be the one to captivate me. With much karma still existing between us from prior lifetimes, as if in chains, she stole my heart, eventually became my queen. But I would never find satisfaction in her love.

Gwenevere, preoccupied with her new life at the castle, breezed down the corridor past our chamber door.

"Dear," I called. Several moments passed, then I heard footsteps returning. Gwenevere stood in the doorway.

"Yes, love?" she answered.

"Do you have a moment?" I asked.

"I am quite busy," she said, almost annoyed by my interruption. "Is it urgent?"

"No, it isn't urgent. I would just like to spend some time with you," I replied.

With her thoughts focused elsewhere, she turned her head to the side, "Arthur, you know I am busy. I'm entertaining all day."

"But you entertain everyday," I told her.

She sighed, "I am the queen."

"And a very good one, I might add. But you could make time for us."

"Arthur, please. I don't have time for this. I must go. You've already made me late," she complained, throwing her hands into the air.

"Go then, I am sorry that I've bothered you," I answered.

Rolling her eyes, her frustration rose to the surface, "I can never please you. I can never please anyone here."

"It's ok. Really it is. I will be fine. Just go and do the things you must," I smiled.

Slowly turning toward the corridor, she stopped and sighed, her head turning back toward me, her eyes edging toward distrust, "Arthur."

"It is ok. I assure you," I promised.

*

An old druid by the name of Leif arrived at the castle's gate in search of me. With the arrival of the Saxons, our gates had been closed to limit the threat of an assassin, but charming the guards Leif had enticed them enough to send for me.

As I approached the gate, the druids aura clearly identified him, "You must be Leif."

"Good day, Arthur," he replied. His long, but happy eyes revealed wisdom to me, as well as a gentle sense of humor.

"This one is always welcome here," I called to the guard, before turning back to Leif, "You are very welcome here. Merlin has spoken of you often."

Holding his hands clasped together while resting against a slightly rounded stomach, Leif entered the courtyard. The dark Lenin of his dress was accented by the light skin color of his hands.

"Is Merlin well?"

"Is he ever?" he replied, pretending to be serious.

"Good question," I smiled.

Still standing near the entrance, the sun low in the sky, cast our shadows several times the length of our bodies upon the ground.

"I have wanted to meet you for a long time, Arthur. You see, I met you in a dream, several years before your birth."

"Destiny cannot be altered."

"Are you in need of a seer?"

"Perhaps, Leif. Perhaps."

"I would be happy to assist you in any way."

"I do appreciate your offer," I told him. "Merlin has often spoken of your gifts, and you are welcome here."

He nodded.

"It is very close to the eve," I told him. "Will you stay the night?"

"If you wish."

"Good. I will have quarters made ready for you later, but it will be soon time for the feast. I do hope you are hungry"

"Always," he smiled.

With Leif at my side during the feast, we shared a light meal, speaking with very little candor. But late in the evening, as we were about to depart, he asked, "Arthur, may I have a private moment with you?"

"Of course."

Gesturing toward a corner where we might sit, I took a seat across from him at a long and worn feasting table. I reached for an empty goblet and plate, still remaining from the meal and set them to our side.

"Arthur," he took a deep breath, exhaling as his face changed expression, "I have had many dreams, many visions. Some I believe, are not destined to reach into this dimension. They may not become true. But others, I'm afraid . . ."

I listened, silently wondering to what degree Merlin had influenced him.

"I came here for an important reason. I want to help you, if I may," he told me.

"I know that you speak with Merlin and that he believes we are doomed."

"But we do not share all of the same visions," he interjected.

Our expressions shifted as a momentary silence offered a deeper reflection.

"We really don't have as much free will here as we might believe. Certain futures are needed, however tragic, to force us into growth," I told him.

Leif eyes softened as he sadly agreed, "I know. It is very hard for me, Arthur. To see visions of what might be and to have little effect upon the future. But you have the power here to make a difference."

"You have more influence than you might realize," I told him.

"Perhaps, but it is you that can directly affect outcomes in this world," he reached for his goblet and took a sip of wine.

"I can only do what the people will allow," I told him. "But you can help me. I see it now. Your words can influence others, to help them see a higher vision. Many in this country that barely know me—trust you. You can help them to see what we are trying to do."

"I will do what I can."

"I have a good feeling about you, Leif," reaching across the table, I grabbed his hand and squeezed it. "Who knows Leif, maybe we will change the world!"

Leif's eyes sparkled as he placed his other hand atop mine, grabbing it tightly.

"And if not, the world is certain to change us."

*

Waking from a powerful dream, my head was still dazed from its energy. My thoughts drifted back to a word that I saw inscribed above our castle's entrance—*Camelot*. Upon Merlin's next visit, I inquired about its meaning.

"It is an ancient word the Celts once used to describe a gathering to raise one's awareness of the God and Goddess. Their meeting, was called a *Camelot*," he explained.

Believing it to be the perfect definition of our life, I named our castle—Camelot. It first seemed that naming the castle would be enough, but this vision was too important to limit to ourselves. With the entire land accepting this name for our country, the people of Briton received the power of its energy.

And that was a beginning. Another piece to the puzzle, another step taken, furthering the awakening of the God energy in our world.

*

Concluding a celebration honoring the harvest, Vivianne and her friend waited for me, having edged their horses off the main road. Patiently remaining within the cool shadows provided by the forest, her intuition had told her that I would find her guest interesting.

"Hello Arthur," she called to me, as I passed.

"Hello Vivianne."

"Do you have a moment, my King? I would like you to meet a friend of mine."

"Always, dear Vivianne," I told her, adding the slightest pressure to the reign, as Bay, Pellenore's gift to me, moved in her direction, stopping at her side.

"Please meet my dear friend, Morgan—Morgan Lafay."

"It is a pleasure," I told her, admiring Morgan's beauty. By most anyone's standard, Morgan's striking features and possessing eyes were beyond intrigue and I could not help but feel her allure. Vivianne paid close attention.

"She has just recently come to us and knows very few people here. Perhaps you would know someone that might be a friend to her?" she suggested.

"I'm sure I do," I answered.

Sitting on her horse, quietly reserved, Morgan's aura suggested she was seldom short of words. Her long black hair caressed assertive shoulders, concealing the right side of her face. Entrancing and enchanting—Morgan was a power to behold.

"Perhaps you would come to Camelot for Michaelmas. You would be most welcomed," I told her, feeling the kindling of an ancient and unexplained passion.

Smiling gently, Morgan allowed Vivianne to speak for her.

"Perhaps she will," Vivianne answered.

Nodding, I lifted my reigns, while tapping my heels against Bay's chest, "Good day."

Only days later, Michaelmas arrived along with my ancient love, Morgan. One who had both hated and loved me, her entrance into my life brought with it an unusually passionate embrace. The deep love we had once shared, left us with little control over the future that lay before us. And with passion ruling our bodies, we became lovers as the challenges of a destined future lay at our feet.

"Morgan," I whispered upon waking, "I must go now."

"No," she sleepily answered, reaching her arm around my naked body pulling me closer.

"I must, dear," I told her gently, pushing the linens down as the cooler winter air breezed across our skin. "I have kings in the library waiting for me this minute."

"Let them wait," she said, the depth of her resolve unforgiving.

"You know I cannot do that. I must go," I insisted, trying to ease my body from her grasp.

With a great sigh of discouragement, she pulled her arms away as if to punish me for my disobedience.

"I want to stay," I said, trying to ease her frustration.

"Just go and play King," she insisted, still half asleep.

"We will have another time to sleep in. Just not this morning."

"Leave me be."

Having only been lovers for months, Morgan's need for control already overwhelmed her. Although my love for her was great, something inside of her found no satisfaction. As if she knew we would not be together forever, she reached for an unattainable sense of security.

Waking from another powerful dream, the God light seemed to be still searing the skin of my face. Surprised by the vision, I could not deny the powerful feelings that I had experienced—seeing the vision that Morgan was not my great love. The dream had clearly shown the one dearest to me had not yet entered my life, but was waiting for our meeting in the immediate future—a Lady of King Lionel's Court.

Feeling Morgan's tight clutch upon my life, I resisted seeing the entire vision I had been offered, understanding how this would upset Morgan's dreams for a life at my side. But I also knew the importance of meeting the key figures destined to come into a life. The dream of Camelot existed because we had refused to withhold energy, because we had remained open to receive all that God and Goddess were prepared to give to us. I knew that if I closed to greater possibilities, I risked the failure of everything.

Wrestling with the dream for several weeks, my resistance gave way when an invitation to visit Lionel arrived. Realizing that time had run out, I prepared to take the trip with the company of only a few of my knights, while leaving Morgan behind.

It was during the first evening at Lionel's, at the feast when our hearts were revealed to each other, her radiant blue eyes capturing my attention as she momentarily glanced in my direction. Seated at a table opposite of me, I yet had no chance to speak to her, but the delight held in her eyes told me of her longing. For me, there was no longer any doubt—my dream had revealed the truth.

Sneaking up behind her after the feast as she left the common room, I leaned forward, my lips moving close to her ear, "You are very beautiful," I whispered. "May I ask you of your name?"

"Louisa," she smiled, turning her head back toward me while reaching her hand to free locks of her chestnut colored hair entangled in her gown.

"A pleasure," I nodded, touching my heart with the palm of my right hand. "I am Arthur."

"Yes, I believe I knew that," she smiled.

"I suppose one loses obscurity when they accept a Kingship," I replied.

"I think so."

"One of my favorite things to do at Camelot is to spend hours wandering through the grounds," I told her. "There are an endless number of trails woven through our gardens."

"King Lionel's gardens are among the most beautiful in the land."

"Really?" I asked, noticing that after exiting the common area, we were walking along a path beside one of the gardens, the fresh flowers bathing us with their scent.

"Yes."

"I am quite certain that you have more important things to do—but I don't suppose that you could show me some, or at least one of Lionel's gardens?"

"I have some time," she shyly replied.

"I don't wish to impose."

"It is all right, I do have the time," she insisted.

"Wonderful," I said, reaching for her hand. "May I?"

"Yes."

Squeezing my hand in return, she clasped it in a way that felt as if no other lifetimes had ever separated us.

Although few words were exchanged, there was no silence as we walked down the path leading into the garden. Our hearts had already begun to soar with the forgotten memories of what we had once meant to each other.

Stopping in front of a bench positioned in front of a vine of crawling roses, we sat down. The calm we felt told us that nothing could take this moment away. We sat quietly until a thought arose inside of her.

"I see that your Queen did not make the journey," she said.

"She is quite busy and does not greatly enjoy travel. She has quite a grand life at Camelot," I replied.

"Do you love your her?"

"Well," I began.

"I am sorry to be so rude," she apologized.

"No, a fair question, and Yes, I do," I answered.

Looking away, she searched for more roses among the vines.

"And I'm sorry that she has no heart to give me. I wish that she did," I told her.

"Why would she not give it to you?" she picked up a rose petal that lay on the bench.

"Gwen is a woman of the world. She has little time for romance."

"That is sad, you have much love to give," she said.

"And what about you. How could one so beautiful as you have no lover?" I asked.

"I can say the same thing for you," she insisted.

"The we've reached a stalemate—I concede," I said, as she gently laughed to herself.

"I know," I began. "I proclaim as King that from now on, all will see your beauty as I do now. So be it."

"Don't tease me," she said.

"I'm not—it is now so," I assured her.

"Maybe I should proclaim something?"

"Please do," I encouraged, attentively waiting.

"Okay. That from this day forward, you will helplessly charmed by me forever more," she stated.

"It is so."

"I don't believe you."

"No, it's too late now. It is the law," I assured her.

Pulling my arm toward her, she put it around her waist. My body relaxed, lost in an eternal embrace.

Escorting Louisa back to her chambers, I stopped in front of her doorway, her sparkling eyes holding me in trance.

"You know that I must return tomorrow."

The soft glow in her eyes faded slightly as I squeezed her hands in my own.

"Will you promise to visit me at Camelot?"

"You will forget about me," she said, leaning toward the door.

"I will not. I can promise you that."

Wise for age, she hesitated, "I don't know."

"Yes you do. Do you wish to see me again?"

She nodded.

"Then you must come. You can't let me leave like this."

"We'll see," she answered, her voice unable to conceal her desire.

Leaning forward, my lips grazed her cheek, softly dragging across her skin until finding her moist lips. Stopping, I took in a breath, inhaling her scent while losing myself into the remembrance of this passionate and familiar kiss. She opened the door and pulled me inside.

Having just arrived at Camelot, I turned Bay over to my squire while retrieving some of my personal items from the saddle. With little awareness of my surroundings, my thoughts were still with Louisa as Morgan snuck up behind me. Grabbing me around the waist, I jumped as she began to openly laugh at me. Then she looked into my eyes.

"You bastard!" she yelled.

"Morgan, wait," I said, trying to console her.

"You God damn bastard!" she yelled again. "I trusted you!"

"What's wrong?"

"You unfaithful bastard," she continued, her eyes unleashing her rage upon me.

"I have met someone. That is all," I said, reaching for her hands.

"Don't touch me."

"I was just being myself. What do you want from me?"

"Nothing. Not a damn thing," she told me, forcefully pushing her hands against my chest, causing me to take a step backward.

"I knew better than to trust you," she vengefully added as she turned, quickly leaving the area.

After Bay was taken care of, I walked to my chambers to find many of my belongings scattered across the floor. Noticing that all of her personal items were missing, I realized that she had left. And with her, still beyond my knowledge and conceived without blessing—my own unborn child.

*

Often visiting the castle, within a few months of our meeting Louisa took residence with me. Light hearted and whimsical, she found much of my work bothersome. One day as I sat in a chair in our chamber brooding over the war, her body lay across our bed as I carefully studied maps, finalizing my war strategy. Petite, but voluptuous, her exquisite body was more than tantalizing. With her head resting on her folded arm, she teased, "Lancelot is such a great knight. Is he stronger than you?"

"Louisa!" I said as I humorously glared at her for a moment before returning to my work.

"I suppose he probably is," she added.

Looking up again, "You are so mischievous!"

"I don't know what you mean," she said, coyly.

"Well, I'll show you what I could do to Lancelot," I said as I rushed toward her. Already beginning to laugh, she screamed as I grabbed her. Raising her over my head, I began to tickle her.

"Stop! Stop! Please!" she screamed.

"Take it back!" I told her.

"I take it back! I take it back!" she yelled.

Laying her on the bed, she tightly held to my hands, pulling me near.

"Lay by me," she told me, trying to catch her breath.

"Enough?"

"No more," she breathily answered.

Hearing a knock on the door, I opened it and was greeted by a courier.

"The Saxons broke through our defenses," he began. "We've lost several knights, twenty or more."

Continuing to listen, I was barely aware of his words as recounted the details of the battle. When he finished, I uttered, "Thank you." Walking over to Louisa who was now in tears, I dropped to the floor, laying my head in her lap, "This can't be."

Momentarily lifting my head, I looked to her for comfort. Seeing the distant look in my eyes, she became frightened for me, and leaning her body closer, pressed her chest to my face, rocking me in embrace. Agonizing briefly, I stood up to join the others, now assembling in the library.

Several of my most promising knights, I later learned, had fallen that day as grief overwhelmed a still innocent heart. Now playing grown up games with real consequences, the world was forcing me to grow up.

We solidified our positions easily enough, sending the Saxons into retreat and although their days in our land were numbered, it would still take a strong unified effort to send them away in defeat. Our loss compelled me to rigidly focus my mind upon their removal and for a time, I became consumed by the war.

*

Christina and Katrina, sisters to one of Camelot's knights, had been recruited by Vivianne to be part of a plan that she had devised to gain influence over me. Having lived at Avalon since the death of their parents, they were indebted to Vivianne and she had instructed them to visit their older brother at our castle, hoping they could manage to gain my attention and remind me of their traumatic life situation.

Upon hearing their story and believing it a pity they weren't able to grow up with their brother, I invited them to move into the castle. But within a few days of their arrival, the keys to one of my personal chambers came up missing. Immediately suspecting them, I listened on the internal plane and was told that Christina was the thief. She was immediately sent back to Avalon.

Returning to my chambers a few days later, I found Katrina searching through my belongings. Leaning against the doorway, I waited for her to notice me. She never looked up.

"Hello, Katrina."

"Hello!" she answered, startled by my unexpected presence. "I was just looking for you."

"I am a bit large to fit in a drawer," I told her.

She forced a laugh as I waited in silence for her to explain. When no words came to her, I asked, "Tell me, what is it that Vivianne has you looking for?"

"I don't know what you are talking about. I was just hoping to find you," she insisted.

Walking over to her, I placed my arm across her shoulder, pulling her to my side, close to my body, "You think me to be a fool, yes?"

"Arthur, I am here in innocence," she insisted.

Shaking my head, "Have you no mind of your own? Does Vivianne command every move you make?"

"I don't have to take your insults," she answered, her mock disgust, unconvincing.

"When you're in my home, as my guest, you *will* follow my rules," I told her. "This mission you're on is quite ridiculous. I know Vivianne believes I have an object somewhere that I rely on to bring me power. Has she instructed you to find and steal it?"

"I don't take orders from Vivianne," she answered, trying to move away from me as my grip upon her shoulders tightened.

"I know that you do."

"I'm leaving," she said, trying to break free from my hold.

Tightening my hold further, I reached down to her wrist, "Yes, you are."

Taking her by the hand, I escorted her to her chambers, "Gather your things," I told her, and sent for a guard to have her removed from the castle.

*

After a long seven years of war, the great Saxon invasion finally came to an end, and peace to the land was restored. Still a dark time in Earth's history, the volatile anger that remained within our hearts would continue to seek expression. No longer with an enemy to hate, if we were not careful, our tensions would be released upon ourselves. A new challenge—one that required me to seek higher truths, now confronted me. I returned to my home, the forest, to walk among the ancient oaks until a new vision arrived.

Quite accustomed to Earth's energies that danced with me amid the evergreens, I knew that within only a few hours of solitude, new wisdoms could penetrate my state of darkness.

Looking up at an old, familiar oak, I allowed its stability to slough off the confusion from my body. Sitting down beneath it, I leaned my back against its trunk, while memories of Beltane surfaced within my consciousness. I saw the stag facing me, seeking a fight, and then for no apparent reason, turning to walk away. It was as if he only sought expression, a desire to show his power to me. Then, moments later I could see—visions of organized games—competitive games that would allow the men to use their skills, once used in our defense, now as a source of expression.

An acorn fell from the tree above me, landing a few feet to my side and I looked up at the squirrel that had chewed it loose from its branch. I suppose he wished he hadn't dropped it, now he would have to wait until I left to retrieve it. Staring down at me, I watched him closely. He climbed over to the next acorn, and began nibbling away, while dropping bits of bark and acorn fragments onto my head.

"Hey," I yelled, standing up to avoid the rain of the unwanted pieces of his lunch. Walking over to the next tree, I sat down, keeping a close eye on him as I began to imagine the games.

Within the tournaments, I saw the men challenging each other and being ranked according to their level of skill. Jousting, swordsmanship, archery and knife and ax throwing, all skills that had been honed during war, could now be used to channel their physical aggression.

Glancing upward again, I saw my friend scurrying away, and bringing my attention back within myself, I could see that my questions had been answered. With the solitude of the forest providing needed answers, my mind was once again clear. Now it was time to return to the castle and make preparations to bring the games into our dimension.

*

After falling asleep late in the evening, I awoke within a dream to find myself standing effortlessly beside my bed. Looking to my side, I could see that my physical body, still lying in bed, was sound asleep. I immediately expected something spectacular.

For an unknown reason, I felt a strong pull toward the great hall and giving into the desire, drifted through the stone wall of my chamber. Passing effortlessly through floors and ceilings, I finally penetrated the great hall's main wall, a wall decorated by the colorful banners of our kingdoms. Hovering in the air, I was awestruck by my travels through what seemed to be impenetrable surfaces, but was equally impressed by feeling the grandeur of the halls natural energy. With my senses intensely acute, it felt as though the air whispered to me, "Anything is possible."

In this night a gift awaited us, one that had not yet arrived in our dimension. A huge feasting table created with a simple shape, although uncommon by size: a circle. Standing quietly before the stage, it waited for me to notice. It's importance I easily felt as I watched, allowing its knowledge to come to me—a table where no one could claim superiority, where no seat could be owned—a table to honor my greatest knights, ones who could sit with me at this high circle of hope as long as *our* truth allowed.

"My God," I said to myself, leaning up from bed as my body continued to awaken. I could still feel the dream's power coursing through me, "My God."

Beyond a dream, I witnessed this vision at the same level as the God energy that had created it, and with the spiritual light still numbing my face, my body worked to adjust from the shock. I sat in awe until my body's need for sleep overwhelmed me. In the morning I would search for further meaning.

During my sleep, I began to understand more about the table, for when I awoke, I was completely prepared to have it built. Later that morning, I walked out into the forest to choose the trees that would be used for the table's creation. Remaining very aware of the vision throughout its construction, the dream's energy began to descend upon the castle.

When finished, its width reached twenty-two feet in diameter, so large, that steps were crafted and recessed into the top, allowing servers to access kings and knights from the center. Hewn from thick oak planks, it would take craftsmen a year to complete before finding its home in the great hall. And there, an additional six months would pass before allowing it to be used. Wanting to raise our awareness of its importance, I ensured that the table stood idle while our respect for it grew.

In time, twelve knights and myself would make many important decisions seated around this glorious oak circle. My only concern now was in bringing all of its power into this dimension, allowing the table to make its rightful impact upon our world. Perhaps a heavy responsibility to bear, but the God and Goddess still walked nearby as the Roundtable began to leave its mark in our world.

*

"Arthur, you cannot hide from me," Merlin demanded, after forcing his way into the library. Sitting alone in my chair, next to a long wall, floor to ceiling with shelves that contained many volumes of books, I had been waiting for Louisa.

"I am here, right in front of you," I answered. "How can I be hiding?"

"You are so ill tempered. I don't remember you this way when you were a child," he whined.

"You were much more agreeable then," I replied.

"Damn you, Arthur. You need me."

"Things are very good in our world now, Merlin. It's time to enjoy our abundance."

"You have no idea what lay in your future, or you would listen to me. Why do you no longer seek my help?"

"Well, Merlin," I began, no longer withholding my patience. "Things are well and I haven't needed your help recently."

"Don't toy with me boy. Do not forget, I made you King."

"When we need your help, I promise I will seek your counsel," I assured him.

"When you need my help? And did you not need my help during the war? If you would only take a moment and look, you would see your future is doomed!"

No longer believing in him or his visions, I still somehow found myself tied to him, "And what do you suggest I do? How can I prevent our doom?"'

"You can listen to me," he answered.

"I'm listening."

"Your job is just to do as I see fit. I can prevent you from making the errors that your future holds," he told me.

"Merlin, if that is my job, you might as well leave now," I said, my eyes focusing in disinterest through the garden window.

"God damn you, boy," he yelled. "Had I only known, I would never have made you King. Let me tell you something, Arthur. You will listen to me. One day you will come to me, pleading for my help."

Returning my gaze to him, he could clearly see that I had no interest in our conversation.

"You are a doomed king, Arthur, doomed," he yelled as he walked toward the door, forcefully slamming it as he left.

*

At the eve of a lengthy stay with Louisa's parents, in her childhood home, she grabbed my hand and led me to the barn where Bay was stabled. There, she placed a bridle in her mouth and jumped upon her back.

"Come on," she said, reaching down to me.

Grabbing Louisa's waist, I slung myself up behind her and pulled close.

"Where are we going?" I asked.

"To a secret place," she whispered, guiding Bay out of the barn and onto a trail that led into the trees.

"Will I be safe alone with you?"

"I don't think so," she answered.

Riding off into the dark, we followed a trail through the forest for close to an hour. Leaning back, toward me, she pressed her body against my chest, whispering, "This is my secret."

With the trees opening up, a bright moon had found its reflection across a small body of water.

"It's where we swam," she told me. "When we were children."

After tying Bay up, Louisa walked toward a large stone that leaned out over the water. Slowly removing a piece of clothing with each step, the subtle moonlight washed over her shapely body. Even in the dark, her radiance could not be denied. Then looking toward me, she smiled, "Are you coming?"

She turned around and dove off the edge of the stone, shattering the silence of the night as her body penetrated the water's surface.

Removing my own clothes and diving in behind her, I swam to her side, playfully tugging at her arm as I hovered in the deep water. She began to swim away, "Come on," she said, swimming to the other side and taking a seat upon a partially submerged stone.

Following her, I stopped, floating above her body as my hands rested against the stone beneath the water. Then taking a seat by her side, together we admired the moon's radiance, noticing its energy pouring upon our surroundings.

"I'm happy now," she told me, as she leaned her shoulder into a void beneath my arm.

"Me too."

Absorbing the fragrance of the pine held by the motionless air, I felt a special moment of freedom as we listened to the crickets methodically singing their cadence.

"I thought we'd never get to be alone," she said.

"Me too."

Taking a deep breath, she inhaled the night air, "I would often spend time here as a child, thinking of a man I believed I was destined to meet," she told me. "I was certain that he'd one day find me. I never doubted."

Remembering the confusion that had surrounded me as a child king, I began to feel bad about my choices.

"No, that is not what I meant. I didn't have the same challenges," she said, intuitively comforting me, speaking of the doubt that had brought me into a marriage untrue to my heart. "I only care that we are together. Nothing else matters."

Leaning forward, her movement sent a widening circle of ripples across the water toward the opposite shore.

"I made a mistake."

"No, no, my sweet," she told me as she pulled me closer. "The world asks so much of you. Don't feel that way."

"It can be confusing at times."

"There are many demands made of you," she said. "I sometimes feel so distant from you."

"I wouldn't have the desire to do this without you."

"Do you ever wish we could walk away from everything and be alone, just us," she asked.

"Yes I do," I nodded.

"We could live in the romantic Highlands," she imagined.

"It would be wonderful, living close to the earth, connected to the cycles of life."

Turning her head to the side, she sighed, "I do love Camelot, but castle life—too many people concerned with promoting their causes."

"Here, here."

"It's true," she insisted.

"I'm not disagreeing."

Louisa, relaxing again returned her eyes to the moon. That is where we should live, the moon."

"Let's go."

Louisa smiled. Camelot now seemed to be less of a burden and our hearts grew closer together. Touching her forehead with my cheek, I dragged my lips down her nose, momentarily resting them upon her mouth, then further down to her neck.

"As long as we have each other," she whispered.

Giving into each other, only a deep sense of trust controlled us now. Our love, having waited an eternity, flowed freely as its passion united our bodies.

* * *

The first knighting ceremony of Roundtable took place in the recently enlarged great hall. With candidates representing each kingdom, all of the kings within the alliance were present, proud to have their own men knighted within the order. Jasper, Heath, McCoy, Galahad, Faye, Alden, Lionel, David, McKay, Percival, Hanguis, and Lancelot were the first Knights received into the Roundtable.

Always finding these ceremonies to be humbling, I never felt I could meet the expectations of the people in attendance. And as always afterward, I took time to be alone with Louisa. Grabbing her hand and a blanket, we snuck out of the castle and into the night.

Walking toward the stream at the head of the lake, we headed toward one of her favorite spots. With the full moon's light charging the night's air, the trees cast long shadows on the ground in front of us. When nearing the water's edge, I spread the blanket on the ground, and lying down, Louisa rested her head on my stomach. Although we had barely spoken since leaving the castle, we felt very close to each other.

"How did you know what to say?" she asked, referring to my words during the ceremony.

"I don't know."

"It was so powerful," she added, referring to the feelings she felt during the ceremony.

"I hope everyone was pleased," I replied.

"They were," she assured me.

She lay there contemplating the evening for a time, then stood up.

"Come," she told me, tugging me with her heart.

Already beginning to disrobe, she was completely undressed by the time she reached the water's edge. Stopping when the water was up to her knees, she reached backward, exposing her bare breast to me. Bathed by moonlight, the outline of her body cast her silhouette across the surface of the water.

"Come, sweet," she pleaded, her hand still reaching for me.

Undressing, I joined her and together we walked out into the deeper water. When our feet could no longer touch the bottom, we began to swim. I stopped just before reaching the opposite bank while Louisa nuzzled up behind me, putting her arms around my waist.

"It's cold," she said.

"I know."

With the water too cold for us to find comfort, I asked, "Do you want to get out?"

Nodding her answer to me, we swam back to the shore and returned to the blanket. Laying her body next to mine, she trembled from the cool night air breezing across her wet skin. As I pressed my lips to her shoulder, I noticed the softness of her skin and felt the strength of her arm. Kissing her neck, I leaned up and traced my fingers across the side of her breast, down to her belly, stopping just below her navel. Softly caressing her stomach, she began to cry.

"What's wrong?" I asked, as she began to deeply sob. "It's okay. Nothing could be that bad."

Waiting for her tears to free her, I asked again, "Tell me, sweet."

"I'm afraid you'll be upset with me," she breathily answered through her tears.

"I don't think so," I softly replied.

"I didn't mean for it to happen. I really didn't think that it would."

"What, love? What has happened?"

Gathering herself, her face revealed her frustration with herself, "I'm with child."

"Are you certain?"

Nodding, her tears finished, but her eyes could not rise to meet mine.

"What is so bad about that?" I asked.

"I'm afraid it's not what you want," she answered.

"No, Louisa. Don't do this to yourself," I insisted. "We can handle this. It would not have happened if it were not to be. You are very important to me—much too important to have you upset."

Feeling her heart becoming lighter, she could not yet trust that my love for her would remain constant. Leaning down, I placed a kiss upon her stomach, "You'll see."

"You will want us both?" she asked.

"Yes."

"And never push us away?" she asked.

"Never," I promised.

*

Of my most troublesome knights, William was among the worst. Believing I had the best of everything, he spent large amounts of energy lusting after the life I lived. Endearing friendships, romance and particularly my Kingship, fueled his obsession. One of his recent fascinations had become Louisa.

While I visited Pelly, William stayed behind at Camelot with a plan to steal her affections. Speaking privately to her, he told her that I was having an affair with a young girl in Pelly's court. Already feeling vulnerable with the pregnancy, Louisa grew deeply distressed. And when I returned from my trip, she was livid.

"I know about her," she informed me.

"Who?" I asked, still innocently unconcerned.

"You know who!" she demanded, her stern expression surprising me. "I know why you go to Pelly's so often. You're lady friend."

Seated squarely in the lavish armchair beside her bed, the certainty shown from her face was unnerving.

"Who have you been talking to?" I asked, wondering who might have done this to me.

"Why would that matter?" she asked, looking away from me.

"Because it is a lie," I answered, taking a seat upon her bed.

Pausing in thought, she then asked, "Why would anyone make that up?"

"I can think of a thousand reasons. Who told you this?" I insisted.

"One of your knights."

"Perhaps William? The one that continually lusts over you?"

"Yes," she reluctantly volunteered.

"I think it's obvious he would like to have you for himself."

"How could he say those things?" she said, as her anger toward me began to weaken.

"Some people are in a different place than we are," I answered.

Feeling the truth coming from me, she became embarrassed by her accusations. With his energy so deliberately disorienting, she would have to understand his suffering and his pain if she was going to find protection from him. It was hard for her to understand anyone being so desperate.

Part of the challenge in creating Camelot was to be conscious in the midst of darkness. And as part of the group that was bringing light to a place where it had not existed, if our love was to endure, we would have to find deeper trust within ourselves.

*

Finding it very difficult to interact in the world with such a firm hand, while remaining gentle enough to be touched by my dear Louisa, I felt myself becoming vulnerable in our world, and in my relationship with her. In mid conversation, while alone with her in our chamber, I changed the subject.

"I am so overwhelmed," I confessed, taking a seat across from her. "I just cannot deal all day long with these petty complaints."

"What's wrong?" she replied, surprised by my confusion.

"These Kings – they cannot maintain peace in their lands. I'm finding it very hard to help them and to maintain my vision," I answered.

"I wish you wouldn't invite them here so often."

"I only invite them to prevent them from warring with each other. They can hardly wage war against each other when they are here."

"I wish they were more self-sufficient," she told me.

"I don't see that as possible." Thinking to myself, I added, "I hate what their energy does to me."

From her seat upon our bed, her soft eyes drew me closer and I took a seat by her side. With long sweeping motions the length of my spine, she caressed my back.

"I must go to the forest."

She nodded an agreement.

Moments later, I found myself walking through the groves of trees in *our* lush and magical forest. Prepared for a lengthy stay, I decided to abstain from food, desiring to make a deeper connection with Earth's energies while sorting out the uncertainties that had been placed in my life.

Walking beneath the tree canopy, I found my seat of stone, sat down and looked across the meadow. With no deer in sight, I looked up to the aged oak towering above me, still seeing no sign of life. I waited.

By the end of the day I had grown hungry and my body was beginning to weaken its connection to the physical earth as my mind expanded toward the spiritual dimension. As dusk arrived, an owl landed on a branch above my head and called out, "*Who Whooo.*" I began to feel alive.

Feeling my vision returning, I took a seat on the ground, wanting to be in touch with the earth while drifting half-awake, half-asleep throughout the night. As the sun crested the horizon, the moon released its pull upon me and I stood up, deciding to walk deeper into the forest.

With my body growing weaker from the lack of food, I could feel myself entering into a heightened state of awareness as the forest began to breathe life back into me. My mind was once again expanding and with my hope returning, I began to feel very tired and decided to rest. Upon reaching the entrance to a grove of Pecan trees, I took a seat on a thick bed of leaves beneath a towering Pecan. Feeling slumber reaching for me, I lay down and drifted off to sleep.

With my physical body asleep, my mind began aligning with the spiritual dimension, and as I became more conscious, I realized—that I was listening to Jesus speak.

"You have been born into a world of desperation, but you do not have to become desperate," he told me. "Never forget, the petty quarrels here are illusion. Don't believe in them. Remain focused on the creation of your vision."

In this state of being, with my spirit aligned with higher vibrations, my ego was non-existent. Remaining open, I desired only to be fed by his truth.

"This sanctuary is a magical place," he continued, speaking of the forest that was so dear to me. "Here, you will find healing. This place will whisper truths to you in times of greatest need—Never forget."

Finding myself drawn deeper into the grove, it seemed I was floating as I moved toward the sounds of life, love and laughter that emanated from its center. Stopping, the moment I saw visions set amongst the Pecans, my eyes focused upon an ethereal castle, one that seemed to drift in between the dimensions, and—one with *no exterior* walls.

With many interior partitions and levels to distinguish individual rooms, the perimeter was open to the forest—and had even become a part of it, with vines growing along the tops of the inner walls, cascading down into the rooms. Long Pecan branches helped to form floors, having grown into the structure.

In front of a grand archway at the castle's entrance, many people stood in a receiving line. Dressed in formal attire, they seemed to be awaiting my arrival. And as I traveled toward them, I heard a distant voice, *"You may stay for a moment."*

Stopping at the head of the line, a man reached for my hand, shaking it, "Arthur, we are so happy that you have come." Nodding to him, I felt the woman at his side reach over to touch my arm, "I know you have forgotten us, but we have never forgotten you. We are always with you."

Elegantly dressed in a long and flowing ruby gown, her eyes sparkled, revealing to me the unearthly quality of hope that a being from beyond this dimension carries. Returning her smile, I intuitively made my way down the line as the man next to her began to speak, "Arthur, I've never left your side, not for a single moment."

Glancing down the line, my eyes revealed to me an endless number of faces, all looking toward me as they offered their hope and blessings. Then feeling an overwhelming pressure, my spirit was pulled back to where my physical body lay. In an instant, I was back inside my body, although I did not yet wake, but instead remained in an unconscious and restful sleep.

A cardinal landed upon a low branch just a few feet above my head. Singing his morning song, he called with his heart as my eyes opened for the first time since falling asleep. Perched on an opposite branch, were two of his mates. Hearing a sound on the ground to my left, I lifted my head to see a doe grazing, barely twenty feet away. Then turning my head up to the sky, I closed my eyes as the memories of the dream state reached for the surface.

In awe of what I had witnessed, I was weak from the absence of food, and barley aware of my physical surroundings. More focused in the world of spirit than in the physical realm, I knew it was time to return to the earth. Time to eat food and time to pull the power of my visions into this dimension. Laying still for a moment longer, the cardinal again called, *"Wake up, Wake up, Wake up."*

Realizing I had received my vision and feeling all of the support the spirit world had to offer, I stood up, and began the long walk back to Camelot.

*

Still only twenty-two years old, and just months beyond the creation of the Roundtable, I had already encountered many life experiences when Louisa's pregnancy came to full term. It was late in the evening, during one of the coldest months of winter. Standing by the fire in the dim birthing room, I watched over her, as she lay in bed, the midwife standing by her side.

Keeping the room at a comfortable temperature, the fire was the room's only source of light. Shadows from the flickering flames danced across the low ceiling.

Louisa, perhaps not completely secure in bringing a child into a chaotic world, seemed to be resisting.

It was not an easy birth. Louisa's head tossed from side to side as the agonizing contractions wrenched her body. Her face pale and dripping of sweat, she reached for my hand. Grabbing a stool, I took a seat by her side allowing her to squeeze my hand, "I'm here, love."

Forcing a smile, she returned to her focus of bringing our child into the world. Caressing her forehead, I pulled the stray locks of hair away from her face, "It won't be long now."

Hearing a knock at the door, a small shaft of light entered the room as the midwife cracked open the door. Jasper, standing in the corridor, handed her towels and a large pot of water. Nodding to me, he turned away as the door closed behind him and the midwife walked over to the fire, adding the water to a pot already hanging above the flames. Then she turned toward me as Louisa moaned—our child was ready.

Handing Louisa a towel, she gripped both ends, twisting it into a knot as the pain of birthing moved through her body. But just moments later, our son found his way into our world. Taking his blood-covered body into my hands—I raised him high into the air as the firelight bathed his body.

"Denby, my love, you've made it," I told him.

Lowering him to my lips, I kissed him and bringing him close to my body, walked over to Louisa. Kneeling down beside her, I laid him upon her breast.

"There you are," she smiled. "Did you not wish to come?"

Reaching for the chair, I took a seat as the midwife left the room. Feeling our blessings, we realized that we had been touched—by a beautiful child whose mere presence brought more of *our* energy into the earth.

* * *

Along with one of the brightest moments of my life, a dark challenge of the future entered. Vivianne's hatred, continually seeking expression, often caused her to act in ways that were irrational and unruly.

Having seen weakness in my relationship with the church, she despised me for not restructuring the tax law. And with her greatest desire to see my kingship fail, she devised a plan to help me toward what she believed to be an unchangeable future. By striking at me very subtly, she wished to injure me from the inside, focusing her attentions in my life, on what she believed to be a great weakness—love.

Knowing that I loved and cared for my people and family, Vivianne saw opportunity. By taking my dearest love from me, she finally reasoned—I would be rendered powerless.

Shortly after the alliance had been created, Pope Titus' heart had turned against me. Believing that I had formed a platform from which he could speak, his initial enthusiasm for me turned to hatred when he realized that I had no plans to help him exert his authority over the country. Personally condemning me, he swore to find a way to cause me anguish.

By herself, Vivianne could not bring her plan into full fruition, but there was a wealthy benefactor who might be interested in her scheme—Titus.

Although he refused any direct association with her plan, he did agree to fund any worthwhile project that would cause me to suffer. And together, they decided that if many of my loved ones found their untimely deaths, I would be weakened in such a way that another could take my place—or so they hoped.

*

With my spiritual life and power still continuing to expand, I began to reach a very high internal state of being and daily trips to the forest were needed to keep me grounded in this world. Slowly transcending the earth's dimension, I perceived the physical world before me, to be an illusion.

Standing in the forest, I felt a deep sense of trust as I looked across to Camelot's meadow. As if a sound wave was enveloping me, my body seemed to be vibrating to an invisible pitch. My vision relaxing, another dimension opened up into my awareness. Although everything in the physical earth remained within my sight, it now seemed penetrable, almost transparent. Looking to my side, now within my conscious vision, stood the woman dressed in the ruby gown.

Nodding, her eyes sparkling endearingly, "And now, Arthur, you have accepted your power."

"What?" I asked.

"You have joined us, in our dimension," she told me. "You are no longer limited to the illusion."

The intensity of the energy felt overpowering, "I feel dizzy."

"It will take time for your body to adjust to this level—in accepting your power, you have allowed a great amount of light to enter your body. But in time, you will find this to be your natural state of being."

Barely aware of my surroundings, I was only focused upon her, "I have left the earth?"

"You are still part of the earth, and have the same work here—You have not died—just transcended the earth's dimension," she explained.

"I can live in both worlds?"

"Yes, that is what you have done, agreed to live in both worlds. You have done this in many lives, so you needn't be upset," she smiled. "We can speak directly with you now."

Kneeling down upon one knee, I placed my hand upon the earth—still needing more connection; I took a seat in front of her and pushed my hands beneath the dead leaves, digging them into the soil.

"You will be fine," she assured me. "It will just take time to adjust."

I began to grind my teeth together.

"We must go now, our direct meeting is still a challenge to your beliefs," she explained. "But as I have said, we are always with you and always will be. We will meet again soon, when you feel more comfortable."

Nodding to me, she released me back into the earth's dimension, where I was no longer able to perceive her existence.

*

Knowing the depth of Louisa's love for me inspired me to give her more of my own. And with her twenty-third birthday approaching, I held a banquet in her honor. All of our closest friends were invited—it began with a toast.

"My dearest Louisa. This evening is to celebrate your birthday. You've only experienced Camelot with your presence and cannot know what impact you have made upon us. But we see your gifts to us," I began, my arm outstretched, holding a goblet of wine. "Your presence lights us up, gives us hope and your gentleness lifts the hearts of all who enter here. I am, we are, grateful that you have chosen to make Camelot your home," I told her, lifting my glass.

Feeling a hundred blessings being bestowed upon her at once, it was more than she was prepared for, and a flood of emotion overwhelmed her. Her tears washing away all the doubt she carried about my love, she could, at least for this moment deeply trust in herself. With her petty fears seeming ridiculous, her beauty radiated outward. Then she asked to speak.

"I don't know if I deserve this, but I will at least pretend that I do," she tearfully told us. "Few of you knew me before I arrived here. You don't know what impact you have had on me. But I have never felt so accepted; I have never known so much joy. That is your gift to me. I think I must have made the better deal," she said, laughing through her tears. "It is a dream beyond a dream to be here. I can only thank you for making me a part of it."

Then she added, "And I adore all of you."

Flaming arrows, fired by archers, flew over our heads, toward targets secured in the ceiling—and the games began. Knife and ax throwing competition were first, before the effects of the ale could be felt, then we listened to the beautiful melodies of the Celtic musicians.

A powerful time in Camelot's history, it seemed that our battles with darkness had finally been completed, that there would never again be a need to fall from the great spiritual heights that we had achieved. For us, heaven and earth were becoming one.

Late in the evening, I grabbed Louisa's hand and we snuck away into the forest. Tonight, I had a special gift for her.

The darkness remaining in her own body had prevented her from completely understanding what we were about to do. But the tears she shed had cleansed her, opening her up to greater possibilities.

"Do you trust me?" I asked, standing beneath the ancient oak in Camelot's meadow.

"Yes."

"Just know that we are completely safe," I reassured her.

Her trust allowing her to feel my feelings, when I relaxed my vision, she followed, allowing us to open a doorway into a world of light. Walking through the dimensions, we stopped on Glastonbury Tor.

Gasping, she pressed the palm of her hand against her chest, "What happened?"

"We became light."

"My God," she replied, still dizzy from the power.

"It is shocking," I said. "It's not like anyone ever speaks of this possibility."

Looking across the water, she allowed her energy to ground.

"I guess not many people become this open," she said.

"One day, it will be quite common."

"It will be a beautiful day."

Walking around the Tor, we enjoyed its beauty, as the light filling our bodies allowed us to feel the highest spiritual truths. Our openness had made us more aware of the God energy than of the earth, and we needed a moment to become more aware of our physical surroundings.

Taking off her shoes, Louisa walked to the water's edge, her foot disappearing below the surface with each step. Louisa loved the water.

"Would you like to travel anywhere else?" I asked. "It is your night."

"This has been quite a lot," she answered, carefully placing each step in the water.

"I hope it's not too much?" I inquired.

"No, just enough—an evening that I could not possibly forget. One I will never forget it," she said.

"I'm glad."

"Our world is filled with such extremes," she said. "In one moment, we are in the midst of petty liars and tragic events, and in the next, we're almost in the presence of God."

"It is very disorienting," I agreed.

Shaking her head from side to side, her hair brushed free from her shoulders, "But it is the only world that has been given to us." She smiled, "There must be some purpose to it all."

Reaching for my hand, we walked in silence admiring the night sky's constellations, mirrored across the top of the water. And seeing that her eyes were tiring, that her body was beginning to desire sleep, I eased her into the real world of light and back to our illusion—Camelot.

*

With our dream of Camelot existing at its peak, the consciousness of the world was very open to the magic of God's hope, as it often is during the beginning of a new millennium—and yet another gift for our world was about to arrive.

A surprise for the people, although they truly had been prepared—the mythical lost sword had returned, bringing with it a boy king. And many events throughout the ages had come to the earth, as our consciousness would permit. Now, it was time for another.

It was first seen in the early morning, as the dense fog began to lift. Protruding through the mist as they entered into the physical earth, large stones assembled together that had been waiting in a dimension just beyond the earth's awareness, waiting for a time when the people could witness an event that would indelibly imprint in their minds that powers existed far beyond the consciousness of man. The time had now come, and with it, the massive stones of Stonehenge appeared. And the world would never forget.

*

Often spending the afternoon alone in the library, I sat there gazing out the window. One of the few places in the castle where I could find solitude, I used my time there to contemplate the events of the day.

Louisa knocked on the heavy oak door. Walking to the entrance where she waited, I pushed back the round wooden bolt, and swung the door open. Walking in unusually reserved, Louisa signaled to me that something had upset her.

"I've heard you are planning a trip to Pelly's," she told me.

"Yes, that's right," I answered, returning to my chair, allowing my body to deeply enjoy its comfort.

Her eyes widened with a growing mistrust.

"Louisa, you know it's much too dangerous for you to go," I told her before any additional words escaped her mouth. "I could not live if anything happened."

I could easily sense her feelings of mistrust were not dissipating.

"Louisa," I begged. "Please don't ask this of me."

But her eyes found no comfort, "You cannot ensure my safety?" she uneasily asked.

"It's a risk, one I'd rather not take," I answered.

Seeing her heart weakening, she was growing distant.

"Please, it is very dangerous," I assured her.

I found her unspoken mistrust to be crippling.

Unable to find a solution, "You may travel with us," I nodded. "You will find Pelly's home to be of no threat to you."

Warmly received by Pelly, our stay might have been memorable, had I been able relax and enjoy myself. But for some reason, I could not take my mind off of the trip home and gladly greeted the final day of our stay. Riding beside Louisa and ahead of the others, Alden and another knight were close behind.

Slowly walking our horses down the road, already a great distance from Pelly's castle, we reached a bend in the road forced upon us by the landscape. Curving around a mound in the land, the forested area ahead greatly limited our vision. Naturally dropping back with Louisa, Alden and another rode ahead of us. But the moment the road straightened, my worst nightmare became reality. Several men on horseback were riding toward us in a full gallop.

Turning Bay around, I called out to Louisa, "Look into my eyes!" I told her, hoping that she would follow me into the next dimension, certain that Alden could handle this situation on his own.

But it was too late. Louisa's fear, I could do nothing about. She would be held in the earth's dimension and we would have to face this situation directly.

Pulling Bay up, I brought her to a stop as my knights gathered around us, positioning Louisa in the center, to best protect her as we waited for the group to approach. Within seconds, we were surrounded.

Fifteen men walked their horses around our perimeter as they eyed Louisa. Wearing worn and unwashed clothing, they seemed to barely be able to provide for themselves. It might seem unlikely that such a group would be willing to make a challenge, but they were desperate men living desperate lives, willing to risk without concern for the outcome.

"What do you want?" I asked.

The men laughed. One man, heavily scarred upon his cheek and arm answered, "The girl."

Then without warning—they charged. Even though their inexperience cost them heavily, several of them soon falling from their horses, it would only take one of them to reach Louisa, to deliver a wound to her that would turn her white dress—red.

Pulling her from her horse before she lost consciousness, I sat her in front of me and with both arms holding her in position, I urged Bay home. Having completed their mission, the few surviving attackers scattered separately into the forest, while my knights followed me closely.

We were still a few hours from Camelot and I made no effort to slow down, allowing Bay make the trip as fast as she could, although it was a mere formality. I had seen the wound to her stomach and already knew of the result. It was as if we pretended that all would be okay—but it would not. My life would never be the same again. Louisa was only moments from her death, and there was nothing that I, nor anyone else could do.

By the time we had reached Camelot, we held our horses in a slow walk. There was no hurry, no further reason to rush. Walking Bay up to the den before dismounting, I refused any help, carrying Louisa's lifeless body inside to the room where we would share our grief for her.

As word of Louisa's death spread, many people traveled to Camelot to offer their condolences. Joining me in my grief, the knights helped me to prepare for her funeral the following day. Even William tried to help me find comfort.

"I'm very sorry, Arthur," he told me, as I stood with several men in the grieving room.

"Sorry! Sorry!" I repeated. "Now your sorry?"

"It's a horrible," he explained.

"What are you sorry about? Lying to her, or her resulting death from your actions?" I demanded.

"I don't know what you're talking about," he answered.

"You don't. Do I need to remind you of your lies?"

"Me? Perhaps it was her?" he accused.

"You God damn son-of-a-bitch!" I yelled, jumping on top of him and knocking him to the ground. Violently pounding my fists to his face, "I kill you, you son-of-a-bitch."

With several knights pulling me from his body, he continued to lie on the floor for the moment, trying to regain his consciousness.

"I'll kill you, that I promise!" I yelled to him, held back by my men.

Realizing he was no longer welcome at the castle, William hastily made his way to the stables, and finding his horse, traveled far away from Camelot.

Grieving for Louisa, I often found myself at her gravesite, laying on the huge black block of granite that had been carved into her headstone. Ten feet in length, its large letters read, *Louisa 984*.

Months had passed and unable to get beyond my suffering—a large part of my soul left the earth—leaving my body barely alive. Having been my inspiration in countless lives, I was refusing to go on without her—it was just that God had not agreed. For some reason, I had been left here—alone, surrounded by many soulless wanderers of the earth.

With my faith in God shattered, I could not believe that any further good could come to me. I struggled for months, barely able to make the choices that each day required of a king.

But finally coming to the realization that I must continue with my life, I pushed my pain far from my consciousness, while unconsciously magnetizing many difficult life lessons as a result. In need of healing, the worldly pressures remained upon me.

With my ego strengthening itself around my wound, a sense of power did return, although I was different now. I did not smile so easily, and my innocent wonder had become far removed my life. My forgotten anger tainted all of my actions, sending me on a collision course with the world as its harshness moved closer into my life.

* * *

Lott had a son who might be described as impulsive, manipulative and by some, perhaps even half crazy. Another soul whom I shared karma with, it was inevitable that he would one day find me. And after the loss of Louisa, I was ready for a challenge, something to make me forget how much I still suffered. Magnetizing such a person to come to me as if I were a wounded animal, within a year of Louisa's death he arrived.

Very much the charmer, Gawain quickly captured me. Wanting to forget my pain, I desired to give away some of my power. It was a great burden for me now, with my sense of self-trust so badly damaged. In his own past lives, he could never hold onto a kingship and he now sought the next best thing, an influencable king, and one who could give him the sense of the authority he desired.

Although we had only just met, our past connection made it feel as if we were brothers and feeling very hopeful around him, he could sense that I wanted him to be a part of Camelot. He promptly expressed his own sentiment.

Sitting on the verandah, after sharing a private meal, he told me, "I'm finished with my father."

"You're welcome to stay here."

"At Camelot? You would allow me to live here?" he humbly asked.

"Certainly. You are very deserving, just to have endured this long with your father is a great accomplishment," I laughed.

Sharing my laughter, he added, "It would be a great honor."

"Then it's settled."

Expecting Jasper to be pleased about Gawain's arrival, I was shocked by his reaction.

"You did what?" he yelled. "God damn Lott's boy lives here now! Have you have forgotten where this castle came from! Well I can assure you Lott has not. Gawain is part of his plan."

Having done what felt natural to me, I didn't know how to respond, but silently thought about Gawain's sincerity as Jasper continued to curse my action.

"This boy will take all that you have! Mark my word, Arthur, he is not your friend!"

"I can't just send him away," I said.

"And why not? You have no idea how vicious those people can be," he demanded, referring to the Lott family.

Having never seen Jasper respond like this, I was confused by the choices presented to me.

"I just need some time. I'll watch him closely and if he makes even the slightest error, he's gone," I assured him.

Finding little comfort with my answer, Jasper inwardly fumed, "Arthur, you cannot see what you are doing."

"He seems sincere. Am I suppose to judge him differently than everyone else?"

Shaking his head, "He will be the end of Camelot."

Jasper's influence upon Camelot ran deep—our courage depended upon him. He was the one who taught us how to defend ourselves in the physical world and his contagious self-confidence brought us protection.

To ensure our safety, Jasper regularly challenged us at arms, making certain that we were all well skilled. With the honing of our fighting skills his full responsibility, I seldom turned down an invitation to train with him.

On one particular day, he had invited all of the knights to gather in the courtyard for a demonstration. Wishing to engage two knights in combat, Alden and myself, we knew that he would likely defeat us both.

The three of us walked into the center of the courtyard as we held an audience of perhaps a hundred. Jasper, raising his sword, signaled the competition began. Walking in circles around us, he still found time to keep his eye on Gawain. A small amount of dust from the dry ground began to rise into the air.

Keeping Alden wedged between us, he seldom gave me an opportunity to directly face him. With a large amount of energy directed at Alden, who was already weakening from the exchange of many blows, Jasper would have to finish him soon if he was to have any energy remaining for me.

In haste, Alden made his error. Stepping too far forward, Jasper grabbed his arm and first pulled him off balance, then to the ground. In an instant, he had tapped him on his backside with the tip of his blade, signaling his death. It was now between Jasper and myself.

If Alden had weakened him any, I could not feel it; he seemed as strong to me as during any of our many previous sparring matches, our swords often clashing during the years he had spent preparing me to be King. But now there seemed to be a sense of urgency existing that I had not felt before— and it fueled our sword fight.

After close to an hour of constant battle, we had both grown tired. The heavy swords refused to be lifted so easily and our pace had slowed.

I felt something that I had never known before—the weakening of Jasper's heart. Deeply disturbing, I somehow felt responsible.

Easing the intensity of my sword, I prepared to accept defeat.

"I believe you have me, Arthur," Jasper told me. Obvious to me that we had not seen all of Jasper's ability, I could also see that he could not access it.

"And I was just about to concede," I told him. Walking to his side, I placed the tip of my blade into the ground, leaning the hilt against my armored leg. Reaching for him, I wrapped my arms around his body.

"Well, let us remember this day," I laughed. "Not likely to happen again."

"It was only a matter of time Arthur, I am an old man."

I could feel his heavily winded breath rushing by my ear.

Jasper's strength was needed within our order, and to see him weakening, terribly frightened me.

Upset by what she had seen, Jasper's young girlfriend decided that she could settle the matter for us, cornering me in the corridor as I walked to the den. Her hardened and angry eyes had no patience for me.

"What do you think you are doing, Arthur?" she demanded, her thin body appearing much less threatening than her voice.

"I'm walking to the den."

"You know what I'm talking about! Why have you brought Gawain here?" she demanded, the top of her head several inches below a candle sconce hanging from the stone wall.

"I believe this matter does not concern you," I told her, trying to make my way past her.

Standing in my way, "Doesn't concern me?" she yelled, my words sparking her rage. "It God damn does concern me if it involves Jasper. And it should concern you!"

"I will not discuss this," I said, feeling weaker by the moment.

"Oh yes you will!"

Listening to my grandfather's lover tell me how to run my affairs, I became speechless, unconsciously opening myself to more abuse.

"You tell Gawain to get the hell out of here and to go back to that son-of-a-bitch he left!" she demanded, her curses extending to Gawain's father.

Just a few feet from the den, Jasper easily heard her yell above the roar of the men's voices, and walking up behind her, reached around her waist and lifted her off the ground.

"I'm very sorry, Arthur," he told me, as he carried her toward their chambers.

"God damn it, Jasper!" she continued. "I'm not yet finished with that little bastard! Someone will have to . . ." her voice began to trail off after turning the corner, although she could still be heard cursing me for several minutes.

I stood alone in the corridor briefly, then continued to the den, trying to deny the reminder—that my heart had grown weak.

One who needed a degree of control over his environment to feel safe, Jasper became uneasy with all of the changes taking place at Camelot. Too many people came through our gates now for him to feel comfortable, and with the addition of Gawain, his life had become almost unbearable. A part of him knew that I was less able to protect myself now and with the passing of each day, his anger grew until it could no longer be hidden. Boiling to the surface, it found Gawain.

His karmic memory of Gawain fueled Jasper's growing hatred of him and more often, he found fault with him. Gawain's hatred for Jasper had no choice but to grow.

Feeling barriers growing around Jasper's heart, many began to feel his betrayal. Unable to understand that much of his hatred had followed him from the past, from lives prior, Jasper's hatred magnetized more conflict for the future. I felt helpless. And with our karma holding us together like a knot—we could only accept our fate and be forced to face yet more life changing events.

*

Months since he had left the Roundtable, William's conscience deeply troubled him. Having pretended that his life at Camelot was unimportant to him, he was still haunted by its memory, a memory that would finally bring him back to us, to face me and to try to make peace.

Apologizing, William stood before me in defeat, as if his life had been taken from him. I listened.

"I'm truly sorry, Arthur," he told me. "I had no idea what might happen."

I waited and listened.

"I'm not asking for anything," he shook his head.

"My life mate has left. Do you know how weak that makes me?" I calmly asked.

"I'm sorry," he said. Seeing his face deeply grieved, I could no longer find any hatred for him. And believing that he had committed an error so horrible that redemption was not possible, he turned to leave.

"Stay for the feast," I told him. "You've been missed."

Unable to take his hope from him, I allowed him to remain. With others around me far more dangerous than William, sending him away seemed to be of little importance.

*

Gwenevere's love, traveling in many directions, had perhaps found its greatest match with my knight Lancelot. In him, she knew a familiarity that did not exist with me. It was the distance of her heart that had caused me to search for greater love than she could offer—and why shouldn't she seek a romantic partner better able to suit her? I had.

Accepting what love she had for me, I allowed her the freedom that her soul needed to thrive, although I did fear for her, feared the law that made infidelity to a king, an act of treason. Even though she was not my greatest love, she was a love that I needed.

Understanding that many in the kingdom did not share my sentiment about Gwenevere's affairs, it was troubling for me to hear rumors of them. Knowing what the church was capable of doing, of how they might find offense with her, I could only pray that she would be left alone, to live her life in peace.

*

After receiving an invitation to visit King Pelly, I left for his castle along with several knights. Approaching his lands that evening with a desire to surprise Pelly with fresh meat, we spent the last few hours of daylight hunting. Alone with Jasper, we had just taken a deer for our meal when a powerful knight approached. His presence, otherworldly, made me consider that he was here as a test.

"Great King, I challenge you," he called out to me. Pulling the reigns to the right, his horse followed, making his way around a tree in forest before stepping over a fallen tree that lay between us.

"We have no quarrel knight. Leave us be."

"I cannot do that."

"You have no free will?" I asked.

"I only reflect the choices that *you* have made. I wish to engage your knight."

Looking toward Jasper, I shrugged my shoulders. Confidant in his ability to protect himself, I watched as he prepared to receive the knight's attack. Heavily wooded, there was barely an opening among the trees to permit a joust.

With their horses in full gallop, their poles met at the base of the ravine, destroying my sense of well-being. I watched Jasper fall to the ground. Walking up to Jasper, he held his sword above him.

"Great King. I will spare his life if you will accept the challenge," he said.

Nodding, I walked my horse over to where Jasper lay. Leaning across the saddle horn, I reached for his hand and pulled him to his feet. Taking his jousting pole, I edged Bay through the trees, seeking a good distance before beginning.

Pulling Bay's reigns to the right, she wheeled around to face the knight. With my eyes meeting my aggressor's, I eased Bay into a gallop and when I reached a clearing in the trees, I urged her forward. Digging her feet into the soft dirt, she flew toward the knight. If my pole were to even graze him, he stood no chance at this speed.

Deflecting his pole, mine landed squarely in his chest, sending him tumbling to the ground. At her leisure, I allowed Bay to turn around and return to where he lay. Except for the sounds of the winded knight and Bay's feet softly pressing into the earth, the forest was quiet. I dismounted and walked over to him.

"So knight, what choice have I made that would cause you to risk your life?"

"Choices that have yet to show your err," he answered.

"You are free to speak," Burying the tip of my sword into the earth, I sat down on a large stone in front of him.

"I ask *you* King, why risk your knight? If I had not shown mercy, he would not now be with you."

Turning to Jasper, I felt remorse for my actions, for unnecessarily risking his life. Appreciative of the wisdom offered by the knight, when I turned back to him—he was no longer there, having disappeared into the ethers.

Abruptly turning toward Jasper, I paused, "We need to get to Pelly's."

The encounter with the knight left me stunned, his words haunting me throughout my stay. Unable to feel safe in his court, I only desired to return to Camelot. And as soon as Pelly would allow, we left.

Within hours of our departure, challenged again in the forest, a voice called from a distance, "I challenge you King, to a test of arms."

Leading my horse down a large forested hill, I saw the knight through the trees. Feeling unusually protective of Jasper, I carefully considered my options.

"We have no quarrel knight," I told him with resolve.

Understanding that I had no intention of fighting, he was not yet ready to concede his challenge.

"Then grant me a challenge of words," the knight insisted.

"Speak your mind."

"It requires the telling of a story, one that I believe you will find endearing."

I nodded.

"It is not an unusual story, a story of a land ruled by a king unworthy of his people. The king, having forgotten that his people had given him the crown, acted without concern for their welfare. In time, his crown was lost," he paused. "Then the crown went to a promising young king who had a heart for his people. For a time, he remained strong and was greatly loved, but truth began to slip away. Desperate ones around him caused him to forget his beliefs and the truths that once ruled his heart grew into only a faint memory."

"Your point?" I asked.

"His people felt betrayed by him," he answered, stopping as he focused all of his attention toward me.

"It is a sad story," I said.

"I promised you a challenge King, and this it is," he paused. "Why will you betray your people?"

Again momentarily stunned, I turned away. When I looked back toward him, he had disappeared.

I had come to the earth in these dark times because I believed that I could make a difference. Knowing many mistakes would be made; I accepted the opportunity to be a part of Camelot's creation, a chance to help create a history that could inspire generations into the future.

And now the spirit world was challenging me, trying to help me to stay conscious of myself and of what I felt to be my purpose. But my pain was anxiously tugging me toward sleep.

*

It had been during a prior lifetime when the church forced me to drink poison, for teaching spiritual secrets of the earth, when the karma between us had been created.

Even in this day, Titus, my enemy from the past and now the Pope, remained my adversary. Believing that I was getting in his way, he saw me as the one stopping the creation of his vision. I didn't need him to create *my* vision, but his, required my obedience. And because I would not oblige him, as he demanded, he remained determined to destroy me.

With the church demanding large amounts of tax revenue from the people, Camelot was pressured into mediating many unnecessary battles. I was in the castle when word came to me of a skirmish that had taken place in a small town. Jasper, along with Gawain and several others had been dispatched there to resolve matters with the church, the town having thrown their tax collector out.

While I was in the earth, I would never know the truth of what had next occurred, but it was a day to deeply grieve me.

No one noticed anything unusual—until Jasper fell from his horse. Having snuck up from behind, an enemy had run a sword through his side. Jasper was killed.

Immediately upon hearing of his death, I slumped to the floor. Almost throwing up, I felt too much pain to withhold my tears. For a brief moment, I could feel the mistake of my actions, of allowing the church to influence my Kingship—then I went numb.

Completely unprepared for Jasper to leave, I still heavily relied upon him. And realizing that I didn't have the confidence to continue without him, my fear turned to terror. Managing to drag myself up the stairs and into my chambers, I bolted the door, laying in darkness for several hours before finally drifting off into a black and dreamless sleep.

Awaking the following morning, I was forced to face the reality of what had been created. Jasper was gone—and I was left alone to deal with violent men and violent tempers. What we had together created was now my responsibility alone. Having not fully understood his gift to Camelot, anxiety began to take control of me as my ego hardened, soon convincing myself that he was never really needed.

It was very hard for me to face Jasper's murder and I never understood how it could have happened. Murdered from behind? It was not conceivable to me that he could have erred in such a way. But I would not see the truth until I left the earth. Jasper was not at fault. He made no mistake, at least not in that moment. His murderer, one that I believed could be trusted, was one of our own group—Gawain.

The loss of Louisa had splintered my soul. The loss of Jasper crushed it. With the largest portion of my energy forced from body, what remained in the earth was not enough to maintain the dream of Camelot. Even though my body continued to function, I was fast asleep and my heart, no longer free to lead.

* * *

Similar in nature to the House of Avalon, Merlin's residence was a home and sanctuary where many druids lived and practiced their earth-based spirituality. With one of our knights missing, rumors spread that the men of this home had murdered him. Doubting the rumor, but still weak from my losses, the knights could feel my lack of resolve.

Gawain, outspoken after the loss of Jasper, created a breech of trust within the Roundtable. Privately convincing several knights of Merlin's guilt, he rallied the necessary support to take the matter into his own hands. The men, having found Gawain to be of greater heart than myself, followed him in an attack of their home, to avenge the death of our knight. Heath, Galahad, McCoy and others made their charge, entering their home, leaving no man alive. Merlin, along with many of his apprentices—killed. Leif had been at Camelot during the attack.

With the loss of the key figures of our dream, control of the Kingship was almost non-existent. With no time for me to heal, and the land needing a strong king to act immediately, Camelot demanded that its destiny be controlled. Swallowing my pain, and closing the door to my greatest wisdom, I found the smallest remaining piece of my soul. Gathering the knights at the Roundtable, I forced my vision upon them.

"You have no idea what you have done," I began, my eyes showing signs of fatigue—my mind only able to see the impending doom. "This injustice that you have created, that we have created, is the birth of a nightmare. You cannot create desperation and expect peace. Our days are numbered. Do not expect this peace we have been blessed with to remain. We will soon return to the sword."

No longer in a state of being to see all of my choices, clouded by depression, I made the choice to teach the knights of the error in their actions. Allowing *all* of them to remain at Camelot, I devoted my energy into making them live their lives more truthfully. My destiny now was to fight myself, and the knights that were within my own home. Camelot's expansion into light was over.

*

Although the greatest potential for Camelot's hope had been extinguished, occasionally bright moments did still exist. I did have Igraine and my son, Denby. And there would be others to enter my life—some which would return from their untimely deaths, being reborn back into our world. But even so, my injuries had left me paralyzed and believing that I must fight darkness, and that no peace could exist as long as it remained a part of our world. Holding onto the world's darkness, I held onto my own pain as suffering reached further into my being.

Determined to control my environment, I began to turn the failure of Camelot around. Forcing unruly people to live more truthfully, my constant vigilance over them caused many to turn vicious.

Josephine, a niece to Lott, had arrived at Camelot just days before Gwenevere. After hearing of Lodegrance's plan to send Gwenevere, she was Lott's attempt to have his own blood live and grow within our castle.

The long dark locks of hair, often adorned with ribbons, reached well beyond her shoulders. Her soft and open eyes, marked with wisdom, triggered my memory of her. An ancient friend, I intuitively invited her in.

Although, I loved her immediately, it had been the danger surrounding Gwenevere that held my attention and Josephine happily found her place within our court, never returning to Lott.

A source of inspiration, she often found ways to lighten things up—once telling me a story about the witches. It seemed they had come to the belief that they could willfully make their house disappear from the earth's dimension. Having heard many stories about dimensional shifts around Camelot, they believed this was a power they could own. Alone with her in the library, she related her story, "Vivianne placed each one of the girls at different places in and around Avalon."

"You're making this up," I teased.

"No! I swear it's true!" she laughed. "She did. They were all supposed to imagine that the house disappeared."

I laughed openly.

"And Lancelot . . ." she said, breaking into laughter.

"Lancelot!" I said, lightly slapping my palm against the table. "Was he there?"

"Yes, poor Lancelot had the job of watching to see if it disappeared."

"No."

"I swear! The witches were furious when he broke the news to them. He was so shaken that he changed his story, saying that he thought it might have started to fade for a moment, and suggested they just needed a bit more practice."

"I don't believe this," I told her, pretending disbelief. Through her laughter, she promised, "I swear! I swear it is the truth!"

Laughing much of the morning over the witch's charades, I was thankful I had Josephine to spend time with. She was always a delight.

*

Occasionally spending the last few hours of the evening alone in the library, I spent my time there reflecting over the passing day, and in preparation for the new one.

Sitting at my desk, I was writing about the sense of loss I felt without Jasper, as I reached a moment where my ego had weakened. Sensing the air in front of me moving, I watched it take shape. Transforming, I began to see the outline of a man. Colors and textures filled the space until a clear vision of an unmistakable friend stood before me. His face marked with the compassion of God, he looked at me with all the sorrow of a cold and cruel world.

"Jasper?" I asked, in disbelief.

"I have never left your side," he answered, walking closer. "You've only now seen me."

"I can't believe it," I said, standing up from my chair as I walked toward him. "I couldn't believe you left. I never suspected that you could be taken."

"It was time—time for you to feel the full responsibility of this creation."

"I don't want it. I don't want to be here without you," I told him. "I've made such a mess of this life . . ."

"You have done what no one else could have done. You cannot be hard on yourself for that. It is all within the plan," he assured me.

Feeling pain inside of my chest, "I don't want to be here. I want to go with you."

"This is your place, Arthur. The people here are barely surviving. Without you, Camelot would crumble and the world would never know of your dream. It's so important that the earth remember the hope that has been created here. They will draw strength from it for centuries," he said.

"I don't see how I can live with such loneliness," I insisted, taking a seat on a stool by the bookshelves.

"There are others coming, you won't be alone forever. You'll see. Even your dearest Louisa has already returned," he said reassuring me.

Breaking down, my watery eyes pleaded, "Louisa?"

"Yes, of course she will return. But not immediately, she is still young."

Lifting my heart, hope returned to me as he reached over to touch my hand, "Don't give up. We are by your side."

His image fading, "I must go. But do not forget, I walk with you now, as always."

Disappearing, he returned to the world of spirit, while leaving me sitting alone—although more hopeful for the future.

Very open to the spirit world, my energy allowed beings from the other realms to interact with me in direct exchanges. Along with Jasper and greater beings of light, I knew that Merlin ached to return. It was no surprise to me when he turned up. Our exchanges, often distasteful, were like a relationship with a torturous sibling.

"Hello Arthur!" he commanded, his image appearing to step out of the library wall.

Looking up from my chair, I showed no surprise, "How have you been?"

"Well, I was doing fine until things got a little out of control over here at the castle," he said with contempt.

"You can't put the blame solely on my shoulders," I told him.

"I can't! And whose knights carried out that murderous rampage?" he demanded, his arms waving in the air.

"I'll take some of the blame, as I must, but you are the one that got yourself killed. Why did Gawain hate you enough to do it?" I answered.

"I will not listen to that!" he argued.

"Of course! Anything but the truth! You had an aversion to it when you were here, why change now?"

"You little bastard! How can you treat me like this? I've come here to help you and you can't even offer a simple apology," he whined, taking a seat upon a stool near the window.

"How about this? I'm sorry I don't want your help," I told him.

"You little shit! Well, you're going to be helped whether you like it or not, I will now assure you," he informed me. "I just don't understand. My place is with you, helping you. And you won't allow it."

"You're place was in the earth. You got yourself killed and now you come crying to me—because I'm the only one that can hear you!" I told him, feeling the burden of his presence.

"I guess it is true," he said, patronizing me. "No one wants me. Are you going to turn an old man away? I have nowhere else to go."

"Merlin, you do what you want. You always do what you want, regardless of anything that I might want. You're going to hang around here and annoy me and there is nothing that I can do about it," I answered.

"Oh thank you, thank you!" he teased. "You won't be sorry!"

And as quickly as he had entered, he was gone.

Knowing Merlin to be a mischief-maker, I knew before long, he would dramatically test us all. But something about this meeting brought comfort to me.

*

On a hot afternoon, I sat brooding alone in the library, feeling greatly overpowered by the knights. Unhappy with the Roundtable, I had yet to find resolve. My expression turned to surprise, as I heard the sounds of a warhorse entering our dimension.

Stepping through the library wall, entered a heavily dappled gray horse carrying a bold knight. Covered in armor, the great horse pranced in place, his reigns tightly held.

"Ah you King Atha?" the knight asked, in a heavily accented voice.

"I am," I answered, surprised by the presented adventure.

"Your knights need a King," he stated.

"Am I not a King?"

"Your knights have no discipline," he answered.

"Knights present problems to all kings," I answered.

"But these are the knights of the Roundtable. They should act with nobility," he demanded.

Irritated by his attempts to influence me, I asked, "Tell me, knight, what would you have me do? What would occupy a knight's mind during a time of peace?" I asked.

"A *Quest*!" he exclaimed. "Send them on a quest—to find something that they do not have."

Wheeling his horse around, together they leapt back through the wall, and back into their world of light.

Pondering his words, the advice from this unknown warrior sounded genuine, although I could not help doubting its merit. But as the days passed, a clearer vision was presented. And with it, the great Grail quests were born.

Believing that in searching for something of great value, I hoped the knights might find something much more precious—peace of mind. I prepared a third of my knights to immediately depart for the quest, seeking the Holy Grail. The rules were simple. One, they must treat each other and everyone they met with respect; and two, leave no stone unturned in their search.

At the end of two months, one group of knights would return and the next would depart. Proving in time to be successful, it exhausted the knights of excess energy that they might have otherwise used against each other or myself.

Alone in the library, I directed my thoughts upon the welfare of the country. Merlin, becoming bored with me, changed dimensions. Standing with his arms crossed, his head was tilted to the side, "You can't live in this box forever, Arthur. Why don't we go for a walk to the lake?"

"Yes, let's do," I agreed.

Walking through the courtyard and out the gate, I was a little disturbed that no one had acknowledged me. Having passed several people along the way, no one had even looked in my direction.

"Don't be so sensitive. They can't even see you," Merlin scolded.

"What?"

"When I appear to you as being fully physical, you have joined *my* dimension."

"Oh."

Following the winding road through the castle's meadow, we walked toward the lake passing beneath several ancient oaks scattered along the way. These were the grounds where I often played as a child and it was near here where I had first met Merlin, as my spirit began to free itself from the confines of earth.

Approaching the edge of the meadow, I could see the lake just beyond—a place that breathes magic to me. Tucked within the forest, its tall moss draped trees lined much of its shore, preventing winds from reaching the water, often leaving its surface almost mirror smooth.

Reaching the water, Merlin continued walking as if he hadn't noticed he'd left land several steps earlier and called out to me, "Won't you join me?"

"I prefer dry land," I answered, walking along the shore.

"Its just water. What are you afraid of?" he asked.

"You are a spirit," I told him, reaching down to the earth and picking up a small flake of quartz crystal.

"And you are not?" he asked, lifting his hands, palms turned upward.

"Merlin, I can't walk on water," I insisted, turning my head.

"How do know? Have you ever tried to?" he asked.

Slightly annoyed, and realizing he would persist until I had at least made an attempt, I lifted my foot. Feeling my senses double in intensity, I shockingly realized this was a *real* possibility. Stepping out onto the water, I rested my full weight upon its surface.

Shaking his head, "Why are you so obstinate, Arthur?"

"Why are you so annoying?" I answered.

Still afraid the water might not support me, I carefully took a step while looking toward Merlin.

"Are you coming?" he asked.

Very carefully walking toward him, I joined him at his side.

"Can you not see how powerful you are?" he asked.

"I didn't realize. . ."

"What you are able to do?" he interrupted.

Standing upon the water with Merlin allowed the God energy to flow through my body, giving me a perspective far higher than even the hawk had taken me.

"There is more to life than worry," he told me.

Taking in the moment, I tried to understand and apply this mystical moment to my life. Remembering the sense of doom that waited for me at the castle, my focus wavered.

"But how does it help the world?" I asked. "Will it prevent the Saxons from attacking?"

"Perhaps it will," he answered.

Feeling the supporting energy beneath my feet weakening, I headed for the shore. A few steps later, I found myself standing, knee-deep in water.

"You must believe, Arthur. It is you're only hope."

"And what do you know about believing. You're just telling me something you read in an ancient text! You couldn't do these things when you were in the earth," I scolded him, wading through the water toward the shore.

"Maybe I couldn't . . ."

"That's right, you couldn't. And I'm tired of your pious attitude, pretending you have all the wisdom in the world," I told him.

"I try."

Reaching dry land, I turned to face him, "You try? You try to what?"

"To help," he said.

"You don't try to help. You only try to annoy me."

"I enjoy your company."

"*I am cursed.*"

Tired of his games, my frustration with him and the world reached the surface.

"What do you want me to do?" he asked.

"I want you to control your mouth!" I said. "Why must you believe you're so smart?"

"I can only speak what I know," he said.

"But so many of your words are theories. You can't have wisdom that you've not yet lived. I could tolerate you a lot easier if you wouldn't pretend to be so wise," I argued.

"But I speak what I believe," he reasoned.

"That is what I'm saying! You don't know if what you believe is true or not," I told him, growing more frustrated by the moment.

"I believe it is," he answered.

"It is no use. I am cursed and that is that," I told him.

"I don't know why you're so angry."

"It's not your fault," I told him. "You just can't see."

"I don't know what you want from me."

"What you can't give me," I answered. "I need to get back to Camelot. Everything is fine. I just need to be alone."

Walking back to Camelot, I left Merlin at the lake. Unable to hold the higher vision of truth that Merlin wanted me to remember, I was forced to become aware of power that I could not yet accept. But because I lacked confidence in myself, his unwanted and often bad advice kept coming to me. He felt compelled to try and help.

*

Although my heart was now withdrawn from much of the world, for Denby it knew no bounds. A joy, my love for him was a great inspiration. Quickly growing, and at the age of nine, he was beginning to experience the world. Having been amazed by the beautiful music that came from the minstrel's mandolin, he wanted to experience its creation for himself. He was alone when he found the instrument leaning against a wall in the great hall. Picking it up, and expecting it to play for him, he soon found that the beautiful sounds would not flow through it for him as it had for the minstrel. Growing frustrated, he smashed it against the ground, breaking it into several pieces.

His nanny told me what had happened when I came for an afternoon visit. Walking into his playroom, I sat down.

"Hello Denby," I said. "Have you had a good day?"

Waiting for a reply, I found him unable to answer. With his eyes drawn downward, he looked displeased with himself.

"Why so sad?" I asked. He shrugged.

Leaning back in the oak seat, my eyes scanned the wall's surfaces, admiring the intricate herringbone pattern of the stonework it contained. For a brief moment, I considered all of the labor that had gone into the creation of our home, of the years of sacrifices that had been made and of the protection it now afforded. Then my mind returned back to Denby.

When I was certain that he could not find the courage to speak, I looked toward the broken mandolin that lay on the floor nearby.

"What happened?" I calmly asked. "Someone really smashed it up."

Remaining quiet, his eyes were long and drawn.

"They must have been very angry," I said. "I wonder who did it?"

Turning toward him, his gaze shifted to the floor.

"I wonder why they were so mad? Do you know?" I asked.

He shrugged his shoulders.

"Well I bet they probably feel bad about it now. Do you think so?" I asked.

He nodded yes.

"You didn't do this, did you?" I asked.

He had no reply

"Denby, did you do this?"

He finally nodded.

"I see. It was you. Why were you so mad?" I asked.

"It wouldn't play," he answered, wrenching his hands together in frustration.

"It takes lots of practice to play the mandolin. The minstrel has been playing for years," I told him.

Sitting quietly, he pressed his hands, palms down, onto the floor.

"We all do things that we regret, but after we do them, we have to make amends for our mistakes. If we strike against someone, it hurts their feelings and they will be mad at us. We'll have to do something to show them that we really do like them. Do you understand?" I asked.

He again nodded in agreement.

"We must go find the minstrel. His feelings will be hurt and we'll have to redeem ourselves."

Grabbing his hand, we walked out the door.

* * *

Usually reserved only for special occasions, it was not typical that we held the pass meal at the Roundtable, but this day contained a unique air. After consuming venison from a recent hunt, all was quiet, except for a noise growing in the distance.

"*Clip, clop, Clip, clop, Clip, clop, Clip, clop.*"

Hearing the sound of horseshoes striking stone pavement, our attention peaked as it became obvious that this horse, was *inside* the castle. With our attention directed toward the entrance, a heavily armored warhorse soon made its way into the hall, headed toward us carrying a very unique knight—a *Green* knight.

Stopping in front of the Roundtable, his clothing, armor, sword, even his skin and disheveled hair was green. But his face was one that we all knew too well—the face of *Merlin*.

"I have come for the murderer!" he demanded as he leaned forward still seated in the saddle, resting his hands upon its horn.

We all remained quiet.

"Do you think I have come all this way to be turned away by silence?" he added. "Give me the murderer."

"Does your murderer have a name?" Alden asked.

"Yes, several. But for now I seek the one called Gawain."

"I am no murderer," Gawain called out to him.

"Then why am I dead?" Merlin asked.

"We served justice," he replied with resolve.

"Good. Then your God will protect you again today—surely yes. He would not allow me to come back from the dead to claim you, if you acted in truth. Stand and fight," Merlin demanded.

"I will not fight a ghost," Gawain replied.

"Then a ghost will remove you from this world," Merlin assured him, laying his palm across the hilt of his sword.

Standing up, Gawain answered, "I'll send you back to where you belong."

Merlin, dismounting his horse, walked over to an open area in the hall and waited. His confidence unshaken, Gawain curiously eyed him as he walked closer, stopping safely a few feet away.

"Are you ready?" Gawain shrugged.

"We shall see," Merlin nodded, raising his sword to meet Gawain's. And the challenge began.

Merlin, having gathered many new abilities since leaving the earth, seemed now to have mastered swordsmanship and as the match wore on, we all became concerned for Gawain's well being.

Enduring every blow that Gawain delivered, Merlin remained strong, even as Gawain began to show signs of weakening. Then, as if out of character, Merlin made the simplest of mistakes, stumbling, and unnecessarily exposing his neck. Gawain not wasting a second, took full advantage, and with a single blow severed his head from his body, sending it rolling to the ground.

Giving the appearance that he had just been shaken, Merlin's body stood first stood still, then slowly began to take steps toward his head, stopping directly in front of his face. Kneeling down, he reached toward his head. Just before his hands made contact, his eyes popped wide open.

"Excuse me!" Merlin snapped, through the mouth of his severed head. Then lifting his head into the air, he placed it back upon his shoulders, while his body, acted momentarily disoriented. We stared in disbelief.

"I am truly sorry," Merlin apologized, as he prepared to resume fighting, once again lifting his sword.

"Is anything wrong, Gawain?" Merlin asked, lifting his bushy eyebrows. "Let us continue."

Well, Gawain's heart had all but died, but forced to resume the contest, he soon found himself pinned to the ground with his throat beneath the cold steel of Merlin's sword.

"Should you live or die? What will it be?" Merlin asked.

"Spare me!" he answered.

"I am sure you wish to walk away free, and that I cannot allow. If I am to spare your life you must agree to my terms," Merlin told him.

"I agree."

"You've not even heard me out. Perhaps you'd rather die?" Merlin said, as he pressed his sword forcefully against Gawain's throat.

"Tell me what you ask," Gawain gasped.

"It is something that will be very difficult for you. I don't believe you can do it," Merlin told him.

"I swear I'll do it!" Gawain pleaded.

"Well, since you swear," Merlin taunted. "You must immediately leave Camelot."

Gawain pausing, Merlin pressed the steel deeper into his throat.

"I agree," Gawain's voice cracked.

"And why should I trust you? You *are* a murderer," Merlin responded.

"I will leave. I promise," he told him.

"That is not the only condition, there is more."

"I will do what you ask."

"For one year you must quest—quest alone, with only the company of your horse. And you must find an answer for me," Merlin said. "Can you do this?"

"Yes," Gawain answered.

"Liar."

"I will do it," he promised.

Merlin paused,

"In one year, to the day, I will meet you here. If you come without the answer to my challenge, you will owe your life to me. If you have found the answer, your debt will be paid.

"Do you agree to my terms?" Merlin asked.

"Yes."

Merlin stood, and released him before continuing.

"Listen closely, for this rhyme will guide your life. You must find it's answer or your life will be mine."

"To who whom does truth belong,

when lives of innocent have been wronged."

"How can one live so bold
with a heart so distant and violently cold."

Then, as he reached his horse, Merlin remained quiet. Finding his seat in his saddle, he secured his sword.

"How can a heart ignore the cost, when a dream so great . . ." he paused, spinning his horse toward the corridor, the horses hooves loudly striking the floor. Then casting his powerful eyes upon Gawain, he finished,

"Is almost lost."
Along with his horse, he instantly left our dimension.

We all simply stared in disbelief. But Gawain, thoroughly intimidated, did immediately leave Camelot. And for the first few weeks, lived up to his promises. But eventually, finding the isolation to be unbearable, he reasoned to himself that it would be good to visit his father for a time and returned to Lott's castle. Having convinced himself that he would only stay a few days; he instead remained with him a full two years, having no intention of ever facing the green knight again. But even Merlin knew that Gawain would eventually return, and soon enough, he did.

Having only been within Camelot's walls only for hours, Gawain had joined us at the Roundtable when we once again heard the chilling sounds of a horse's hooves.

As the warhorse turned the corner and entered the great hall, all eyes cast upon the druid Merlin seated upon him. Approaching the Roundtable, he called out to Gawain.

"Why have you missed our date?" he demanded, as Gawain's heart instantly weakened.

"I had no way to keep track of time," Gawain nervously explained, his eyes shifting from Merlin back toward me.

"Lie," Merlin called out. "You were hiding with your father,"

"I was with him . . ."

"Shut up! You waste my time and I will not have it. But I will forget your absence, for I am a very forgiving person," Merlin told him, his tone changing as he patronized Gawain. "But you must still answer the rhyme, if there is any hope for you."

Merlin, waiting for him to begin, grew impatient when Gawain did not respond.

Stepping down from his horse, he walked over to where Gawain was seated and stood behind him, "To whom does truth belong?"

Gawain's head hung low, "Not I."

"You're doing well," Merlin replied as he crossed his arms, stepping a few feet back. Gawain remained quiet.

"How can one act so bold?" Merlin asked.

Gawain paused, as if seeking someone to rescue him from his fate, "I don't know."

"Well, you are still alive," Merlin told him. "I will give you that one. It *is* the truth."

Merlin, enjoying the power he held over the table, walked around its circumference as he one by one cast his eyes upon each knight of the Roundtable. Reaching his hand up to his chin, he scratched.

"Do you believe this to be an honorable man?" he asked, questioning us of Gawain's integrity. "Are you this easily duped?"

No one replied.

Stopping behind Gawain, Merlin reached for his sword, "How is the dream almost lost?"

Gawain shook his head, "I don't know."

"That is right, you don't, and now you owe your life to me," he told him. "Stand up."

With no heart remaining, Gawain pushed his chair backward. The armor upon his legs clanked as he moved from beneath the table and standing up, turned to face him.

"On your knees!" Merlin ordered, pointing his sword toward the cold stone floor.

Slumping to the floor, Gawain waited as the tension in the air thickened. With all of us prepared to witness Gawain's last breath, Merlin reached down and grabbed the long dark locks of hair that lay upon his back. Allowing the sharp blade of his sword to descend, he severed Gawain's hair close to his scalp and tossed the strands upon the floor. He then rested his sword upon Gawain's neck.

"Do you feel the steel?"

Gawain nodded, unable to move the rest of his body.

"You owe your life to me," Merlin told him. Turning his stare back to the knights, he closely eyed Hanguis, then Lancelot and the other members of the Table, as if looking for something. Waiting to see the growing belief in our faces—that *we*—had to answer to *him*.

Slowly moving the sword across Gawain's neck, he softly caressed the skin with its blade. Deepening his voice, "Murder again, and I'll be back to collect."

Then walking over to his horse, he stepped up and seated himself in the saddle—and without making a single move—disappeared into a flash of light.

Gawain's life had been spared.

*

For six years, the Grail quests had continued and peace reigned in the land. But it was no surprise to me when Tintagel's messenger arrived with the news—the Saxon's were invading. Having made many mistakes, we had created too many desperate acts in the world to remain unchallenged—it was time for war resume.

Very organized in our execution, I was anxious to end this challenge and sent all of our available knights into the front lines. Determined to quickly send the Saxons into retreat, I joined Gawain to fight by his side. Pushed into a vulnerable position near the forest's edge, the enemy, waiting within the forest, met us with full force.

With two soldiers attacking me, I was in a vulnerable position. Having little choice, I faced one enemy, forced to leave Bay momentarily exposed to the other. Before I could turn around, the other soldier had run his sword through Bay's side.

My heart sank as I turned to witness his action, my resolve turning to anger. Delivering a forceful blow to the shoulder of Bay's aggressor, I removed his arm from his body. Gawain finished the remaining soldier

Bay, already staggering, began to lose her footing. Jumping down from her back, my face was ashen as my heart grieved. Grabbing her head, I forced her to the ground. And seeing the severity of the wound, I knew I could nothing but wait for her to pass from this world.

As her physical body took its last breath, it relaxed while her spirit body sprang into life with unmarked beauty. Following her into the spirit world's dimension, she jumped up and snorted loudly. Spreading wide her front two legs, she dropped her head at the sight of her lifeless body and began to back away. I grabbed her reigns.

"Whoa Bay," I said, through my tears, "You're okay now."

After giving her a moment to collect herself, I pulled on the reigns, "Let's go."

"You're okay now," I insisted, as we walked into the trees and away from the sounds of desperation. With each footstep, I considered my loss. The peaceful sounds of the forest seemed accentuated now. My foot slipped off the edge of a stone as its lichen covering broke loose. Bay jumped.

"Whoa, Bay," I reassured. "It's all right."

Reaching a clearing in the trees as we approached the adjacent meadow, I could see a unicorn waiting for us in the distance. My heart was bleeding. Realizing this as Bay's escort, we walked toward her new companion.

The powerful unicorn raised his head as we entered the meadow, directing his attention toward us. Stopping, I took the bridle from Bay's head.

"Okay. You've done your job," I told her. "Go on now."

Bay remained still, uncertain of my request. She knew that her place was with me.

"It's ok, go on. I will see you soon enough," I reassured her.

Lifting her powerful front feet from the ground, she lightly spun around and made her way toward the unicorn.

Agonizing, I forced myself to leave and return to Gawain knowing he might take an unnecessary risk if he could not quickly find me. Walking back to the sight of Bay's physical body, I wiped the tears from my eyes and returned to the earth's dimension. Reaching down to her body, I took the bridle from her mouth and straightened her head, the tall green grass concealing much of her body. Gawain quickly rode up.

"Where were you?" he yelled.

"I had to take care of one of the Saxons in the forest," I told him. Without hesitation, he pulled me up onto his horse and together we rode further into our own perimeter, the violent metaphor deeply troubling me. For me, Bay's death marked an omen.

*

A week into battle, I could see the importance of becoming more unified in our efforts. Needing the full cooperation of the other kingdoms to end this war, I decided my efforts would be best spent at home, rallying support and meeting with kings. Returning to Camelot, I left Gawain in charge of our campaign on the front.

Only days after my arrival, an error reached my awareness, hearing the Saxon's had made ground in Lott's kingdom. With the majority of our knights on the front lines, Camelot was left vulnerable. Hours later, the Saxons had reached and surrounded our castle—Camelot was under siege. With not a minute to waste, I traveled on a beam of light through the dimensions and back to Gawain.

"I only have a moment," I told him, after finding him seated a makeshift table in the center of our camp.

"When did you arrive?" he asked, looking up in disbelief. "We've seen no one enter in days."

"I just arrived," I assured him. "But you must listen closely. Camelot is under siege. It will be only moments before the castle is overtaken and our enemy is likely to have fifty or more men beyond our numbers when all of the fighting has ceased. Do you understand?" I asked.

Although he still seemed confused, I continued, "I have no time to explain anything else. But you must take all of the men you can spare and go directly to the castle. There is not a moment to lose. I'll return ahead of you," I said, looking into his eyes, awaiting confirmation.

"We'll leave immediately," he assured me.

"I will be there waiting for you," I insisted, as I began to walk away. Turning my head back toward him, "Just get there, Gawain—Now.

Walking away from him, and beyond his sight, I shifted my focus as I walked back through the corridor of time—instantly finding myself standing inside the walls of Camelot. Searching through the long halls of the castle, I looked for my friends, instructing each one I found to take cover in the secret passages. I had plans of my own for dealing with the Saxons.

Realizing the enemy had already scaled our walls and were fighting their way toward the entrance gates, I had only moments to act. Walking into the courtyard, I climbed the series of ladders leading to the platform below the gate's giant pulleys. Standing above our entrance, I yelled down to the Saxons still outside of the castle.

"We surrender!" I waved to them. "I will give the order to open the gates if you will come in peace."

"Just like that?" a Saxon voice replied.

"We have no protection. All of our knights are away in battle," I yelled.

"Ha, Ha!" an invader yelled. "I knew it! Fools! You bunch a damn fools!"

Turning around, he yelled to his men, "Come on! We got 'em now. Bunch a damn fools. Ok then, open up! We are takin' your castle now!"

"All right, but you must come in peace," I reminded him.

"Peace," he said to himself. "Whatever you want to call it," he yelled, laughing to himself. "Just open up!"

Very confidant, the Saxons already believed the castle was under their control. Turning around to speak to my men, "Lay down your arms. We are going to surrender. It's our only chance."

With Camelot's heavy gate lifting, a roar of men's voices rolled into the courtyard as the Saxon's rushed in, taking control and assembling all of our men in a line. Their plan was very simple—murder everyone they found.

After a brief search of the castle, and holding fifty of our men, they were ready to begin. Standing beside their executioner, in the fifth dimension, I waited just beyond their vision. He grabbed his first victim.

My sword was swinging full force, headed directly toward the executioner's neck as I changed into the earth's dimension. Before anyone could understand what was happening, it sliced through his flesh, severing his head from his body. I returned to the fifth dimension.

"God Damn! What the bloody hell happened!" a Saxon yelled. With several of them crowding around the executioners body, they tried to make sense of what had gone wrong.

Their leader, shaking his fist in the air yelled, "You will not take this castle from us!" Perhaps believing dark forces were trying to intervene in the capture, added, "We will have our way!"

"This place is haunted," another Saxon whispered to the man at his side.

Convinced that their blatant arrogance had overpowered the opposing forces, they resumed their plans. Their new executioner, understandably hesitant to accept his job, looked over both of his shoulders. Picking up his ax, he instructed our man to kneel.

Again, returning into the earth's dimension with my sword forcefully in motion, I quickly removed the head of the new executioner.

"Son of a bitch!" a Saxon yelled in horror. "God O' mighty! This is the house of the devil!"

This time, I remained standing in front of them—the Saxon's, frozen in disbelief.

"I am the King here and these are my people—I will not allow you to harm them. And if necessary, I will do to each one of you what I have done to these gentlemen before you."

Within minutes, not one Saxon remained within Camelot's walls. I hadn't believed things would go so well.

*

Walking toward the lake with Merlin, the sun, high in the sky, had removed all traces of the morning dew. Approaching a favorite oak beside the bend in the road, we were still within Camelot's meadow and Merlin, making conversation with himself, seemed completely entertained. Barely aware of his words, I had let my mind wander back to the castle—until the moment we walked beneath the oak's great branch. My body was jolted.

"*Damn*!" I yelled. "Where the hell have you taken me?"

Merlin began to roll with laughter.

"Damn it Merlin! You take so much pleasure in shocking me," I scolded, as he began to laugh even louder.

"I must admit; it is true," he happily confessed.

Shaking my head in disgust, I began to look around at my new surroundings. The feel of earthy energy, the musty smell of soil and the dim light, made it seem as though we were underground.

"We are deep in the earth," he told me. "In the cave of crystal."

As my eyes began to adjust, I could see a slight glimmer in the darkness. We *were* surrounded by huge quartz crystals—*walls* of them.

"Is there any purpose to this visit? Or was it just an excuse to shock me?" I asked.

"We've come to find you're crystal," he said.

Knowing better than to ask *Merlin* too many questions, I just followed him. Walking through a narrow passage, we entered a cavern—it's ceiling as high as Camelot Castle—all covered in quartz. Merlin continued as I stopped to stare at the walls glistening in the dim light.

"Come Arthur, you act as though you've never been here before," he said.

"Well, I don't remember it."

Following a trail along the largest wall, we reached a platform, all formed from quartz crystal. At its center, and within a knee-high crystal trough, lay a uniquely shaped hand sized crystal. Reaching for it, I placed it in the palm of my hand. It fit perfectly.

Looking toward Merlin, as if seeking an explanation, I saw his eyes softening as he waited for me to feel the cavern's power. Its smooth vibrations caused me to feel light headed. My eyes returned to the transparent surfaces of the cavern, as if looking for something that was still beyond my perception.

"It has the memory of all that you have ever been in the earth," he told me, directing my attention back to the crystal I held in my hand.

"It will help you to remember who you are," he paused, waiting for me to grasp his words. "And all that you can become."

Staring at the crystal, my focus began to weaken. The earth's powerful energy was overwhelming me.

"We mustn't stay here long. This place is very hard on a third dimensional body, unless you are very pure," Merlin warned. "We must go."

"All that I've ever been?" I asked.

"This crystal knows you better than you know yourself," he answered. "But we must go."

Returning to where we had made our entrance into the cave, we instantly reappeared beneath the oak. Blinded by the bright light, I held one hand above my eyes to shield the sun while glancing to down to my other—my hand still held the crystal.

"Yes, Arthur. It is yours," Merlin told me. "It can *only* be yours."

Deeply ungrounded from the infusion of light into my body from the cave, I silently stared into Merlin's eyes.

"You needn't make sense of everything. The crystal will work with you, its energy reminding you of who you are. While it's not necessary to understand—never underestimate its value."

* * *

Denby, entering my chamber, walked out onto the verandah interrupting a private moment I held just after finishing breakfast. His brow tense and behavior unusually reserved, I could see an important matter weighed heavily upon his mind.

"Is something troubling you?" I asked.

Denby took a seat across from me and gazed out across the meadow. It was early and the soft sun still hung near the horizon.

"No, it's just that I've been thinking."

Waiting for him to relax, I angled my chair so that I might better see the grounds. A thick bank of fog hovered near the edge of the forest.

"We have a beautiful home," I told him.

"Yes, we do."

Tall and handsome, Denby was already reaching into his teenage years. From a distance he looked as though he was an adult. But his eyes told the story; in them, you could see that he was still a child.

Returning his attention to me, he was direct, "I've decided to become a priest."

My mouth opened slightly.

"I've been thinking about it for quite a while," he added, fidgeting with a spoon from a table setting. "May I have a cup of tea?"

Unable to find any words to say, I could only stare in disbelief.

"Are you ok?" he asked.

Remaining quiet, my head turned slightly as I took in a deep breath and slowly exhaled.

"I don't expect you to be pleased," he added.

Forcing myself to talk, "Denby, you don't know what you are saying."

"I do. I know exactly what I'm saying," he assured me.

"Those people are my enemy. They are *our* enemy, and have done nothing but create hardship for our country. Wars are fought in their name, for their beliefs. They allow atrocities to occur," I pleaded. "Surely you see this."

"They teach people of God," he answered.

"They know nothing about God, only about greed and their own lust for power over the world. They frighten the world into submission for reasons of their own, not for God," I told him.

Looking into his eyes, I was grievously pained as I realized I had no power over this situation. It was his destiny. He did not yet understand the church's desperation, and drawn in by their overpowering fear, he was losing control to them.

"I want to do this," he told me.

Taking in another deep breath, I sighed. Having focused so much of my hate upon the church, Denby could not help but be magnetized by them. As if trying to make peace between us, he was drawn to become one of them. Perhaps it was the only way he could feel safe.

"I need to do this," he insisted.

"Can we think about this for a while?" I asked.

"I've already spoken with the Abbot and he has found a place for me," he answered.

"When do you leave?" I asked.

"Tomorrow."

"Denby," I said. "Denby," my voice trailing off.

"It is not so bad."

"Is there nothing I can say?" I asked.

"I will visit," he replied.

Reluctantly giving him my blessing, Denby left for the Abbey the following day. But in my eyes, the world had stolen yet more love from me.

*

It seems Vivianne believed that with the loss of Denby, I might be more open to listening to her. Her plan had all along been to weaken me to the point that I would give into her, satisfying her lustful desires to influence the country. Now she felt it was time to make an aggressive move. In a desperate attempt to claim power, sent me a message.

Bridget, one of her girls, arrived at Camelot unannounced. Meeting with her alone, in the library, I read the note that Vivianne had penned to me. In it, she implied responsibility for the deaths of both Jasper and Louisa.

Staring silently for a moment, I looked up, "I have a message for Vivianne. Will you take it for me?"

"Of course," she answered.

"Tell her that am going to kill one of her witches for each member of my family that she has had murdered. Do you understand?" I asked.

Her face reeked with horror.

"That is all," I said. "You may go."

Bridget ran from the room.

My anger growing with the passing of each second, I remained still while considering my options. Believing that she must be stopped, I stood up and walked toward the library wall, the same wall that had so often brought visitors to me from the next dimension. Stepping through it, I traveled to Avalon, and appeared directly in front of Vivianne, seated in a room with several of her maidens.

"Did you really think a bolted door could protect you from me?" I asked.

"You are not welcome here," she demanded, powerfully standing up to confront me.

Amused with her, I stepped away, closely eyeing the beautiful girl at her side, openly sharing my thoughts.

"Well, let's see where we are. You have claimed the lives of two of the ones most dear to me. So, I believe you are in my debt. Which two witches shall you pay with?"

Immediately hearing shrieks of horror from the girls, I waited for Vivianne to answer.

"*No!* I will not have this!" she viciously told me, her face wrinkling with anger as she inwardly reached to control me.

"Not have it? You have bought and paid for it. It is no longer a question of what you will or will not have. Tell me which ones! Remember, they must be the ones that are dearest to you," I added.

Her rage turning to desperation, she almost began to plead, "No, no, you cannot do this," she cried.

Lifting my sword, I pointed toward one of the girls, "This one?"

"*No, No,*" she pleaded, now clearly begging.

"How about this one?" I asked, lifting my sword toward another.

"Please, Arthur!" she cried, her hands wrenching against each other as her desperation grew.

Allowing the tension to build, Vivianne's face turned pale, as a sense of powerlessness saturated the room.

"I tell you what Vivianne, I will give you some time to think about this. It is not something that needs to be rushed," I said, shrugging my shoulders. "You will have three days. Then I'll return. Is that fair?"

"No!" she yelled.

"Well, I think it is," I said, and stepping back through the dimensions, returned to Camelot.

Vivianne, overwhelmed and horrified by her predicament immediately fell sick. And with no other hope than to find peace, she sent Bridget back to Camelot, in a desperate attempt to seek forgiveness.

"You tell Vivianne to leave me be!" I told her, feeling no pity. "I will spare her maidens for now. But if she takes one more action against me, I'll return to Avalon and show no mercy."

"I will tell her," she promised, her sense of relief apparent.

But back at Avalon, Vivianne's body, overwhelmed by stress, had already begun to weaken. Forced to face the mirror of her desperate actions, she had lost her sense of power in the world. And knowing that at any moment I might seek revenge, her heart had been lost, preventing any recovery. Within a few weeks, she died from the duress.

*

A voice, growing louder as it approached, pierced the relative quiet of the library. Seemingly originating in a distant corridor, its messenger was drawing nearer. Interrupting a chat with Gawain, I asked, "Is that Leif?"

Gawain shrugged.

"I think so," I told him. "He's really upset."

Obviously headed in our direction, we could now hear his concern, "The damned witches!" he yelled, just outside of our door.

Unlatching and pushing the door open, I found myself face to face with him, staring into his eyes, "What's the problem Leif?"

"It's the damned witches! They're going to kill us!" he screamed, turning to run. Terribly upset, it seemed he had the intentions of informing each of the castle's inhabitants of his horrible vision.

"It's the witches!" he yelled, having already traveled to the end of our corridor. Turning to Gawain, I said, "He's gone mad."

Hoping to intersect him traveling through the courtyard, we walked outside believing he would eventually pass through on his way into the other areas of the castle. By now, many people had come outside to see what was going on. Surrounding the courtyard's perimeter, we all waited for him to enter.

The twin doors of the den swung open, and Leif, like a madman, ran into the center of the crowd.

Beneath the full afternoon sun, he stood poised, almost proud of himself, while admiring the sizeable audience he had accumulated. Strangely now, he appeared quite normal, even calm.

Staring at us for a moment, certain he had gained all of our attention—he began to laugh. Then he laughed harder and louder. Laughing from the depth of his soul as he forced us to realize—we had been had. Soon we were all laughing with him.

Leif, the lighthearted and delightful old druid was a master of deception and relished opportunities to use his craft. With the cold war at Avalon putting a black cloud over Camelot, Leif was forcing us to see our fear, all the while freeing us from it. Refusing to allow us to wallow in desperate thought, Leif made his mark upon us. This was his invaluable gift.

*

Even though much of my eternal memory and power had been lost, my ancient friends, as promised, were still reentering my life. Having completely forgotten Jasper's promise of Louisa returning, I had forgotten what it was like to be in her presence. But the time for our meeting was approaching. And in this day, she was carried a new name—Nimue.

Meeting during the summer solstice at a festival in its celebration, she was an unexpected surprise. As fresh as a flower, she was more beautiful than she had ever been as Louisa, and gracefully carried a sense of peace and power that she had only recently come to know. In this life, she carried more life force, her physical presence the combination of several souls, her wisdom and power much greater than Louisa had ever known. And with the death of Vivianne, she had become the stabilizing force at Avalon, its great power now resting with her. Just as Camelot had once made a transition into light, so now was Avalon.

Moments after our introduction, an image of Louisa flashed in my mind as I forced myself to hold my attention upon her. Looking attentively toward me, her sparkling eyes were beginning to penetrate my hopeless despair as her presence began removing layers of my pain.

My eyes, delicately refraining from growing attached, looked away for a moment, back to the rolling hills of the countryside and then into the deep recesses of my memory. A feeling came to me, of a memory still locked away.

"Have we met?" I asked.

"I think so," she smiled, her eyes revealing her wisdom to me.

An unusual sense of comfort existed between us. Standing in the fairground's walkway, we were in the way of the passing crowds. Feeling the need to move, I could not willingly leave her presence.

"I was about to walk the grounds. Would care to join me?" I asked.

Nodding, I held out my arm for her as we began our tour.

Walking next to her in silence, I began to realize what the years had done to me. She had become the epitome of beauty while I had spent the last thirty years wrestling with the darkest energies in our land. My heart could not so easily open now and I found no quick way to freedom.

Spending the remainder of the day with me, it seemed she found my company enjoyable and late in the day, upon my invitation, returned with me to Camelot. By evening, we had become close confidants. Feeling very comfortable in her expressions to me, she asked, "Arthur, do you find me attractive?"

"Very much," I assured her, beginning to feel self-conscious. "I should have made that known, my dear. I find your presence very comforting."

"Comforting?" she asked.

"A delight to be with. You have captivated my attention," I added.

"Perhaps you have other things on your mind," she said.

"I'm just not used to being around one so beautiful," I told her. "I don't know how to behave."

"You do not need to pretend around me," she said.

I smiled.

Over the last several years, I had become more comfortable being with women of much less grace than she so easily carried. But within her heart flowed an endless source of love for me, unmarred by time, and she desired to feel the same from me. After several meetings without being able to fully feel the depths of my love, she eventually questioned me about my feelings. Late in the evening, we shared a moment alone in the alcove of the library, overlooking the grounds.

"Arthur, do you love me?"

Knowing that I did not have the answer that she wanted to hear, I began to think about how I might best respond.

"Nimue, you are as beautiful as anyone I have ever known but great love no longer flows from me," I told her, unaware of what impact my words might have. She broke into tears.

"Please, please. Don't cry. It is not about you. It's just this world has taken away almost everyone that I love," I tried to assure her. "I am afraid for anyone that becomes close to me. They must pay the price for it."

"I am not crying for myself," she said. "It is for you."

"Don't cry for me. I'll be fine," I told her.

"No you won't! You are not fine," she demanded. "You can't even feel what you've lost."

Becoming very uncomfortable by our discussion, I turned away, looking though an opening in the wall that framed the world beyond the castle. Watching the groundskeeper light the torches that lined Camelot's outer walls, I felt her uneasiness and apprehension. Then turning my attention back to her, I tried to reassure her, "Everything is fine."

"No, Arthur. It is not. You are at risk," she insisted.

Wanting to escape the conversation that we were having, she refused.

"I don't know what to do," I told her.

"Get away from this life you are living. How can your soul heal when you are so close to danger," she said. "Return to the forest. Seek your highest wisdom."

"I wish it was so easy," I replied.

"It is Arthur. Take time for yourself and return to the forest," she pleaded.

As the layers of pain encompassed my soul, I had stopped feeling the gentle guidance the forest had shared with me. Having become caught up in the trappings of castle life, the forest no longer held my interest. She was right; I couldn't remember what I had lost. But now it seemed senseless for me to try to recover.

"My dear, it is in God's hands," I said. "Can we talk about something else?"

"It will not go away," she insisted.

"Then let's go for a walk in the forest," I suggested.

Unsatisfied with my answer, she sighed deeply and turned toward me, her arm resting upon the back of the chair.

"This will not be ignored, Arthur. It is something you must face, now—or later.

"Perhaps then, I will find the forest comforting?" I suggested.

Nodding, she reached for her coat that lay beside her, and stood up to join me.

Feeling ashamed and embarrassed, Nimue continued to pry into my wounds. Seeming so pure next to me, I believed my sadness could only drag her down and I desperately wanted to hide my suffering. But she felt differently. Unafraid of my pain, her intrigue and interest in me only seemed to grow.

Walking near the lake where Merlin used to take me as a child, a memory of hope returned briefly. I told Nimue about Merlin. He seemed curiously familiar to her.

"Do you know him?" I asked.

"Yes," she answered.

"How?" I asked.

"I've met him in the dream world," she answered.

"He is a tricky fool," I warned.

Smiling, she asked, "Tell me Arthur, what one thing do you want more than anything?"

My mind momentarily escaping Camelot, "Peace. To live in a world where fighting no longer existed."

"Yes, it would be so wonderful," she agreed, her head leaning back as her eyes searched the night's sky for stars. "How can we survive till then?"

"I don't know," I answered.

Sitting on a rock by the edge of the water, we looked into the sky that had now become quite dark, the sun setting shortly before leaving the castle. The stars seemed to be reaching out toward us.

"Look for a falling star," I said.

Searching for a time without any luck, Nimue finally raised her hand to point toward the sky, "There's one!"

"You win," I said.

"I win? Then what is my prize?" she asked.

"You must choose. Anything in the world," I said.

"Anything. Well I will have to choose wisely, if I can have anything," she said pausing. "Okay."

"Okay?" I asked.

"Yes, I've chosen," she answered.

"Well, tell me," I said.

"Oh no. That was not in the rules. You just said to choose," she insisted.

"You've got to tell me," I pleaded, my eyes growing long.

"I'm sorry," she answered.

Allowing her play, I could sense that she longed for the days when I loved to play, as I had before her death. Looking toward her, my eyes asked again.

"You should know," she insisted.

"You are supposed to tell me. I just didn't mention all of the rules," I told her.

She shrugged, with an apologetic smile, "Take a guess."

Pausing for a moment, "Of course," I replied.

She then reached over, grabbed my shirt and pulled me closer to her as we became lost in a very familiar and age old embrace.

Nimue visited Camelot often, although I had trouble allowing her to gain my deepest affection – my heart still fearful of losing her. Keeping her at a distance, my body still craving the touch of intimacy, I reached to fill that need from women that I did not love, from ones that did not require my love.

Passing Katrina during a chance meeting in town, and then engaging me in conversation, she revealed to me a spark of interest that remained between us. Finding her lusty sense of adventure to be attractive, I invited her to visit her brother at Camelot. She called on us the following evening.

Spending most of her time with me, she remained in the castle late into the night. Eventually, I grabbed her hand and took her into an empty guest's chamber. After my physical needs had been met, I fell asleep in her arms.

Mordred, already inside the castle, was hiding in an adjacent chamber awaiting Katrina's cue. When she was certain that I was asleep, she unbolted the door and snuck into the corridor. Finding Mordred, she brought him to the room. Just before entering, Merlin made a loud noise.

"*Crack*!"

My eyes opened to see Mordred charging into the quarters with his sword drawn. Expecting to kill me in my sleep, he was now surprised to find that his job would not be so easy. Leaping from the bed, I reached for a crucifix, crafted of thick oak that hung on the wall. Grabbing it and holding it high into the air, I caught the descending blade of Mordred's sword, burying itself deep into the oak.

Pulling the crucifix toward me, I pulled Mordred's sword from his grasp and threw him to the floor. Beating his face with my bare fists, he soon lost consciousness.

With his face deeply cut and bruised, and his mind beyond his senses, I had him removed from the castle, my rage marked upon his face, scars that would remind him of me for all of his remaining days.

*

My dark and unconscious fears about a destiny out of control had begun to manifest themselves into my life. Afraid that I might one day end up captive in my own dungeon, I was frightened so badly, that I could barely sit still.

With the attacks coming directly to me now, several additional attempts had already been made upon my life—many, that had been prevented only by Merlin's interference. As my ego thickened further, I wore it like a crown, as if being a murdered king would be an honorable thing. In a downward spiral, I sought more excitement and danger with the passing of each day.

A part of me knew that it was time for me to leave the earth, yet my ego would not allow it. Having forgotten God, I consciously resisted death while unconsciously trying to create it. And Merlin, insisting upon helping, only made things worse. Refusing to let me die, he would tell me in advance of each attempt to be made upon my life. Losing confidence by the day, I began to cling to him.

Always believing that her son would one day become king, Morgan continued to do everything in her power to make the transition as easy as possible for him. Having convinced one of our stable boys to help, she was ready to make another attempt on my life—but Merlin had already warned me.

After returning to the castle after a long day's ride, the boy greeted me in the stable, bringing me a refreshing glass of ale. Standing in front of the lad, I held the glass while looking into his eyes.

"You should really be more careful in choosing your friends," I told him, as I emptied the poisoned contents out onto the ground, handing the glass back to him. With his eyes flashing terror, I turned and walked away. He left on his own accord.

The dance with Merlin was costing my soul, pulling me deeper into darkness with each passing day. Already beyond the day of my intended death, it was time for me to leave the earth so that the healing of my soul could begin—but Merlin kept me chained here. Still refusing to let me die, I needed him to give into his compassion, distance himself, and allow my death come as magnetized.

*

Even though I could no longer be true to myself, Nimue's heart never left me. So distressed by the future she saw moving toward me, she could seldom allow herself to visit. It was just too painful. Instead, she remained at Avalon and watching from a distance, offered her assistance as she could. Still living within Avalon were many witches loyal to Vivianne, which desired only to harm me. Nimue sent word to warn me, when she heard of their plan.

Determined to find a way to put an end to my life, Katrina believed that she could seduce me back into her dark world. Amused by her persistence, I found myself during our next chance meeting, once again attracted to the sense of danger she presented. And even knowing by Nimue's own warning, that her plans included my murder, I found the risk compelling.

Allowing her to tell me her carefully crafted story, of her innocence regarding Mordred's attack, I offered forgiveness and an invitation to visit Camelot. Still intrigued by the danger, it was a dare that I could not refuse.

All the while, another dark moment was moving toward Camelot—Gwenevere was in trouble. Although her relationship with Lancelot had continued with my blessing, our enemies saw it as an opportunity.

A law in the land forbade adultery, and with it existed the severest of penalties—the punishment of death. With Gwenevere's unfaithfulness generally known, rumors of her affairs had been circulating for years. Perhaps the people didn't understand my belief, that I had made peace with it. But many felt it to be a blemish on my Kingship and wanted this act of treason stopped. This was a law that they were forced to abide by and they demanded the same of their Queen.

The Pope writing a decree demanded that Gwenevere be arrested and tried for treason. I refused to honor it, but a large portion of the people had taken his side.

Pressuring me to uphold this law, the people eventually forced me to accept the Pope's decision and allow Gwenevere to be held in the Abbey. Having paid less attention to the country's well being in recent years, Gwenevere's trial had become a means for them to express their grievances, as if punishing me for my lack of resolve.

When it became known that there would likely be no legal release for Gwenevere, Lancelot decided that he must leave the Roundtable, try to rescue Gwenevere, and hopefully escape the country. The day before the trial, he did just that.

The Pope's guard was no match for Lancelot and the few knights that assisted him. In minutes she was free and together they fled to France. But a growing problem was left for me to face, alone.

Obvious to the people that I had allowed her escape, many even believed that I had assisted Lancelot, and the resulting dissent poisoned their minds. The country was splitting apart and there was very little left that I could do to make peace with them. And more importantly, there was nothing that I wanted to do. I had no desire to make any concessions.

In my mind, the world had stolen the ones that I most deeply loved and I refused to freely give anyone else away. I could have never brought myself to allow Gwenevere's death, even if it meant losing the country.

Mordred now found his chance. With his window of opportunity never greater, he was compelled to move quickly toward his claim to the throne. With the country divided, many rallied to support him, as it was believed by some that he was truly my son and the rightful heir to the throne.

After an army had gathered behind him that was large enough to genuinely challenge my kingship, yet another decision was forced upon me. Could I allow this to continue? Let him take Camelot?

Wrestling with the decision, I could see no other choice. If Mordred took the castle, he would surely take my life.

*

Many year's ago, I had lost the power that enabled me to transcend the dimensions, and with it the wisdom I needed to protect myself. Now completely vulnerable to the aggressions of the world, the only vision I could see was one of war—of a violent and bloody battle to come that would completely erase the memory of the peace.

My mother, having heard of the rumors, immediately began searching the castle for me. Entering the library, she found me discussing strategy with several knights.

"Arthur," she breathed, her attentions unusually somber.

"Yes mother?" I answered.

"May I speak with you?" she asked, her ghostly expression troubling me.

"Of course," I answered, momentarily excusing myself from the conversation.

After the men left, I took a seat as Igraine knelt down in front of me. With her long and full dress partially draped over my legs, she held my hands within her own, sobbing. Surprised by her actions, I attentively awaited her words.

"My dearest Arthur," she elegantly began. "You must not go to war."

Silent for a moment, I took in a deep breath before replying, "I have no choice. The castle could be taken from me."

"No, it does not have to be," she insisted. "You've done far more difficult things than this. Go to the people. Talk to them. Find out what they want. They are the ones with the *true* power. No one else can touch you."

"I know exactly what they want. To murder Gwenevere, to take more love away from me. Where will it end? With you? After they have taken you?" I insisted.

"Whom are you listening to? This is not you speaking, not my son. Someone has confused you," she paused, shaking her head and squeezing my hands within hers. "This is very important Arthur. You cannot see what is happening. The people made you King, it is *they* who make the choice. Not one of your challengers."

"I wish I could see from your eyes, but I cannot. There *is* no other choice right now. War is the only answer," I told her.

"Please wait," she begged, continuing to sob. "Please pray for a greater vision of what can be, what can still be. Give the people what they want. They will protect you," she said.

"I'm sorry. I have to stop this. I can spare no one else," I definitively told her.

"You may not survive this battle," she pleaded, her tears dripping from her chin and onto my hands.

"I don't see any other choice," I said, firmly holding to my belief.

Deeply sobbing, she turned her head away. Then realizing she couldn't speak, she stood and began to walk toward the door.

"*No*," she finally said, speaking through her tears as she pushed against the chamber door. "You cannot do this," she cried, as she stepped out into the corridor.

Igraine's intuition had once again been true. Others were influencing me as darkness surrounded me like a cloud. Even Merlin believed war to be the only possibility, already advising me to prepare for battle.

My decision had been made. I would not risk Gwenevere's life and I refused to bring her back to face her crime. These choices were bringing danger closer and I began to sense that Camelot itself might possibly be attacked. And this was something that I could not allow.

Preparing for war, I was surprised to find that many of the knights shared the people's belief in my negligence, refusing to risk their lives for what they saw, as *my* cause. But as the civil unrest dramatically grew, they could see that *all* of our lives were in jeopardy. Mordred, should he overtake our castle, would surely kill any opposing knight. Mustering together all of the willing knights, we left Camelot in search of him.

Three days would pass before our scouts returned after spotting his camp. Stopping immediately, we set up our own camp and began preparations to strike at dawn. An uneventful evening, until a guard escorted an unexpected guest to my tent, Katrina had arrived behind us. Having persistently followed us in our quest for Mordred, she refused to leave without seeing me. Pestering the guard incessantly, he eventually brought her to me. And although I didn't send her away, my attentions for her would have to wait.

At first light, darkness, as if a black cloud, swept across the country. Battle cries stole the silence and our sacred land no longer held meaning. Numb and spiritually dead, our world had turned upon itself. There was nothing now that God could do but to wait and hope for a new age that would once again bring our hearts together—A day that would not come tomorrow, in the next century, or for many lifetimes into the future.

Beginning the battle with 160 knights, we outnumbered Mordred's force by 40. And when the last sword penetrated flesh, forty of our men remained. Mordred's army had been lost. He himself had died in a battle with Heath, who was mortally wounded by Mordred's sword, and only able to hold on for one day before succumbing to his injuries. Then, in a state of numbness, we made our camp nearby in an old defeated castle that had been burned to the ground.

Having planned to spend a few days there, to gain strength before making the trip back to Camelot, we shared the duties of hunting for deer and caring for the wounded.

But Katrina, having hidden her disappointment from me, was smoldering inside. The fact that we had won the battle only made her more determined to once again try to take things into her own hands, her dark desires, kept secret. Night had fallen and with her at my side, I lay asleep in the bell tower.

My next moment of consciousness came to be as I was jolted awake by a sharp pain in my left side. Looking down to my stomach, I saw my sword fully penetrating my body, Katrina, having pushed it through me from behind as I slept.

Turning toward her, I saw the hollow eyes of an empty soul and yelled at the height of my voice, "You bitch! You god damned bitch!"

Running down the tower steps as fast as she could go, she disappeared into the thick grasses that overran the courtyard. On a moonless night and with no perimeter walls remaining around the castle, darkness concealed her escape. She was gone and I was left dying.

Gawain, hearing my curses, ran up the tower to find me. Standing in disbelief, "Who did this to you?"

"Katrina," I painfully grimaced, my mouth and lips turning the fiery color of blood.

Seeing the severity of the wound, "Arthur, my God," he stammered. Slightly weaving to one side, he reached for the stone header to steady himself. "Tristan! Alden! Get up here!"

After removing the sword, they carried me down to a long and narrow feasting hall, the only undamaged room left in the entire castle. Laying my still conscious and breathing body upon a large oak feasting table, I continued to resist the pain. Everything else was in the hands of time, the wound, much too damaging to find any hope for my recovery.

Occasionally I would speak to one of the knights, telling them of things that might help the country after my death. The remainder of the time, I agonized, viciously hating myself for what I had allowed to occur. Now, at the edge of death, I saw the grievous mistake, one that made me seethe with self-loathing.

"Galahad!" I called out, wrenching my body to the side while trying to lift my head.

Standing up from his seat at the end of the hall, he walked toward me. Reaching my side, he knelt down, bringing his face within a breath of my own.

"Yes, Arthur?"

"I need you to do something for me," I told him, pushing the words up from my throat.

"Of course, anything," he promised, his eyes revealing his expectance of loss.

"I want you to take my sword to the lake. Throw it as far as you can across the water and never look back. Do you understand?" I asked.

Sighing, he leaned closer, his lips just a few inches from my ear, "Arthur, this sword means nothing now."

"*No!*" I yelled, wrenching my head toward him while reaching for the woolen shirt that covered chest. With our eyes just inches apart, I pleaded, "Galahad, if you can find any loyalty for this lost soul of a King, you will grant me this request."

"Of course Arthur, I will do this," he nodded.

"It must be returned to the earth. Do not look where it rests, for you do not want to know. It is a cursed thing," I told him, resting my head back against a folded saddlecloth, my teeth clamping tightly together. "Please hurry."

"I'll return soon," he assured me.

My appreciative eyes became distant again as my thoughts momentarily drifted away, but a sudden jolt of pain shot through my body, reminding me that my time in the earth was not yet complete.

With a Lady from Camelot's court, Nimue stepped through the narrow doorway, momentarily blocking the morning sun that was filtering through the hall's only opening to daylight. When she reached my side, her tears began to flow. The others in the hall came to her side, sharing their grief, but I could not bear to witness.

"Get away from me!" I demanded. "Take your god damned tears and get the hell away from me."

"Please Arthur," Nimue begged, her face mournfully pained. "There is no shame is death."

"I will not have this!" I yelled. "I began this life alone and I will die alone!"

Heartbroken, Nimue walked to the opposite end of the hall, sobbing deeply as she clasped tightly to the arm of her escort. Until that moment,

I had not understood how deeply I had been cared for during my time as Arthur, but I was in no condition to accept the love now. Suffering in silence was my only comfort. Wishing to be alone, I was deeply ashamed of the conditions I had created for myself and I forced the others to remain on the other end of the hall, where they mourned and prayed for me.

"Gawain! Come here, please!" I yelled.

Pulling a chair up beside me, he took a seat.

"The alliance no longer exists," I grimaced. "You must make peace with your father. He's the country's only hope."

"I will try," he assured me, his expressionless face attentively focused upon me.

"And protect Nimue for me. She is my greatest love," I told him as my vision in the physical dimension beginning to blur.

"I will," he promised.

Returning late in the evening, Galahad brought to me a sense a peace and completion. Leaning close to me, he whispered in my ear, "It's done, Arthur. I've thrown the sword into the lake."

Opening my eyes, but barely aware of my surroundings, I cleared my dry throat to speak, "That is good."

Knowing that the sword had been given back to the earth, my spirit felt closer to releasing the body that still imprisoned me.

"Thank you, Galahad," I told him. "I could not leave until that was done."

While in the physical world, my body lay still, but in the internal world I was very busy, searching for the strings that still held me to this plane. Considering my life choices, I thought about my mistakes as I wrestled myself throughout the night. Jasper, Merlin and many others in the spirit world would visit me as my consciousness drifted higher.

"Let go," Jasper pleaded. "The nightmare is over now. Come home."

My head turning back and forth, the self-judgment was unable to give me a moment of rest.

"You have done well," Jasper insisted.

Then I drifted off into a deep and soulless sleep.

The early morning sun, streaming through the doorway, stirred me awake as a shadow fell across my face. My eyes opening to the mixture of light and dark, I focused upon the face of the huge creature standing before me. My beloved horse Bay, now a unicorn, pushed her nose against my hand. Believing that I had died, I looked down to see that I still lay upon the feasting table. My friends, half-asleep, were still seated at the other end of the hall.

Bay moved her head to my chest, took in a deep breath and snorted loudly. Reaching up to touch her head, I ran my hand across the horn on her forehead, lightly wrapping my fingers around its base.

"I knew you wouldn't be far away," I told her. Leaning my head forward, my eyes struggled to focus upon her. "Is it time to go?"

With her powerful vibration over powering me, pulling my body closer to her dimension, I began to release.

"Then take this wretched power from me," I whispered to her, as I slipped back into the world of spirit.

"I find – no peace with it."

And then, I died.

But I had been given the opportunity to live a truly wondrous life. From the greatest of spiritual heights, to the hopeless depths of darkness – this is *my* story – of a life that witnessed the greatest love, the greatest hope, and all of the *magic* that once lived at Camelot.

Although this marked an end to my life as Arthur, my work in the earth was far from complete—just the end of an experience in time. And with life and consciousness in the earth still expanding, I would soon return to continue the work, as do all that enter this dimension, of purifying and healing my soul.

A Second Chance

Having endured many desperate lifetimes since loved as Briton's Arthur, I had now turned into one of her worst enemies. Continually challenging her darkness, she despised me for my efforts to make her live up to her people's desire. After the fall of Camelot, desperation had swept over the land and I returned to challenge her from within during many lives—I led wars against her in others. Along with many other beings, I gave my best effort to make her return to the truths that had once ruled her heart. And when she began to stand on her own, I felt freed to move on, and to heal myself so that my power might once again return.

Reborn into the earth, I began with an unusual and powerful awareness of the world. Jasper was once again my grandfather, the father to my mother, and a few of my enemies had been placed in positions very close to me. I didn't completely like my new life, but Jasper ensured that I was well taken care of. He made certain that my emotional needs were met and that I was able to find to find the necessary expression a growing boy needed.

After marrying, my parents moved from their small hometown to a rather large city to raise their family, preventing me from seeing Jasper as much as I would have preferred. When we were apart, I often longed for his presence and when we were together, he spent great amounts of his time introducing me to the world.

During a visit to his home he might take me fishing, or to the fire station where he volunteered. Some days I'd just ride around in his truck with him as he made his rounds at work, working for the highway department he was in charge of all of the road repairs in his county. He seemed to know everyone in town and it was obvious that they held great respect for him.

Jasper was always very attentive to me, but my life away from him was very different. My mother was very demanding, unable to demonstrate love and constantly finding fault with me. It was very difficult to be around her and would have perhaps unnerved me immediately, but knowing my grandfather was not far away kept me calm.

Making his living in the sound business, I often listened to my father speak about vibrations and frequencies. They seemed to me, magical things that I couldn't completely understand. He once showed me a frequency on an oscilloscope. Speaking into a microphone, visible waves of sound would appear on its screen, a low voice created wide fluctuations in the line, while a high voice showed narrower ones. I learned that some frequencies were so high that the human ear could not even hear them.

Although there seemed to be little purpose in knowing these things as I learned them, they would later become very important in helping me to understand my own vibration, and in remembering my ability to transcend beyond the dimension of earth—Just another small step toward the expansion of my consciousness.

Into this life with me, came many memories of the past. Once I interrupted my father while reading a bedtime story to me about Samson.

Leaning up from my pillow, "When I was Samson," I told him. "That didn't happen."

"You weren't Samson," he uneasily replied.

"Yes I was. Mom remembers," I assured him. Getting up from bed, I walked into the kitchen to find her.

"Wasn't I Samson?" I asked my mother.

"Were you Samson?" she repeated, washing the last dish in the sink.

"You know, before this," I said.

Shaking her head in confusion, "You weren't Samson. You were just born a few years ago."

Instantly frightened, I wondered why my parents wanted me to forget this, my own past? I also wondered—why had they forgotten their own? Holding reservoirs of trust and confidence in the past, their inability to remember made me feel tremendously weak. If I were to deny my own memories, I would have to forget many things that I had already learned.

No different than most of the people in our world then, my parents were living lives of relative darkness and were only able to teach me what they believed about their world, making my challenge very difficult. But this was the test that lay before me. The question was, "Would I be able to remember truth under such pressure?"

Sitting in my front yard, I stared up into the night sky, feeling as if my heart was out there waiting for me, far in the distance. Watching the moon, I wondered, "For what reason do the stars exist?"

With my mind becoming confused, my body tensed as I thought back to my life's conditions. How was I supposed to find inspiration living with ones that could not understand me?

Never finding anyone to answer my questions, I began to grow frustrated. My chest seemed to hurt when I looked into the night sky for too long, even making me a little angry. Needing to grow in understanding, there was no one to teach me, leaving me with no other choice. I was forced to turn my focus back into our physical world and wrestle the ones around me for my life's meaning.

My parents did a very good job of providing for my physical well-being, but I looked to Jasper for all of my other needs. It was horrible shock when he unexpectedly passed from this world. Our entire family was thrown completely out of balance.

I was only six at the time when we got the call. My grandmother had returned to the city with us for a brief stay and had left him alone. He was taking a nap, as he often did, on the floor in their living room. This time he did not wake up.

I couldn't believe it at first even though all of our family members there were crying. My brother and only sibling turned to me when he figured out what had happened.

"Pa-Pa's dead!" he exclaimed.

"No he isn't," I insisted, refusing to believe him.

Within a few moments my mother made her way over to us. She had been busy trying to calm down my grandmother, whom was now hysterical. I can only remember her tearfully telling us, "Your Pa-Pa has died."

That was all it took to send me into waves of uncontrolled tears. As young as I was, I immediately understood that he would no longer be able to visit me. This was something that could not be—I still needed him.

He was held in such esteem in the town in which he lived that there were several memorial services for us to attend. I threw up at one of them and my grandmother would spend the next few weeks drifting in and out of consciousness as the shock made it's way through her body. Jasper had made most of the decisions regarding their life, as my grandmother had always been very sickly. She was not prepared for the loss.

Perhaps it was all of the chaos that caused me to become sick, but for the next couple of years my doctors would try to understand the nature of my illnesses. Without warning, I would break out into a cold sweat and become nauseas. Jasper's death had stirred the unconscious memory within me of his loss at Camelot and I became obsessed with dying. I couldn't stop thinking about the rest of my family members too. Surely they will all soon die, I reasoned.

We did our best to keep going but my illnesses persisted. I had secretly become preoccupied with my fears and I began to believe that I could possibly die from poisoning. When playing alone in my backyard, I had a vision.

Sitting on the ground, with my legs beneath me, I stared out into space. Seeing a chalice being removed from a box, I heard the words, *"Much of your difficulty is about this."*

Returning within the vision to a past life, I remembered when I had been forced to drink poison from the chalice that was now before me. Feeling the feelings that I had achieved in that time period, I knew that I had been very powerful.

The spirit world, trying to help me with my present fear, gave me this information as if to say, *"This was from the past – not the future."* I was comforted.

Making a mental note of this, I walked inside and continued with my play. In this early part of my life, visions were nothing out of the ordinary and I never felt the need to mention them to anyone.

My health problems remained constant and for the next couple of years I became plagued with stomach cramps, in addition to the nausea and vomiting. The spirit world, ever present in my life, felt the need to reach out to me and surprised me one afternoon as I walked into our living room. Two men and a woman sat there waiting for me.

"There he is," one of the men said, gently.

"I didn't hear anyone come in," I told them in surprise, abruptly stopping near the room's entrance at the end of the couch.

"We've been here for a while. We're friends of your mothers," the same man added.

"Where is she?" I asked, still untrusting of our new guests.

"She is needing to do some house cleaning. But why don't you come and sit with us," he answered.

Hesitant at first, I looked into the eyes of the woman—eyes that I had known forever. I immediately walked over to her, soon leaning my body against her leg. She held my hand.

Merlin, sitting next to her, did most of the talking trying to comfort me, speaking about my mother.

"She's having a very hard time now," he said. "She depended a lot on your grandfather and really misses him."

Although I could hear Merlin's words, it was Igraine that held my attention. Around her, I felt more love than I had ever imagined. It was quite intoxicating.

After several minutes, they informed me that they had to leave. Not wanting to be separated from Igraine, I asked her, "Will you take me with you?"

A distressed look crossed her face as she turned to Merlin for help.

"We're going to come back to see you very soon," he assured me. "We have some things to do now, but we'll be back."

His confident and trusting demeanor reassured me, although it was barely enough to keep me pacified. It seemed as though I belonged with them. They did leave, but kept their promise of visiting me regularly.

With the loss of her father, my mother seemed to find it more difficult to cope with her life. Her compulsions intensified and she became even more critical of every choice that I would make. I had also become more desperate as I had lost many outlets of expression. My immediate family couldn't understand my needs and just didn't have the energy to help. Beginning to cling to my mother, she began to push me away. Soon we were at war.

Sharply criticizing me, she began excessively punishing me when she believed that I had made a mistake. One time she told me about something she wanted me to do. It wasn't something that needed to be done, just an activity that she wanted me to be involved in.

I answered, "But I don't want to." She viciously replied, "You have to do a lot of things in this life you don't want to do."

Believing that she was powerless over her life, she was trying to teach me the same.

In order for me to reach the medicine cabinet in the bathroom, it was necessary for me to use the toilet as a step. Once when trying to reach the cabinet my foot slipped into the toilet, my sock and shoe were soaked. I was punished, forced to wear my pajamas for the remainder of the afternoon and evening, not allowed to go out and play after dinner. It was not that this was so horribly cruel, at least by some standards, but that these things occurred on a regular basis, preventing me from living my life free of worry. It made me become preoccupied with avoiding all errors. And this made me even sicker.

I began to throw up more often and the doctor whom cared for me decided that additional tests were needed. I spent several days at the hospital with minimal food as they examined me and drew large amounts of blood from my body. They also took several kinds of x-rays. In the end, they found nothing wrong with me. Psychosomatic, was their diagnoses. It was all in my head.

*

I never understood that the three people that visited me in the living room, Jasper, Merlin and Igraine, were from the spirit world. Embodying their same physical appearance from their lives at Camelot, they seemed as real to me as anyone else. And it had never really occurred to me that I had not seen them at the same time with my mother until one day when she walked through the room as we were speaking. She called out my name.

"I'm right here," I said, somewhat confused by her inability to see me. Looking at my friends, I jumped up and followed her into the next room, afraid she might become angry if she could not quickly find me.

"Here I am!" I told her, as I turned the corner into the dining room.

"Where were you!" she demanded.

"In the living room," I said.

"I didn't see you in there," she replied, doubting my word.

"I was in the chair, taking to those people," I told her.

"What people? There's no one here," she insisted, becoming uneasy at my suggestion.

"Your friends," I answered.

"There is no one else here," she firmly told me.

"Yes there is. They're right here," I told her, as I leaned back to peer into the *now* empty living room. Surprised, I turned back to my mother, "But they were just there," slightly stunned. "They must have left."

Appearing troubled, she dropped the subject and began busying herself preparing dinner.

Reasoning to myself that they had walked out the front door, a part of me knew that to have been impossible. Only seconds had transpired since I had last seen them.

My favorite toy as a child had been a beautifully painted plastic woodpecker. With suction cups for feet, rotated by a spring inside, it had the power to walk along or up a smooth surface. I most enjoyed putting him on an opened bedroom door. Taking about a minute to get above my reach, I stood beneath it, waiting for it to run out of walking surface after reaching the top and fall. I loved this toy and knew that it was special, it giving me very powerful feelings. Perhaps it reminded me of Camelot's forests.

One day, I remember no longer being able to feel the woodpecker's power. Extremely frustrated, I told my parents I no longer wanted it. They said fine and told me to put it in my toy box. But I told them that I didn't want to have it at all and upon waking the following morning, I found that it was gone. Although it was painful to know that the woodpecker had been taken, seeing him everyday only caused me to become more conscious of what I was losing. I didn't want to be aware of what was happening to me.

*

Walking into my backyard, I tried to get away from feeling my mother's overpowering energy and her need for me to believe in the world in which she lived. Feeling like I only had a few moments to be alone, I hurried, taking a seat upon the grass, staring up into the open sky.

Thinking about the pressures I was feeling, I began a conversation with God.

"Do I forget about my world of magic? The people here don't even know about it. Maybe I can pretend that I don't believe? They become mean when I try to tell them about it."

Having no answers to the pressures that I faced, I could feel memories of my past slipping from me. Reasoning with myself, I came to the conclusion that my life would be in danger if I tried to hold onto what I believed. To me, it seemed that the only way to protect myself—was to forget myself. And that is what I chose to do. Within a few weeks I had a plan.

I decided I would take my powerful feelings and put them into my dresser drawer, to hold them there for safekeeping. There, they would be well protected and beyond the reach of anyone's grasp. And then I could go into denial, and never let anyone know who I really was. It seemed to be the only solution.

Walking up to my dresser, I pulled out a drawer, the second from the top, as I began to feel my power. Imagining myself placing my power within the drawer, I considered all of the facets of its energy. Beliefs that I cherished that had come to me from many lives of seeking were directly before me in my conscious mind. It had been my desire to live these truths that caused me so much discomfort in my world. Wanting to live them openly, my life was dictating that I could not. Yet I could not allow another to ravage through what was so precious to me. I had to protect my power and this was the only solution I could see. So I put it away and closed the drawer, then ran outside to play.

At first, I remained conscious of what I had done, having remembered how I could once again regain my power. Whenever I felt a need for it, I would just walk over to my dresser, open the drawer and begin to feel very powerful, often knowing the truth of a situation. But with my vibration edging lower, I was rapidly forgetting myself and soon, I would forget that I ever had any power at all.

But for the moment, I could still remember my life as Arthur, the visions within my mind that brought me very powerful feelings. What I remember most were the horses, as many as the eye could see. All suited in armor, carrying their knights, lined up in pairs on the winding road that led to the castle. It was a powerful sight.

It would still be several more years before I would learn about this life in school, and by then I would have totally forgotten its memory. But this was a seed that would be held inside of me until it was time to remember, many, many years into the future.

A high fever and stomach virus had kept me in bed for days. After receiving a visitor, my mother became upset and walking into my room, demanded that I get up and go into the bathroom. Feeling very faint, I managed to walk the short distance to its door and entered. Following me inside, I heard her angry voice behind me. I am really not sure what occurred next, it's all a blur. But I can remember throwing up on myself, and eventually being allowed to go back to bed.

This event seems to have been a traumatic one for me, as from that point on I didn't like to go into the bathroom. Upon entering, I would remember something that frightened me so badly that I had difficulty coping with being alive.

Just after entering the bathroom a few days later, I heard one of my guides speak through as I considered the frightening memory.

"Forget about it. We'll deal with it later," she said.

Afterward, I sat down next to the toilet and began to spin the thoughts in my head, in a circle. After several moments, I'd stop and check to see if the memory still existed.

It would take me a few weeks of practicing before I was able to keep it repressed, but it did eventually disappear although the fear and anxiety from the memory remained—I just no longer knew of its source. After this experience, my presence became greatly diminished as it now took large amounts of energy to keep this memory from my consciousness. It would also require me to stay very busy, else the memory might return.

*

My next-door neighbor, having found a baby bird in his yard after a storm, brought it over to my house to show me. A newborn, it's still wet fuzz gave it the appearance of being bald. Instantly frightened and magnetized to the responsibility for it's survival, I asked if him if I could keep it. He gave me the bird and I took it into my garage to make a home for it.

With its mouth remaining open, it continually squawked for food. Not knowing what to feed it, I began to give it drops of milk from an eyedropper, at the suggestion of my father. I was warned that it probably would not survive, but that was a possibility that I could not allow.

The baby chirped for more food even though I could see that it's belly was full. I had watched its stomach rapidly grow with each drop of milk it swallowed.

I tried to stop feeding the milk, but it still cried for more, leaving me feeling I must do something to help. Pacing around my garage, I slowly became dominated by my fear.

Nervously, I gave it one more drop, hoping to ease its sense of desperation.

But that was too much. The baby's head then fell to the side and its body slumped over. Seeing a ridge forming just under the skin of his stomach, I realized that it's stomach had burst. The baby had died.

Still having the sensitivity of a young child, I went into a terrible shock, pacing around in my garage while trying to convince myself that it was still alive. But I knew. My choice had killed the bird – the choice to allow it to swallow too much.

* * *

The fear that my life was showing me continued to lower my body's vibration and my ability to make direct contact with the spirit world was slipping away. During the evening while walking through our home's hallway, I stared into the dark, unlit living room. My eyes focused upon the silhouette of someone seated on the couch.

"I need to talk to you," Igraine told me, the tone of her voice solemn.

Walking closer to her, she continued, "We may not be able to see you for a while."

"Why not?" I asked, feeling very rejected.

"It's not that we want to go, we must," she answered.

"I don't want to stay here," I told her, standing with my leg pressed against the front edge of the sofa.

"But you have to. We will not leave you forever, just for a time," she explained.

I began to feel very disheartened. Their visits with me were the only thing that brought me real joy and I could not imagine wanting to live without them.

"There are some things I need to tell you, things you will one day need to remember," she began. "You are not from this place. You have just come here for a time. And your beliefs are very different from most of the people that you will know."

"I don't like it here," I told her, tracing my fingers around the seat cushion's buttons.

"I know, but you have to be here for a while. There are things you must learn alone," she insisted.

Thinking quietly to myself, I realized the people I loved the most were leaving or had already left. Seeming as though I would have a horrible life ahead, I was unable to bear the thought of not seeing Igraine regularly. I began to grow angry.

"It will not be so long. You will see," she promised, trying to reassure me.

Perhaps thinking I could overpower her choice, to make her change her mind, I began to sulk and closing my heart—I walked away. When I returned a few moments later, she was gone.

*

Having become an accomplished painter during many lifetimes, this artistic expression that I had earned in the past, still easily flowed from me enabling me to quite naturally draw and create pictures.

My art teacher in the second grade was a young and beautiful female that I would now guess to have been in her early twenties. With all of her physical beauty, there was a side to her that was very injured, as she was quite rigid in her instruction. She would explain to us what to draw and what colors to use. If we were to make an error, we were faced with very strict consequences. And it was not long before I began to dread her class.

Although I could tell the difference between the colors of purple and blue, I couldn't remember which one was which, and would become very upset because of this when drawing pictures in her class. One day I could feel her standing behind me, eyeing my paper. I was about to realize my greatest fear. Unknowingly, I had substituted blue for purple. When she saw my mistake, she instructed me to throw my paper in the trash.

It could have been worse. I had seen others that first had to rip their paper in half, before throwing it away. But fear began to dominate my artistic expression and although my abilities would remain with me for a few more years, I would never have the courage to voluntarily sign up for an art class, or at least until much later in life. And by then, my artistic abilities would have already deeply submerged into my subconscious.

*

Even though I had spent much of my childhood sick, I still occasionally reached states of being where I could sit quietly for lengthy periods of time. These were very powerful moments for me where I was very close to the knowledge of who I was and what I could become. But family dynamics would play a great role in undermining my confidence.

My father, helpless to the injuries of his own early life experiences, spent most of his waking hours at work. Without a rich emotional life or communication skills to draw love closer, his facade conveyed a sense of well being, but he still somehow seemed incomplete. Unable to find expression, or perhaps even understand his life so far, he could not spiritually support a child, and along with my brother, I was left on my own to develop emotionally. He did provide the physical necessities, but the richest portion of his soul had either already left the earth, or perhaps never arrived. He did not escape his adolescent years without dramatic life changes and suffering.

His father, passing from this world when *my* father was only ten, had once been very wealthy, perhaps even the wealthiest man in town. I remember him talking about playing as a child in the bathroom of their home, opening the drawers below the towel cupboard, each full of certificates for oil stocks that had become worthless with the crash of the stock market. His father never regained their wealth.

And my mother, a person of an average consciousness, was also living a fairly helpless life. Instead of standing clear of her internal turmoil, I tried to help make her feel calmer by speaking to her about her frustrations. Not appreciative of my point of view, she became even more determined to teach me to live the life of a victim and to believe that others should be able to control my life. Feeling threatened by my feelings of power, she had no choice but to try to take them away from me. And more and more I found the uneasiness in my stomach preventing me from accessing my ability to feel.

Given enough quiet time, I was able to consider what was troubling me and allow my body to release the fear that prevented me from feeling good about myself. My stomach would settle and I could return to a peaceful state of being. But my problem was that I didn't have enough time. My mother would constantly find something for me to do. So when I heard her yelling for me, I would have to swallow all of the anxiety that I had been trying to release, and run to her. Initially, this caused even more vomiting, but in time I learned to hold it down, no longer needing contemplation. And a great numbness then began to envelope my body.

*

Playing in the back yard, I was amazed to find a large number of tiny baby frogs hopping about and immediately wanted to show my mother. I had never seen such small frogs before but I somehow felt that they were very important to me. She must have felt the same, as something sparked her interest and she told me to collect them, to show the other children at my cub scout meeting that afternoon. I gathered them up and for the time being put them in a box.

All of the kids were delighted even though we only showed them briefly, but after the meeting, I asked my mother if I could play with them. She agreed and I took them into the back yard. Timothy from across the street came over. I showed him the frogs. He picked one up and said, "Let's throw them on the roof."

"No," I told him, trying to understand his strange desire. We were far enough away from my house that this meant their certain death—and I loved them.

"Yea, let's do it," he demanded, with more confidence than I could find within myself and threw one of them at my house. A sickening moment for me, and feeling completely hopeless, I picked up a frog and joined him in their murder. I felt as though I had betrayed the world.

*

Sitting in my front yard that summer's evening, just after the sun had set and all of the light had disappeared from the sky, I looked into my house from a distance. The front door was open but the screen door remained closed in its place. Feeling so different from the rest of my family members, I thought to myself, "*I am Lone Wolf,*" without understanding the meaning behind the words. I felt such an enormous pressure to be like my family and to like the same things they liked. It was a soulless moment of awareness in my early childhood, where no answers were offered to me.

And I could find no comfort on the inner plane. Merlin was there giving me constant and often unwanted guidance, even at times getting me into trouble when I acted upon his urgings. I decided then that I would no longer listen to him. Shutting him out for the most part, I lost my ability to consciously connect with the spirit world. My world was becoming a lonely place.

But my conscious fear remained present and I noticed that I was developing strange idiosyncrasies. As if to take my mind off of the fear, I used these activities to occupy my awareness. If I were to touch something with my left hand, I would have to touch the same object with my right one. I also began to frequently wash my hands, sometimes several times an hour. Still fearing that I might be poisoned, I believed that this might prevent it in the future. I knew these things were not normal and was even embarrassed by them, but I had no control over my behavior. I just tried to prevent anyone else from noticing.

It had been during recent lifetimes that my ego had weakened to the point where it was difficult for me to suppress any fear. And now, I was overwhelmed by it. The ancient terror of being poisoned was at the surface of my consciousness and in a desperate attempt to control it; I began to ask God if the food I was about to eat had been poisoned. It was difficult to tell if I was ever given an answer or not, but there were times when I ate food that I believed to contain poison. Too embarrassed to tell my family of my fear, I just forced myself to eat while believing I might soon die.

*

My brother, a few years my senior, was a member of the Boy Scouts and their troop was very involved in the Native American culture. They performed as a part of their activities, demonstrations of the traditional Indian dances at exhibitions and other special events. I was very fortunate as for some reason I was allowed to participate with them when they went to the local "Pow-wows."

Having my own costume, I was allowed to dance with the Native American elders, as if one of their own. And I was, as I do have the blood of the Native American within my body. But most importantly, all of these cultural interactions helped me to pull the power into this life from my own ancient Native American past and to feel it was part of my heritage. These connections made me more aware of the land, the earth and the animals. Just another seed to help me to awaken later in my life, as it would still be many years from now before I could consciously reach back for the medicine totems to pull me into the future.

Several of my mother's friends had heard about my activities, of Indian dancing and invited me to give demonstrations for groups. But before long, these engagements began to feel like pressure, my mother committing me without my permission. Leaving me feeling very powerless over my life, I couldn't seem to gain control over the situation and eventually lost interest altogether. I just told her I didn't like doing it and wanted to stop.

*

I first met Heath when I was in third grade, sitting across from me during Sunday school. I recall that his most predominate feature at the time was that he really enjoyed smarting off. It seemed he was always able to fit a wise crack into just about any conversation and it seemed strange that he could do so without really offending anyone. At least he seldom offended me. I guess I could feel that regardless of what might come out of his mouth, he really liked me.

Our priest then would have been thought of as being progressive, even today and he really helped us by allowing our spirits to find more freedom than our parents felt safe in doing. And in our parent's minds, as a legal representative of God, he had the authority to do so. He really helped them to relax their tight holds upon the world. His name was Father Mike.

Heath and I found ourselves in an extremely enviable situation. There were at least six or seven very beautiful girls that were members of our church, and for the most part, we were the only boys interested in them. Our youth group sponsored camping trips, sleepovers and several events that allowed us to be near them often. We were in heaven! But the most fun we had would occur at church camp, a few years later where Father Mike would soon become director. This was a place that would deeply influence my life.

I had always adored girls, long before the other boys had noticed them and my heart was greatly lifted by their interest in me. I usually had a girlfriend and my feelings for them were very romantic. But I also found within myself, *sexual* feelings that I did not know were forbidden by our culture. In my innocence, I just let myself feel whatever I felt. And within my feelings, were feelings of sexual attraction for a few of my male friends.

I was not particularly troubled by this, as it all seemed to fit into place for me and I didn't yet question it, as it was still a few years before I would be faced with feelings of self-disgust—when I allowed my world convince me of how inappropriate my feelings were.

But love very easily flowed from my being and for the time, I had fallen for a pretty girl in my class named Rhonda. Loving her greatly, I gave her my bracelet to wear.

Days later, I was shocked and my heart horrified when it was dropped upon my desk by one of her friends. With the bracelet covered in scratches, it was obvious to me that our steady relationship had ended. Heart sick and humiliated, I decided in that moment that this would never happen to me again. I made it clear in my mind that I would never let my heart feel that much love again.

I had been maturing rapidly until reaching this point and I was now at a crucial place in my young life. I was more openly severing my connection to love, something that was solely responsible for breathing life into me. What would I have to live for without it? Bringing me my primary source of hope, I was now losing it.

I remember a voice speaking to me while looking into my locker after school, "*You were once a king and you're now learning to protect yourself without having others doing it for you.*"

I didn't really understand the statement, as I no longer had any conscious memories from my past. But it felt as though it meant I had become accustomed to having others physically protect me. And now it was time for me to learn how to do it for myself—to live a life of expression without magnetizing enough anger to me that someone would wish to hurt me. This had been what Igraine was speaking of when she told me she must go, that I had to learn something that required me being in the world alone.

*

Many of my gifts of expression were still with me during my years in elementary school and I had become fascinated with the sixties era. Finding bright and phosphorescent colors to be extremely exciting, I filled my room with them, covering the walls with fluorescent posters that could be illuminated by a black light. Also enjoying the dress of that era, I wore flashy and colorful clothes. People couldn't help but notice!

Still appreciating the attention of others, I became involved in school plays and often entering the school's talent show. I really enjoyed making people laugh, but trouble was growing inside of me. As young as I was, the life's events had already caused me to doubt myself. Being unable to release the fear that I regularly challenged, I was prevented from maturing and growing in confidence as one might expect.

I walked into my room after to school, finding all of my belongings misplaced and scattered about the room. My mother had invited some of the neighbors over and had allowed their children to play in my room. Misplacing virtually every object that I owned, I felt violated.

Furious at her for having allowed this to occur, she would not listen to me and refused to accept any responsibility for what had happened. I could only feel vulnerable and unprotected. Finding no resolve, I saw no other choice. I gave up, stop straightening up my room and stopped collecting the nice things that brought me feelings of power. My mother was trying to weaken me and I did not yet understand why. I could not yet see how my own anger and our karmic ties were influencing her life.

*

The last couple of years during elementary school marked a change in me, and my feelings about myself began to show the world that something was wrong.

All of the children in the south corridor of my elementary school could hear Mrs. Hershey yell regularly at her students. Everyday her boisterous voice bounced down the halls as she expressed her dissatisfaction, our own teacher often closing the door to our room trying to eliminate some of the noise. Although I intentionally avoided interaction with her, I did feel some sort of attraction to her, but not of fondness—one of fear, as if wondering if I could handle being a student in her class. It really came as no surprise to me when I entered the sixth grade and was selected to be one of her students.

The first day of class began with a challenge. Having found a playing card that had been left inside of my desk, the ace of spades, I was unaware that she had seen it, until she told me to throw it into the trash. Walking to the trashcan, I dropped the card and returned to my chair. Though giving her no protest, I was extremely angered. Perhaps she then decided I'd be trouble, but for whatever reason, I became the source of her greatest dissatisfaction.

Finding it very upsetting to hear her yelling so often, I did my best to withhold my frustrations. I don't think it was my behavior in her class that caused her to focus her anger on me; it was my quiet and extreme dislike for her. Gnawing at her confidence, she took every chance she got to correct me.

It was just not possible for me to disappear from her classroom, but I did try. I was ready to do anything, non-violently, to stop her from attacking me. But the suppression of my feelings only caused me to further lose the ability to express myself healthily. Losing confidence, the ones around me naturally began to attack. Some of the boys from the other classes began to tease me about my clothes and a few of the teachers made fun of me because of my long hair.

"Is this a boy or a girl?" a teacher once asked, as I walked down the hall.

Over the next year, while slowly becoming a perfectionist, I began putting away all of my colorful and expressive clothing. Eventually unable to wear a piece of clothing that would make me stand out in any way, I became so introverted and shy that I could often barely speak without blushing. Instead of allowing my feelings to control my behavior, thoughts and logic took control of me. Severely choking me, I was no longer capable of letting my heart lead me in any way.

*

Denby, returning as a cousin, was very close to our family, so close, that he was welcome to stop by at any time, often spending the night. Several years older than me, he had a job with the railroad that brought him to our city once a week on Thursday, and we always set that time aside to spend with each other.

He liked to smoke, drink—play cards and dominoes and would occasionally come in with a few bruises from a brawl he had gotten into at a bar. My mother deeply hated this part of him, but being secretly fond of him, accepted this as a part of him that she could not change.

Looking back, I remember him as being one of the nicest men that I ever met and it really didn't make since that he'd get in so many fights. But he was very big and could appear threatening to someone that didn't know him. He did say that others had challenged him.

One of the things that I most remember about his visits were the times we spent watching our favorite TV show, a series about two men that were running from the law with a secret agreement with the Governor. If they could just stay out of trouble for a few more years, they'd receive a full pardon for their past actions. But of course the great difficulty in this was that no one else could know about the agreement. And in the meantime, they remained chased men, waiting for their allotted time to transpire.

For lifetimes since Camelot, together we had challenged the ones in the earth that were in charge of the laws. Even though our intentions were to be on the side of goodness, we had accumulated enough enemies to make our lives very difficult. And now we were waiting for them to let us go, so that we might free ourselves and go on to do higher things. The vision that was still beyond me then, was one of compassion for all, even for the ones deeply caught in the illusion of desperation and violence.

But back in my life at school, I could find no interest in meeting the demands to excel academically as required, and my grades had already begun to drop, even getting close to failing. My brother had always been a straight A student and my parents saw no reason for me not to be the same. With my parents growing very frustrated, they demanded that I improve my performance. But there was nothing that I could do about it. I was trying my best and failing because my consciousness had become too fragmented. I was more focused upon the angry people around me than my schoolwork—too afraid of my environment to concentrate. I could sense that the adults around me believed I was a failure. I was beginning to believe the same.

In a desperate attempt to make me conform, she called me into her bedroom to question me about what was happening in my life. She could feel that I had begun pushing her away.

Questioning me about school and my beliefs, she would then explain to me why I was wrong and that I'd one day understand her way of thinking. It would be the same thing every time. Invalidate my feelings and leave me in a very cold and soulless state of being. Our conversations always left me feeling weak and vulnerable.

But in the effort to make peace, I often tried to find a way to please her, hoping to ease her sense of desperation. But it never did. I could never do enough. It wasn't about me. It was about her. My uniqueness frightened her and she could not be at peace with something she could not understand and control. She couldn't feel safe around me and did the only thing she knew—hate me for being different.

* * *

Fascinated with martial arts, together with Heath, I began to study Karate. I'm sure it was the sense of mastery it promised that had attracted us, the ancient memory of power holding our attention.

We had fun for a time and learned many things—many which were not intentionally being taught to us—like what fear can make a person do. I could see that my teachers were angry, that they were even mean. They were not living the truths we unknowingly sought and could provide us with no answers. Eventually losing interest, we dropped out, continuing our path of searching and discovering new things. And there would be many things awaiting us, as if we were challenging each other to find something that we had not yet imagined. We searched the world for answers.

With violence occurring at my junior high school, just prior to the years I attended, I dreaded each school day. Desegregation had begun, resulting in a few small riots leaving the possibility open for more violence in the future. The teachers seemed just as scared, many of them, seeming to be our enemies.

Our two gym coaches, very aggressive and intimidating men, put us through a rigid physical training at the beginning of each year. Very demanding, they often pushed us hard enough to make one of us throw up. I usually just tried to disappear in the class and go unnoticed by them.

One day after showering, a rumor spread that a boy named had been smoking outside in the foyer. The coaches, overhearing the conversations, quickly called him into their office. With their door remaining open, we all stood outside and watched, knowing that he was in serious trouble. Enjoying the power they felt over him, the coaches told him to stand in front of their dartboard.

"We heard you were smoking," the first coach insisted.

"Were you, Dennis?" the other demanded.

"No! I swear I wasn't," he told them.

With his head centered in front of the board, the coaches sat in their chairs several feet away, both holding darts in their hands.

"Fess up," the other coach said, his eyes twinkling of excitement.

"I wasn't," he insisted.

"Okay," the first coach said, beginning to laugh along with the other. Pulling his hand backward, he sent a dart flying toward Dennis' head.

"Thump."

From outside the office, we all watched in shock as it struck the dartboard, landing just inches from his face.

"Are you sure now that you weren't smoking?" the coach laughed, totally entranced by the child's fear and their ability to dominate him.

"No," he desperately pleaded, almost in tears.

"Okay then," the coach laughed, letting another dart fly.

"Thump."

This one stuck in the board on the opposite side of his face.

"I swear I wasn't smoking!" Dennis fearfully begged.

I can't remember how many darts were thrown, although I do know that there were several. But it was the last one that I cannot forget. Flying perfectly true, it was headed directly for the center of Dennis' face. All of us gasping, there was no question as to where it was going to land. And Dennis was too afraid to move.

But half way in flight toward his head, the dart appeared to have been slapped. Initially flying straight, it was now flying almost sideways and slapping his forehead at an angle, ricocheted off his head and stuck into the dartboard.

The coaches then roared with laughter, overwhelmed by their newfound entertainment. With the bell ringing for our next class, we all shuffled out of the dressing room and hurried on our way. Believing that situations like these were to be an expected part of our life, we didn't really see error in their behavior. But they had apparently crossed the line, as one of the coaches never returned to class. Having been transferred to another school, that challenge was now over. I was thankful.

*

It was during these years that I learned about a type of person that was known as a homosexual, an individual that I understood to be a very disturbed person that enjoyed sex with persons of the same gender. Typically male, as I was taught, they were to be hated and abused. Only a part of me could now remember that I had once felt such desires myself, but my fear of being one of these despised types of people overwhelmed me. Unconsciously deciding that I was not going to be a part of that group, I soon joined the cause of hating anyone that was.

A troubling time in my life, I was finding rejection on every front. Nowhere could I find anyone to mirror the very important pieces of my soul to me, and my uniqueness continued to disappear. I stopped all artistic expressions and the self-rejection within me began to grow as my need to conform began to intensify. I had been shown that this was a dangerous world for people that chose to be different. And the only way I could keep my desires and expressions withheld, was to grow in self-hatred. And that is what I did.

It took large amounts of energy to keep myself hidden from the world, but I believed it was my only chance for survival. My vibration continued to drop and disappearing with it, the memory of hope. It would have been too much to bear otherwise. But once a year, I would be reminded.

Going to church camp every summer breathed life into me. A very special place, it influenced many lives by giving the attending children unusual freedoms. Father Mike had become its director.

The main body of the camp sat at the foot of two gently sloping grades of land. An arching bridge, spanning one hundred feet over the creek divided the land into two portions. On one side was a trail that led to an outdoor church standing upon the peak of a hill that was all contained beneath a high canopy of large oaks. The cabins were once on this side of the bridge, in fact they had been there during my first year there, but now all the campers slept in new ones on the other side of the creek.

A larger than Olympic size swimming pool sat at the edge of what looked like a dense forest. It was said to have been there since before World War 2 and had been temporarily filled with dirt then, for safety reasons. It was believed it might become a target if we ever had come under attack.

But far beyond the beauty of the land, this was a special place for other reasons. A tradition had been started long ago to allow the children here to feel a special power. They were allowed during their brief stay, to live beyond the logic that most of us had to endure when at home—the power of love and a deeper self-acceptance—feelings that I had not yet experienced and that I found to be completely liberating.

Even the pious and most contempt filled visiting priests found they could do little to stop the natural camp energy from flowing. They would not be able to dominate the children here and most were intimidated enough to limit their attempts to try, pretending they liked what they were forced to be a part of.

Camp was a place where art and expression were given a voice and we learned of a spiritual freedom there that went far beyond the dogma that was officially taught in our everyday lives. It was an important gift to me and many souls were given hope there and instilled with the memory of what could be.

Jana, a young and very beautiful arts and crafts director, clearly loved her work with the camp. A very dynamic person, everyone desired to be closer to her and I was no exception.

Having decided that our skit for the final night would be a humorous version of Goldilocks and the three bears, it was time to decide who would play Goldilocks. My eyes grew in shock when everyone in the cabin turned to me. All pointing in my direction, I was jolted by their expectation. Having little say in the matter, they insisted.

But to my surprise, I soon found myself sitting next to my beloved Jana as the makeover began. Completely intoxicated, I was mesmerized in her aura.

First she teased my hair, then curled my eyelashes. As she applied full make-up to my face, wasn't paying attention to what she was doing, I only paid attention to *her*.

The play went off well and was greatly enjoyed, even receiving a special award, one that they made up especially for me. The head counselor said that when he saw the fear on my face as I walked out of Jana's cabin having to face the other campers, he had found an unexpected appreciation for my courage. And so I was rewarded, with extra candy at snack time.

With many opportunities for each of us to find greater self-respect for ourselves, we all earned more hope than we had arrived with. And then we were sent back to our own worlds, to once again face the challenges that our karma would present.

Arriving home each year, I would feel devastated, as though I had been slammed into a wall. Unable to deny how miserable my life was, it would take weeks before I could numb myself enough to cope with the world in which I had to live. I counted the days awaiting my return to camp.

Heath arrived at my house one afternoon, a few weeks after camp for a sleepover, carrying along with his clothes, a few extra rolls of toilet paper. Having mapped out a plan to steal the hearts of two of the girls that belonged to our church, we had decided to "paper" their house, to wrap the outside of their home with toilet paper. This was the accepted method of showing your affection to your beloved. That night, we slept in the makeshift room in my garage. With our bicycles outside, we propped the overhead door up so that we could easily slide underneath it when we were ready to leave. Armed with several rolls of toilet paper, we were ready to go shortly after midnight. We had to wait to make sure my parents were asleep.

A daring effort, the girls, two sisters, lived several miles away, even in another city. And we would have to ride our bikes down a well-lit and heavily traveled road after midnight. With a great likelihood that we might encounter police, we pushed that possibility out of our minds.

Midnight arrived and after padding our sleeping bags to give the appearance they were occupied, we were peddling away, each carrying several rolls of toilet paper under our arms. With cars passing us by, we were undaunted and oblivious to any danger, although very grateful when we finally arrived without a hitch. It seemed the girls had known we were coming, had waited for us and were even watching us through the windows. We did an especially neat job, rolling the paper around the tree trunks so that no bark was left exposed. They were impressed.

Somehow we made it home without incident, rode up to garage, laid our bikes down and snuck back in and fell asleep. No one ever found out!

Still drunk off our success, a few weeks later we planned our next adventure. A different pair of sisters that lived much closer, in fact just a few streets away, had also gained our interest. Feeling very confident of ourselves now, we decided to give it another try.

After walking the short distance to their home, we found ourselves standing beneath the huge tree in their front yard. Instantly throwing rolls of paper high into its branches, I was feeling very hurried when Heath whispered to me, "I need to climb up."

"What?" I asked in disbelief.

"I want to get the paper in the highest part of the tree," he said, looking up to the tallest limb.

"No. Just do it like this," I said, showing him how to throw the paper up through its branches. After reaching close to the top of the tree, the roll caught on a high limb and began to unroll itself, leaving a lengthy trail of paper on its way back down to the ground.

"No, I have to get up there," he insisted.

Frustrated, I looked at him in disbelief. Then reluctantly agreeing, he proceeded to climb. Continuing to use up the paper I had brought as quickly as I could, I heard a sound from the front porch. It was the front door—opening!

Bolting faster than I knew I could run, I shot down the street like a bullet and before realizing what had happened, found myself looking back toward the house, from beneath a car parked in the street. Watching in horror, I saw the father of the household walking back and forth across his yard, exactly where I had been only moments earlier, his head only a few feet below from where Heath's feet had been!

Anxiously looking around, I searched for Heath while waiting for Mr. Barton to go back inside, numbed by the flow of adrenaline. I could not return home without Heath.

With Mr. Barton finally going inside, I continued to wait beneath the car, believing that Heath would appear at any moment. But after ten minutes had passed, there was still no sign of him. Seeing no other choice, I decided to return to their yard, even though I believed I was putting myself in great danger.

"Heath," I whispered, after reaching the tree, uncomfortably close to Mr. Barton's front door. I heard no answer.

"Heath," I called again, this time a little louder.

Hearing loud noises from behind me, the crackling of limbs, and the sound of a large weight hitting the ground, "*Thud,*" I was instantly frightened.

Turning around, I found myself face to face with Heath!

"Where were you!"

"Up in the tree!" he said, a smile beginning to flash across his face.

Joining him in laughter, we both instinctively began to run as fast as we could. Almost instantly, we were down the street. Several houses away, and feeling much safer, we slowed to a walk and began to talk.

"You were up in the tree?" I questioned.

"I couldn't just jump down! He was right there," he told me.

"You mean he never saw you!" I asked in shocked.

"He never looked up!" he answered, as I started to laugh.

"Man, I can't believe it! He was right underneath you! You must have been scared shitless!" I laughed.

"If you only knew," he answered.

"I ran down the street and waited under a car till he went in. I couldn't figure out what happened to you," I told him. "That was close."

Although we could have quickly returned home, we still had plans for creating other mischief.

"I was so scared," Heath told me. Having a lot of time in the tree to contemplate his actions, he had come to some profound realization. "I promised God that if I didn't get caught, I wouldn't do anything else tonight. We've got to go home."

"But we could stay out a little longer," I pleaded, not yet ready to return home.

"We got to go back to your house," he insisted.

Not wanting to get Heath's God upset with him, I agreed it was the best thing to do. Sneaking back into my house, this time through a window, we quickly drifted to sleep. We had indeed been lucky.

*

With the tension growing between my mother and myself, she always seemed able to find a way to stop me from pursuing my interests. Feeling as though she had trapped me inside of my body, I was beginning to panic, unable to express myself and please her at the same time.

Refusing to encourage me in anything but academics, I suffered miserably. And my mother, disillusioned with her own life, had no energy to give to mine. Unable to be happy with herself, she could never concede to being happy with me. I didn't know what to do, but felt that I must escape.

As long as I could feel love, I felt empowered in everything I did. But the loss of my grandfather had greatly shaken my trust. It shook the trust of our entire family. And with unconscious demons chasing me, my family's negative beliefs about me were overpowering. My mind began playing tricks on me, convincing myself that I would soon die.

Although I told no one of my secret, I worried about it constantly. And no one knew why I began withdrawing from the world and experimenting with drugs.

Quickly beginning my explorations, I sought freedom from my suffering and soon began to spend a good portion of my life under the influence. Normally smoking pot throughout the day, if I couldn't get it, I was miserable. I would be too conscious and too aware of my suppressed feelings to be able to cope with my life.

Mostly experimenting with marijuana and alcohol, the use of these drugs enabled me to feel again, or at least until their effects wore off. With my emotions completely shut down, the state of numbness I existed in seemed like a prison, and I couldn't remain in such soulless state of being without trying to escape.

*

Included in my life plan was an injury into my ego, much the same as during my life as Arthur. I had to begin again as desperate as I had left when Arthur, working my way backwards searching for all of the pieces of my soul. A crippled ego would make it difficult for me to suppress negative feelings about myself, and would naturally cause me to seek inward. It was very important that I be able to consciously feel every feeling that was within me before I could be completely healed. And this is what happened—I was soon living with the same sense of desperation that Arthur had died from. And this sense of doom compelled me to take more risks.

Having an attraction to a group of kids that were dangerous, I powerlessly felt myself pulled toward them. Unguided, these children admired physically powerful people and even though they weren't particularly strong themselves, they often got into fights.

While in their company, we usually just spent our time walking around the neighborhood without much direction. There were no gangs in our city then and we were pretty much left to ourselves. But we still needed to express our sense of frustration and the group sometimes turned on one another.

Hearing that they occasionally had rock fights in field near our home, I dreaded the possibility that I would one day have to participate. But one evening, I was initiated. The dominant child stopped the group as we walked through the field and assigned teams.

The two biggest guys were on one team, along with two others, while I was sent to a group, obviously deficient in comparison. One of my teammates protested. His terror filled eyes stared into my own as angrily lashed out at me.

"Tell them you don't want to do this!" he demanded, reading my mind while leaving me feeling disgusting.

"I don't mind," I lied, believing that the world could never forgive me for betraying us both.

"I know you don't want to do this!" he screamed, moving directly in front of me. "Why don't you tell them!"

Swallowing my self-disgust, "If that's what yall want to do. . ." I answered, as my voice trailed off.

"Shut up!" the dominant kid yelled back at him. "He says he wants to!"

Scrambling on the ground, the other kids had already begun picking up their rocks as if survival depended upon it. Hearing him tell us the few rules there were, my soul had already disappeared.

"Okay, yall get over there and when I yell, we'll start," he said.

"Now!"

Feeling as though I had become an animal, I had to give up my consciousness to participate in this. Desperately, I began sailing rocks toward the biggest kids, hitting two of them almost immediately. Almost instantly one of them yelled, *"Stop! It's over. This isn't any fun."*

As quickly as it had begun—it ended. Not understanding the cause of their sudden change in plans, I hesitated, gratefully dropped the remaining rocks held in my hands. Rejoining the group, I felt bad, as if I had not provided them with enough satisfaction. But looking back, I guess they weren't used to getting hit.

*

I was still able to find moments of comfort swinging on the porch swing in my backyard. Sometimes staying there for hours, I once fell asleep during the afternoon. With the God energy pulling me from my body, I found myself sitting very comfortably in a small circle with several beings of light. It was very strange to be so comfortable with them, as I had become so shy in the last few years that I could barely look anyone in the eyes. But this place had the soothing energy of the forest and I existed then, as my deepest spiritual self. Beyond our immediate surroundings, I could see only darkness.

They began to tell me of my life in the distant future, things that I would be able to do much later on, as if to inspire me enough to keep my physical body alive. I sat and listened.

"When you become thirty-three years old, you will begin a death of the ego and will soon begin to spiritually awaken," one being told me. Somehow I was able to feel an understanding for the meaning of his words, even though my mind could not. I was able to know things by feeling that was normally concealed by the numbness of my physical body.

"You will talk to the people about the ways of spirit," another said. "And will travel to many lands."

"What if I don't wake up?" I asked, soaking in the calming energy of the dimension.

Remaining quiet for a moment, one answered, "We will send the Blue-jay."

Although I didn't know what this meant, a part of me must have, as it was easily enough to calm my fear. Speaking further, of many things that my memory could not retain, I felt I was about to return to my physical body.

"You will have to forget about this meeting," a being told me.

Unalarmed, I spoke rather calmly, "I will never survive without this memory."

Sitting quietly for a moment, it seemed they were contemplating my dilemma.

Then I awoke.

Leaning up from the porch swing, I slowly opened my eyes, while realizing—the memory was still in my consciousness. I was delighted.

Although I could not retain everything that was told to me, I did remember much and I was troubled by some of their words. Thinking daily about what they had said, "You will have to forget," I was determined not to.

Each day upon awaking, I tested the memory, having decided that when it began to weaken, I'd simply write it down. But after several months, I concluded that I was not going to forget. It was about that time that all knowledge of it slipped from my consciousness and unknowingly, I was back living in a world of darkness.

*

It was the last class of the school day and I couldn't wait for the bell to ring. Feeling a need to get high, I had planned to smoke a joint on the way home from school—*my* plans were about to change. A sick feeling of fear filled my stomach as I looked up from my desk to see two principals standing at my classroom door. In a few moments I would realize that someone had informed them I was carrying marijuana.

Taking me to the boy's restroom, I was searched, later arrested and subsequently kicked out school. Even though that law required me to attend school, as I was only fifteen, they made an exception. They informed my parents that I would not be allowed to return.

A great relief for me, I was terribly stressed as it took all of my energy and focus everyday just to make myself stay in class. With my natural instinct often to get up and run out of the classroom, the marijuana I was smoking was helping me to cope with the anxiety. With my self-worth and confidence so low, I needed a break.

But my parents, unable to accept that I could be kicked out, persisted in finding a way to have me reinstated. Finally negotiating an agreement, the school would allow me to return the following semester, if I were to receive psychological counseling.

Although, I did not feel completely comfortable with my therapist, I was able to tell him about my greatest problem I was aware of at the time. I had no confidence. When not on drugs, I spent most of the day worrying about appearing stupid. And the resulting stress had created a stomach ulcer causing severe pain and making it even more difficult to concentrate.

But seeing my therapist's interest to be genuine, I became convinced that we could make some progress. We began meeting twice a week.

He had a belief that the mind had many hidden abilities that our world had yet to discover. I found this very attractive and much of our time together was spent talking of these possibilities. He even told me that he once had an out of body experience. My interest was peaked.

Talking often about the unconscious mind and internalized self-talk, he was doing his best to help me. I believed at the time that the vast amount of knowledge he gave me was healing and making me more confident. But as I look back, it was coming from another source. He was listening to me and he cared. That helped me more than anything else.

Returning to school the following semester, I now had to face what I still feared the most, relationships with people. And without the use of drugs, it was even more difficult. I still had no outlets for expression and my anger was causing me terrible internal pressures. My fate having been sealed by events in my early childhood and past-life experiences, caused me to fear healthily expressing my anger. I could only release it when I became overwhelmed, when losing control of it in a rage.

My overwhelming anger began to cause me to shut down in fearful situations. No longer able to stand in front of the class, if attention was drawn to me, I would often freeze being unable to utter a single word. Each time one of these situations occurred, I couldn't help but seethe in self-hatred, the resulting self-loathing choking me for days.

But I could never realize the true sources of my injuries, the simple fact that I was so different than what my world believed to be appropriate. I could not be like others, because I wasn't. I had no interest in being taught wisdoms found by ones prior to me, I sought greater ones. And because my grades were so low, my school was teaching me that I was a failure. I desired a simple life, yet my world told me that I was selfish, that I should use my energy to please others. And my physical love knew no gender bounds; my world told me that I was disgusting.

Deeply hating myself, I lived in a soulless void. A place so dark that I believed no love could exist for me, preventing anyone that might love me to come closer. My spirit wandered even further from hope, love and redemption and I became a loner. The most conscious part of my being had to die—just to keep me alive. I would never have stayed in the earth otherwise.

*

With the help of my therapist, I sobered up the following year but the pain did not go away and few of my issues were resolved. Holding my confusion inside of my body, I had little choice but to continue running and begin living a compulsive and overachieving lifestyle. Putting more of my energy into an existing hobby, water-skiing, I believed I could become more confidant.

Already spending much of my time at the lake, I soon began to aggressively train, as if to one day compete professionally. During the warmer months, I would sometimes ski as often as five days per week, my primary focus on the slalom course.

But the pain held within me would undermine my plans to greatly excel in the sport. Even though I had become a very good skier, I unconsciously resisted reaching the next level. And with past-life opportunities, completely satisfying my need to dominate, I would eventually move on to more interesting challenges. Water skiing was only in my life temporarily, to help me focus consciousness upon myself.

*

A friend approached me in the hallway at school as I was hurrying to my next class. Our school was so large that we seldom passed each other and I hadn't spoken to him in weeks. He looked very depressed.

"Is it really better without drugs?" he asked, knowing that I had recently given them up.

"Oh yea!" I assured him, my mind still focused on getting to my next class on time.

"I don't know," he replied, reaching out to me, "Something has to change."

With my body numb and my mind was running, I just couldn't find the time that I wished I had given him.

"Trust me," I told him. "Give them up. It's so much better."

Staring at me through his deep state of depression, my feet were already moving toward my class.

"I hope so."

"Give them up. It's great!" I told him, as I began to hurry away. I'd already lost too much time and would most certainly be late. But I wished I had made the time. I wished I had grabbed Ron's hand, led him away from the school and just taken the rest of the day off. That was the last time I saw him. The next thing I heard was that he had chosen to end his life, having hung himself from a tree in his backyard.

But Ron would not be the only friend I lost. There would be others, some much closer, that would leave from accidents and even murder. We just weren't able to cope with the pressures that were put upon us.

The study of English had always left me feeling very intimidated, as I could never gain an understanding of proper sentence structure. Beyond the basic noun, verb, adjective and adverb, I was completely lost. I just couldn't comprehend it.

After failing English one year, a destined dream of becoming a writer was forced deep into my unconscious. It would just have to lie there, lost with the all of the other hidden pieces of my soul to wait for healing in the future.

With my poor grades leaving my teachers feeling as if *they* were failing, they couldn't help but to be angered by my work. One of them, a football coach, always expected trouble from me. Believing that I was going to cheat, he often searched me for hidden answers before each test.

"I know you're cheating," he told me.

I finally decided if I was going to be found guilty of cheating, I might as well be doing it. So in plain view, I wrote the answers down on my desk. He could have seen them if only he would have looked. Instead, he checked up my sleeves and looked in my pockets, always becoming angered after being unable to catch me. It was quite ironic that my entire graduation would finally depend upon me passing his class, which I happened to be failing, even coming down to the last exam on the last day of school.

On my way home after my last final, I decided to stop by the coach's classroom, to see if he had finished grading my test. He was in the middle of class but motioned me to come in.

"Come on in," he said. "I haven't graded it yet, but I tell you what. I'll do it right now—just for you."

"I can come back later," I assured him. I was far too shy to stand in front of his class, especially under such dire circumstances, knowing that I had to ace the test in order to graduate. I really didn't want to be told that I had failed in front of a room full of people.

"No. I don't mind at all," he insisted, his face marked with a twisted sort of smile. Confidant that I had failed, he wanted his class to see the power that he held over me. He let them know of my situation and all of their eyes became focused on me.

When he reached the second page, he found the final mistake that I would be able to make and still pass his class for the year.

"It's all over now. You don't have a chance," he laughed. "See you next year."

But he still hadn't finished. Turning the third page over, he was slightly irritated that I had not yet ended any speculation about my graduation. Then he became more visibly angered as he neared the end of the test—I had still not made the final error needed for him to flunk me.

"I don't believe it! I don't believe it!" he complained in extreme frustration after realizing that I had met the challenge. *"You are so lucky! I can't believe it."*

Afraid of being kicked out of his classroom, I started moving toward the door. He was furious.

"I can't believe how lucky you are!" he continued repeating, shaking his head and sneering.

Overwhelmed, I was still at a time in my life when just standing in front of a class could cause me to freeze up. And now I was forced to do not only that, but also to allow many people to be witness to what I would have preferred to be a very private moment. We all found out together that I was going to graduate! Forcing a smile, I walked out the door as he continued to mouth his frustration. If I hadn't been so numb, I would have been overjoyed.

*

My body, continuing to face violent internal pressures, could not withstand the pressure. With my greatest fears centered upon survival, my bodies' lower chakras had been thrown out of balance and the resulting dysfunction in my kidneys had begun creating stones.

Still living with my parents, I was walking through the house when I began to feel a burning sensation in my lower back. Now increasing, it turned to pain and I found myself lying on the floor rolling from side to side. Unable to tolerate the pressure, I stood, my back slightly hunched over and walked to the back door of our home. Opening it, I yelled to my mother who was outside, "Mom, I'm sick!" With the need to throw up, I quickly made my way to the bathroom. My face was ashen.

My mother took one look at me and said, "I think you have a kidney stone." We immediately left for the hospital.

After laying on a gurney for about an hour in the ER, my doctor arrived. Making his diagnosis, an hour passed before I received my first pain shot. Having never felt suffering like this before, the moments of waiting to be medicated seemed like days.

Patiently waiting for the shot to take effect, we were all surprised when no relief came. My body, too tense to allow the medication to work, still left me agonizing. After another hour passed, I received another shot—still the same response, no relief. The nurses looked on in disbelief. "You should have been asleep hours ago." But the third shot took my consciousness from me.

Awakening the next day, I could still feel the familiar burning sensation as my body continued to wrestle the stone. Unable to hold any food down, three days passed and my stomach muscles had grown exhausted from contracting. My head ached severely.

Finally given an extreme sedative, I slept for most of a full day and upon waking, realized that the pain had stopped. We soon discovered that the ordeal was over.

This was first stone that I would pass, my body's way of forcing me to throw up pain swallowed long ago. But my body still needed more purification and these attacks were destined to continue until I learned how to release this energy on my own.

*

Fascinated by the ocean since early childhood, I had always found very powerful feelings of peace during our vacations at the beach. Having wonderful memories of being there with my family, it had been Jasper to introduce us to the magic of the sea. And as my interest in the ocean grew, I became fascinated with the undersea world and soon with thoughts of scuba diving.

The karmic memory of once drowning, helped to create my interest in diving, the need to overcome a force that had once taken my life. And challenging fear always brought me closer to myself. Becoming a very proficient diver, I earned advanced ratings, although no sense of confidence could be felt through the thickened walls of my ego. But gaining a degree of mastery over water, my mind released me for the time and my attention was once again drawn elsewhere. There were still many other things that I feared and I needed to face them all.

Making a living in the tire industry, I was transferred to open a new store located directly across the street from an airport. Closely watching the airplanes take-off and land each day, I felt my interest in aviation increasing. I did not yet remembered my last lifetime where I had been a pilot in World War II. Having died in an explosion that occurred just after my plane had taken off from the runway, another deep-seated fear still remained with me. Unconsciously, that fear drew me toward it and another opportunity to further purify my body.

I felt quite comfortable as we taxied down the runway preparing for take-off—until my instructor unexpectedly gave me control of the plane's ailerons and elevator. Grabbing the cradle as tightly as I could, my instructor began to laugh quietly.

"It's okay," he assured me. "Just ease back."

Feeling the desire to panic, I pretended calm and following his instruction, the plane lifted itself into the air. Preoccupied, I found myself nervously glancing down to floor of the plane, perhaps waiting for an explosion. But after a few minutes, the apprehension eased and I began to enjoy the flight.

Continuing with flight school for several months, my mind soon began to look in a different direction. Even though I was becoming proficient at flight, having flown solo on a few occasions, confidence would not come to me. And with the main purpose of training, to overcome fear almost complete, I was soon ready to move on.

Having recently taken up horseback riding as a hobby, I began spending more of my time at the barn where I stabled my horse. A rank old man named Chuck ran the place, and having some degree of interest in me, began to teach me about horses. He was a real cowboy, had once existed off of the rodeo circuit and had even trained horses for the circus. He loved horses and the life of a cowboy, but I think more than anything else—he loved opportunities to harass and poke fun at both his friends and enemies. His unpredictable personality was both attractive and repulsive, and since I needed to learn how to handle myself around this type of a person, Chuck was the perfect teacher.

He was sometimes funny, disagreeable at others and almost always was ready to give someone a hard time, if he could lure them into his game. I learned quickly—Give in. It was the only way. If you were to wrestle with him to any degree, he would try even harder to make you look like a fool. And he could do it! Years of running with the roughest of characters around had conditioned him well and he could always find a way to make you look foolish, if he wanted.

When someone he wished to harass walked up, he would often begin, "You know, ol' so and so told me that you did . . . . . . Is that true?"

He would always make up something really offensive, often genuinely upsetting his victim. Then he'd back off, "Now wait, that's not what I said. I was just wanting to know if it was true or not." How could they be angry with him? At least not for the moment, until they ran across town to confront the person he had named. Then they'd realize they'd been had. He would really stir up a mess and just laugh and laugh about it for days, constantly recounting the story to us.

But when I realized it was just best to admit to whatever he'd accuse me of, regardless of how offensive it might be, and just agree, "Yep, that's right," I was free. It didn't take long until he realized I was no longer a challenge to him and his gaze would go to others more lively.

A carpenter, living at the barn needed help on his construction crew and approached me about working for him. Unemployed at the time, I guess it looked as though I needed work, as I was often at the barn with little to do. Although I agreed, a part of me really wasn't interested. But wishing to one day to build my own house, I reasoned that this was an ideal opportunity to learn how.

Deciding I would just work for a few months, until gaining enough experience, I'd then return to what I believed to be a more respectable line of work. Having come from a field that didn't include manual laborer, I believed this position to be beneath me and I didn't feel great about having taken the job.

Unexpectedly spending the next couple of years of my life learning about horses and working as a carpenter, my heart was given a chance to rest. Having been so shy while working in sales had created a lot of stress, robbing my internal life and preventing me from deeply relaxing. I had difficulty knowing my own thoughts and desires. But now I was finding more freedom for myself and gave in to my growing desire to spend time alone.

I was still far away from releasing enough pain that I might find the freedoms and power known in my distant past. And the beliefs I had been taught about myself in this life still prevented me from finding any trace of my most genuine self. Feeling anxious about the loss made it difficult to stay present while working as a carpenter. I always felt hurried, rushing my work.

"*Rock, Rock, Rock, Rock,*" a bird screeched just outside my window. Barely dawn, my only desire was to sleep.

"*Rock, Rock, Rock,*" it called out again.

Refusing to allow me to sleep, his deafening screech grated upon my nerves. Reaching for another pillow, I pulled it over my head.

"Rock, Rock, Rock."

"Uhhhhh," I moaned, rolling over. Lifting my head, I slid my body across the bed in the direction of the window. My backyard overgrown in trees limited my vision to just a few feet. Unable to see the bird, I convinced myself that this was an isolated incident and pulled the pillow back over my head.

"Rock, Rock, Rock."

I finally drifted off into light and restless sleep.

After two weeks, my eyes began showing frustration. Awakened at dawn each day, I felt sleep deprived as my hatred for the bird reached the surface.

"Rock, Rock, Rock, Rock," he called every morning.

Always able to find me—even if I spent the night away from home, I could never find peace after sunrise, except when considering ways that I might put an end to his life. Lying in bed during the early hours with my pillow covering my ears, I would think of ways to kill him. Considering using a small-gauged shotgun, I decided that would make too much noise. Poison? No. I never carried out any of my fantasies, but they did make me feel better.

Growing up, I had always lived in a new home, in a recently developed subdivision with very little wildlife around. But now I had moved away from my family and into a very old part of the city. As promised—the Blue Jay had found me. And he was here to stay, remaining close to me until I began to find a spiritual direction for my life. Bringing my anger to the surface, he forced purification upon me while giving me the gift of his vibration—the frequency of *intuition*.

*

The horses moved closer toward my life. Purchasing interests in *racehorses,* my direction seemed to be changing. Studying bloodlines and training techniques, I learned as much as I could about Thoroughbreds as my thoughts moved toward a new career. Now convinced that I wanted to train racehorses for a living, the world would soon bring me a simple reminder.

Matters of the heart, long forgotten, seemed completely foreign to me. Although dating regularly, I had not experienced passionate love since childhood and a destined meeting was drawing very near. Not a meeting with my life-mate, but an encounter with a special *one* that would stir the memory of her, and help me to remember what I valued most.

I met Mia when she moved into the vacant house next door to me. Very beautiful, I immediately noticed that there was something special about her. Our first intimate meeting came as she trimmed the bushes in front of her new home. She told me that she had moved from a nearby home and that she would be living there until the house sold. Belonging to one of her friends, it was made available to help her out of a troubled relationship. I was just happy to have a neighbor that seemed so warm and immediately felt love for her.

Losing what she had hoped to be an unending future with a man that she loved, she was still upset. But I was secretly hopeful that she might find love for me.

I suppose that she must have been somehow touched during our meeting, as a few days later in the evening, she rang my doorbell. Knowing that I was a builder, she asked for help with the light in her bathroom. It had stopped working and she was preparing to replace the fixture. I don't know if that was merely an excuse to be with me or if she really was in need, but within a few minutes, we found ourselves sitting on her bathroom floor, in the dark. The only light came from a flashlight that she held as I tried to prepare the new fixture to be installed.

"Would you like a beer?" she asked.

"Sure."

Returning moments later with two opened bottles of beer, it began to seem that we were just trying to make the best of the moment. I certainly did not want it to end, although it would only take me a few moments, going as slow as possible, to install the fixture and restore light to her bathroom. But we were together long enough to make a deeper connection and within a few weeks, we had begun dating.

Having lived a rigidly structured life for several years, I had only recently opened to the possibility of loving someone. She happened along at the precise moment, and although our lives were moving in different directions, we were crossing each other's path in a storm that would leave me forever changed.

Mia was exploring herself and looking around in the world, as if trying to find the pieces of her own distant past, her ancient past. I was just opening to love.

Being drawn to the Native American culture, she took classes to learn about their heritage. Attending sweat lodges, and other ceremonies, she also studied about herbs and alternative healing methods. She began regular massage therapy and joined a women's group where she seemed to find comfort. I just watched from a distance as my love for her grew stronger.

Arriving at her house, she was excited to tell me about a recent idea. Having lived off of her savings, she was feeling a need to ease back into the world of earning money. And in an effort to create an income, she had begun making *Dream Pillows*—very small, square pillows, just a few inches across that would be filled with herbs chosen for their vibration. Beautifully covered in celestially printed cloth, they inspired mystical thoughts. On the front was a pocket that held a card telling of the herbs it contained and the purpose of each. They also contained a very small crystal.

Within a few weeks the first herb order arrived and the fragrance of her home became intoxicating. The pounds of herbs that she kept on hand seemed to pull me into another world, their overpowering fragrances of lavender, sage, and peppermint calling as though to awaken me from sleep.

Often listening to New Age music in her home, I helped her to make the pillows, turning them inside out after she had sown the two pieces of cloth together.

When we met, I was spiritually asleep. Knowledge of God and the memories of my past were not yet available to me and I could not understand the purpose for many of the things that she was now adding into her life. But my love for her was powerful enough that I did not greatly question her about them. She was giving me something that no one had ever given to me before, and this love growing between us, calmed many of my fears. I just watched.

Finding it difficult to sleep one night, I decided to visit her. It was almost Halloween and my skeleton costume lay near the bed. Instinctively putting it on, I walked next door, knowing she'd still be awake.

"Trick or treat," I said, surprising her after she opened her front door.

"Look at you!" she laughed, placing her hands on her hips.

"I couldn't sleep."

"Would you like some tea?" she asked.

"Oh yes."

Thoroughly amused, she invited me in while putting some water on to boil. She had just the cure, herb tea.

Sitting down in her living room, I watched her walk over to me, still smiling as she admired my costume.

"A skeleton," she said.

"Do you like it?"

"Oh yes," she smiled.

The chemistry between us was strong. Just to be in the same room with her was healing as she unknowingly offered me her gift of hope and the feelings of joy I felt when near her were beginning to become addictive.

She told me of the growing interest in her dream pillows and of the many orders that were now starting to come in. I was amazed. There was something about her that inspired others and this pillow that she was offering, was perhaps a statement—she believed in *magic*. And the people she touched also believed.

Hearing the teakettle whistle, she walked to the kitchen. I looked around the room. The house she was living in had set vacant for many months. I had found no life in it before, nor had any prospective buyers, but things were changing now. In just weeks, it had become barely recognizable. Her life's work had been in fashion, although she had temporarily retired, but her imagination remained sharp. With very little money, she had transformed this house into a home and her desires, hopes and dreams were finding their expression here. Her choices of colors, fragrances and furnishings changed the homes vibration and I began to sense that it would likely soon sell.

She brought me a cup of the herb tea.

"Would you like some honey?" she asked.

"Yes, please," I answered.

Returning, she added a few drops to the cup.

"Your house is so beautiful now," I told her.

Since moving in, she had spent much of her time trying to get comfortable there. Her previous home was much larger.

"I hadn't really noticed," she said as she glanced around the room. "I've been so busy."

"Well, I remember what it was like before you came and it's a dramatic change."

She smiled.

"It is amazing about the dream pillows. I never imagined you'd get so many orders," I told her.

"I'm going to need to buy more herbs soon," she said. "It *is* rather amazing. I'm trying to decide how much to order."

Breathing in the wonderful fragrance, my eyes began to grow tired. Perhaps the chamomile had begun to take effect, or that I found her company soothing.

Continuing our conversation, I finished my tea and soon gained the sense of desiring sleep. It was very late, and recently having begun my own construction business, I had several construction jobs to oversee in the morning. Needing rest, I thanked her for the tea and snuck back into my house.

In the following weeks, our relationship continued to deepen. I hadn't realized how involved I'd become, until I suddenly felt her pull away. Something had triggered fear within her.

Time for her to redefine her place in the world, she was ready to make a new life for herself and she had no idea where that might take her. All she knew was that she needed more time for herself and that meant spending less time with me.

We continued to date, although distance had grown between us. She began to sort her life out and to regain her direction. I was hurt.

But our love for each other linked us together and we would continue to support and learn from each other, only now from a distance. Our destinies were different and we had to accept that—I would ultimately have to continue alone.

Before meeting Mia, I had no love at all and without her, I was forced to become aware of its absence. Spending my whole life running from this fact, I had been compulsively trapped in activity to avoid the awareness of my pain. But I could no longer deny it. I had consciously experienced a new world, a life filled with love, and it was now very obviously gone from my life. The resulting effects were life changing for me.

No longer able to keep up the facade, I could not find the energy that my business demanded of me. With my heart bleeding, I could only envision a dramatic change in my life and very abruptly made the transition to a slower lifestyle. Gradually releasing the responsibilities that I had accumulated, if I were going to continue to live, I would have to become closer to my heart.

*

But hope presented itself to me in my personal life. Having recently become inspired to talk about their unexpressed grief, men were beginning to gather in groups all over the country. Finding that they were left feeling empty as they chased the mythical dream, the dream our world told us to desire, many felt they had been deceived. And in their pain and suffering, they reached out to one another.

Entranced by their honesty, I longed to be a part of such a group. And finding that a similar one existed in my own city, I made plans to attend the next meeting. Mordred greeted me on the first night—I was warmly drawn in.

Very charming, he offered me a cushion as we gathered to sit in a circle on the floor of their large commercial office space. Immediately knowing I was in the right place, I listened to the men talk about lost power and their desire to live more fulfilling lives. We also talked about the distance that had too often existed between fathers and sons.

Later in the evening we discussed a weekend retreat that was soon approaching, to be held in the forest. Always feeling more comfortable away from the city, I believed this would be a better opportunity to understand their message. I made plans to attend.

Weeks later, I arrived early at *The Forest for the Trees*, pitched my tent and began to wonder what the weekend might bring. Already, unconscious memories within me were reaching for the surface. Watching others arrive, I wondered of their attraction to be a part of this experience. I don't think any of us were really certain.

Helping some of the other less experienced campers set up their tents, we made the nervous talk that uncertainty brings. So far everything was still routine, as we pretended to be shallow beings that worked very hard to be agreeable with others in the stressful city. It wasn't until after dinner that things changed.

I think there were about twelve of us to gather around the fire that first evening. Although a moderately cool night, the fire's warmth made us feel very comfortable. Being such a diverse group, it seemed strange that we were all drawn into the forest for a ritual that made no sense to the conscious mind. In fact, our gathering had broken most of the rules that our world had taught us. Why were we here? We were about to find out.

Our facilitator stood to speak, "Many of us spend our lives being a part of a world that seems to want to tell us who we are. We're taught what we should believe, what a respectable life is and what will make us happy. But for a lot of us, these beliefs can't support us in a fulfilling life. And we're left feeling that somehow, there should be more," Larry began. He stopped for a moment to allow us to reflect.

"This weekend we hope to build a bridge—a bridge back to who we are. I encourage you to take good care of yourselves, to find your boundaries and to stay within them. You are welcome to take some time for yourself and to be alone here, if that is what you need. And you're not required to participate in any of the scheduled activities."

Continuing with the introduction, I noticed feeling a strong sense of security, something that I had not felt since before my grandfather's passing. Here, it seemed that everything was okay. We were being encouraged to be who we were and to feel whatever feelings we had. And the walls that we each carried in our daily lives began to melt, as they were not needed. No one here wanted anything from us that we did not want to give. My soul immediately began to respond.

We were eventually given the opportunity to speak and tell the other men what had brought us to the forest this night. Usually terrified of speaking in front of a group, tonight I easily found the courage.

"I've been living such a busy and complicated life—I just can't keep this up. I don't want to. I *need* a change. I need to know more about who I am and what I want," I said pausing, the tips of my fingers pressing into the earth. "I've always felt very powerful in the forest and at the ocean. It seemed like coming here might help me see what I want to do with my life. I need to find something that I don't presently have."

Having been unusually aware of one of the men in the group, Faye from Camelot, I waited to hear him speak. Silent all evening, he had traveled from another state, not having the privilege of knowing any of us before tonight. I watched him, worried that he might not feel the same power that I was feeling. My fears were soon put to rest.

"I didn't know why I came here. I've been wondering about it most of the evening and I was even thinking about leaving," he paused, his strong face reflecting firelight. "*But I know now,*" he said with a quiet resolve. "I've been searching for something for a long time, without even realizing it. There is something within me that is missing. It's not in the world. It's not something outside of me that I can achieve, attain or control. I'm not sure what is going to happen this weekend, but I can see it's going to change my life."

Sudden and unexpected for most of us, we all found a trust that we had not anticipated knowing, but deeply desired experiencing—Feeling our vulnerability and honesty among other men—An experience that most of us had never known.

Volunteering to participate in an exercise the following day, I was asked to see deeper within myself. As a part of the Native American medicine wheel, I'd be given the opportunity to sit anywhere inside of a circle laid out before me on the ground. Having little knowledge of the meaning of the directions, I first chose the west.

"The warrior," one man stated.

"So what does it feel like to sit there?" Larry asked.

"I don't need any of these guys," I told them, pointing to the other directions.

"Anger. Do you feel that?" Mordred asked.

"I'm not angry," I assured him.

Feeling the same as I often did, numb, I didn't understand his question. I believed that as long as I could fight, I could survive, so the other archetypes seemed unimportant.

"Why don't you sit in the king's chair for a moment?" Larry suggested.

Standing up, I walked to the north. Feeling weaker by the moment, my pride seemed to be taken from me.

"How do you feel there?" he asked.

"Not well," I shrugged.

"You don't look so bold now. Even your shoulders are slumped forward," he added.

I found it hard to imagine how the influences of these archetypes impacted me. My posture was even different and feeling vulnerable, I wanted to return to the warrior's chair.

"Why do you feel different here?" he asked.

"I don't know. But I feel weak," I told him.

"Why not see how the magician's chair feels?" he asked.

The east was more comfortable, although I still didn't feel as safe as I had in warriors seat.

Then I sat in the south, lover's chair. Sadness was all I could feel and I almost began to cry.

Having me move about the medicine wheel while continuing to ask me questions, Larry was trying to get me to feel as confident in the king's chair as I had felt in the other positions.

After an hour had passed, he said to me as I sat in the North, "Why don't you stand up in the chair, take your walking stick as your scepter and hold it above your head *claiming* the king."

"I don't think I can do that," I told him, shaking my head back and forth in defeat.

"That's okay," he answered as he continued.

"Why do you feel so weak as a king?" he asked.

"The warrior can make it anywhere. The others have to rely on him for protection," I answered.

Pausing briefly, he asked, *"What about a king that could protect himself?"*

Finding his statement intriguing, I asked, "How could that be?"

"A king that did not need to rely upon anyone else to protect him," he answered. Sitting quietly, I contemplated his words as my heart intuitively began to lift.

"The king archetype is the center of power. A true king does not magnetize conflict, he neutralizes it," he said.

Although my conscious mind never completely understood, my heart did, and there was a marked difference in the way I felt. Larry, seeing the difference in my expression, allowed me to contemplate the possibility while watching the power within me build.

Then he asked once again, "Do you think you could claim the king now?"

Nodding, I continued to sit for the moment, allowing my feelings to strengthen. After a few minutes, I stood up and stepped upon the chair. Raising the walking stick into the air, I held it with both hands horizontally above my head.

"Claim it," Mordred said.

"I claim the king!" I cried. *"I claim the king!"* Quickly stepping down and taking a seat, I buried my face into my hands, letting go of tears that had been withheld for centuries.

Another exercise made a similar impact me, "Stands Alone," was conceived on the premise that we would each have to go back into our world soon and be asked to live the truths that we were now experiencing. It would be very difficult for us to do, to remain vulnerable to ourselves in environments that could be hostile. Here, we were encouraged to find our power. But it would be different in our own individual worlds. Many of us were enmeshed in relationships that would not easily accept our newfound truths.

Standing in the medicine wheel, in the east, I was at the edge of a large, shade producing pine tree. With all of the men sitting across from me, toward the west, Larry asked the first question. "What is it, that you need to do, but haven't done yet?"

Not knowing how to answer, I asked, "Could you say that again?"

He slowly repeated it for me.

Thinking for a moment, I replied, "I haven't found a great love," referring to the lack of having a wife to share my life.

"Why haven't you?" he asked.

"I don't know."

"What would it be like if did know?" he asked.

"How could I know that?" I answered.

"There has to be some way to get there," he stated. "Why can't you have that now?"

"I haven't met her," I shrugged.

"Why not?" someone else asked.

Already very open, my emotions were fluid within me and a wave of feeling swept through me as a piece of my consciousness returned. But unable to understand laws of magnetism, their logic didn't make sense—their suggestion that I controlled the existence of the love in my life.

"I've never met her."

"But why?" another man asked.

Around these men, I felt safe enough to feel my pain and to release it. Remembering the bits of the pain that had caused my heart to harden, my tears began to flow.

Continuing to ask me questions, I felt a little taller with each answer I gave. Finally, Larry asked, "What is preventing you from finding her?"

"I haven't allowed her to come. I won't allow her near," I said, once again releasing tears.

Answers that I could never feel before, were presenting themselves to me as if I'd known them all along. And the riddle to my life was beginning to unfold. I had been released from my body's prison. Seeing that she would eventually come to me, the restlessness that my soul felt began to ease.

A Native American sweat lodge had been prepared for us later that evening and Mordred instructed us of its purpose. The lodge was built by lashing small willow saplings together, creating a domed structure very similar in shape to an igloo. Placing fire-heated stones inside, in a pit dug out in the center of the floor, created the heat needed to help alter the consciousness of the participants. Enabling us to see from a higher perspective, the ceremony could create a greater opening for our healing.

We were told that the Native Americans believed that fear was an energy held inside of a person that it could be released. And that this was the purpose of the sweat lodge. The ancients held this ceremony prior to any important activity to purify their bodies, releasing fear so that it would have less influence over their actions.

Entering the dark lodge several hours after the sun had set, my eyes were only able to see the glow from the heated rocks. Slowly, we each crawled on our hands and knees until finding our seats around the rock pit.

As the ceremony progressed, we each were given the opportunity in the form of a prayer, to speak about things that were troubling or limiting our lives. Giving voice to our suffering and sorrow, we released its expression-limiting energy.

Feeling very powerful to be with others that were able to concede their vulnerability and to confess their fear, the honesty was cleansing our hearts. Deeply touched and moved beyond what I had imagined possible, I felt as though I received a blessing from the earth. I was changed – I knew my life would now be different.

Marking the beginning of my conscious spiritual growth, I left the retreat feeling refreshed, hopeful for the future, and carrying a new vision for my life.

*

The great healing that had taken place in the forest had brought awareness of the earth back into my consciousness, increasing my desire to become more present. And wishing to maintain a connection with the spirit world, I began to search for a teacher that could help me to expand my consciousness. It was this seeking that brought me back to Vivianne.

Having received her teachings in this life from a Lakota Sioux medicine woman, she was in the position to help me heal. Playing a large role in taking my heart from me at Camelot, it was now her job to balance the karma between us – to give back to me.

Vivianne began by making me aware of how ungrounded I had become. With my mind wandering and thinking so rapidly, I was often barely aware of my surroundings, even when sitting still. Constantly racing off into the future or back to the past, I couldn't hold a spiritual focus.

She told me to begin a journal, to start writing about my daily activities to become more aware of what I was doing within each moment. Then she told me to look into the past. Not my past from before this life, but for the most part, my present one. Looking back into my childhood at my frustrations and failures, she wanted me to consciously understand the traumas that I had experienced. It was if I was re-circuiting my mind to free the energy I had lost as a child, bringing my awareness back to the present.

At the same time I began to look outside of myself and into the world of metaphysics. I began to explore the possibilities of having lived prior to this existence and began to read about earth's past written histories.

Up until this point, I remained unconscious of my past-life memories and had forgotten the mystical experiences I had been a part of as a child, my vibration becoming so low that their memories had been wiped from my consciousness. But now, approaching the years of my promised awakening, I was slowly beginning to remember.

Already aware of the Native American ceremony known as the *vision quest*, I felt an urge growing to experience for myself and within a few months I began preparation.

Following a Lakota Sioux tradition, I started by tying prayer ties, small amounts of tobacco held inside of cloth and tied on a string. Inside of each tie, I symbolically placed the energy of what I most desired to release from my life, the many different fears that had strangled my greatest forms of expression.

When completed several months later, they would be thrown into a fire just before going out in the forest for my quest.

Months later, the destined day arrived and holding several hundred prayer ties, I made my way to the forest. With my friend Paul at a site about a mile away, together we would quest for an opening to our vision. It would be just the two of us in the forest with Faye overseeing the quest, placing us into the woods and returning on the day of completion.

We had made an agreement the day before to tie a string upon the branch of a tree that stood about halfway in-between our questing sites, each day before sunset. This would let the other know that all was well. We would tie two strings on the branch when our quest was complete.

Standing next to the ceremonial fire, the ball of prayers ties in my hand, I stretched out my arm. A foot above the flames, my fingers released their hold and the ties dropped into the fire. Unsettling the logs, sparks flew into the air. It was now time to enter the forest.

With Faye as our escort, he ushered each of us to our sites. Having already chosen my place, I entered the circle, a small dry pond bed at the base of a forested hill. It was small enough not to present an opening in the trees above and the saplings around its perimeter seemed to afford a special protection. Paul entered behind me, followed by Faye carrying water. A quick hug of encouragement and they turned to leave, headed toward Paul's sight.

For me, the quest had now begun. After stowing the water, I took a seat in the center of the circle and placed my pipe directly in front of me. Looking around, I took in a breath and listened to the sounds of the forest. Breathing in the fresh air, I wondered what the day might present.

Being the first time I had ever fasted, I found its effects to be surprising. My idle mind soon playing tricks on me, I became obsessed with fear. After skipping only two meals, my body was telling me that I had to eat. Although my mind knew that I was safe, to ease the fear, I ate an energy bar and relaxed into the quest.

Wrestling my fear throughout the day, I finally began to relax near sunset. Now I was headed into the night.

Sitting motionless on my sleeping bag, the need for sleep tried to steal my consciousness from me. But I wanted to stay awake, or to at least be partially awake.

It was September and the leaves having already fallen, allowed the full moon to peer through the normally thick canopy provided by the trees from overhead. It seemed to be scalding me with it's bright light each time it moved from behind a limb, casting its energy fully onto my face and whisking me back to consciousness each time I began to drift off. But I couldn't have slept now if I had wanted to and I spent most of the night drifting on the edge of consciousness, a great place to be while seeking vision.

The only sounds were of nature. The coyotes had begun their call just as the moon had crested the horizon and shortly thereafter came the sounds from a huskier animal, one I might presume to have been a wolf. But my focus remained with the spirit world. I had waited too long for this moment to allow fear to steal my awareness of the earth.

I wondered to myself. What will happen to me tonight? Will I be able to make direct contact with my guides? It had been my dream for sometime now, to consciously speak with the ones that watch over me here in the earth. It seemed they held the secrets of my soul and my heart was greatly longing to find the pieces I believed to be missing. Enduring the night awake was not easy, but I was determined as I waited for a sign.

I didn't know what to expect from a quest, and really wasn't sure what a vision was. But I was making clear contact with the spirit world, without even realizing it. Vision, was on its way.

It seemed as though it would never arrive, but once again the sun found me, bringing much comfort to me as its light revealed a world that I was very familiar with—A world of trees, mist, dew and animals. And the birds began to sing as if congratulating me for my effort.

Shortly after dawn, I decided to stand up and walk around in the immediate area of my site.

Walking over to a tree, I leaned against one of its low branches stretching out horizontally from its base. Standing there, I quietly rested my mind, soon noticing the grass moving in the distance. It was a familiar site to me. Only an armadillo moves about with such little regard for his surroundings.

Completely oblivious to my presence, I remained still while watching him move closer. Headed in my general direction, he was moving very slowly as he rooted up the ground in front of him searching for food. He seemed quite content with himself yet still unaware that he was getting very close to me.

This wasn't the first time I had been close to the armadillo, but it was the first time I had been aware enough to receive the message that it's vibration hoped to deliver. Waiting, I tried to understand it's meaning as he passed only inches from my foot.

Shortly after he made his way through my aura, I wandered back to my circle and continued to consider his visit. The armadillo holds the vibration of boundaries, of maintaining personal boundaries and holding your own space and vibration. This was the strength I needed most. I had already spent the majority of my life losing my beliefs and desires to other people in my life. And the armadillo was now speaking to me, trying to give me the protection I needed to hold my own focus and to stay conscious of my own truth.

Many keys were given to me during this quest as the earth began to gently nudge me from my sleep. And even though many years of awakening still lay before me, at least for the moment, I had been refreshed and cleansed by the earth. After a few more hours of silent contemplation, I prepared to return to camp. Standing up to leave my circle through its boundary to the West, I looked down at my feet. A small frog sat confidently, just inches away. Turning around in search of the water that I was sure he needed, I saw no pond or creek nearby realizing—that none existed. My messenger seemed to exist beyond the limitations of the earth. Perhaps he was encouraging me to do the same.

* * *

My consciousness began a dramatic shift after this quest and I began to examine all of the beliefs that had been taught to me. I spent hours each day in contemplation, in the effort of freeing myself from the limitation that had been so forcefully imposed upon me. I could see that one of the first things that had to go was the positive attitude that I tried to maintain—a silent agreement with the world. I found it too limiting and saw how it often prevented me from making changes in my life. When I was unhappy with a situation, a positive attitude caused me to cling to it rather than to release it and move into healthier situations and relationships. It first had to go, and I then began to grow.

I walked into my bedroom after having taken a shower, abruptly stopping as my eyes glanced to my bed. The pillow I had slept on lay there wadded up—it's case removed. Shock rang throughout my body, as I was fully aware that this change took place—while I was in the shower. At home alone, I had to accept that this was not done by anyone in our dimension and I marveled at the possibilities that this simple action could mean.

I was finally becoming conscious enough that I could notice the spirit world trying to gain my attention, and seemingly overnight began to see how they were working upon my unconscious mind. I began to regularly see that objects in my home were being moved about, as if to make me more conscious of my surroundings—to get me to wake up. The impossibilities that my mind had believed in were soon being defeated regularly, weakening my ego as a result and allowing my spiritual awareness to rapidly grow.

I had always held some degree of interest in the Camelot that I learned about in school, but I had missed out on the opportunity to trigger any memories. With my mind usually far away from school, it was only my body that remained in class. But now, my interest was peaking and I found myself at the library, very innocently reading about medieval cultures.

Before long, I began to entertain the thought that perhaps I had been alive in the earth during this era and even considered the possibility that I might have visited Camelot, perhaps even been a knight. But I still had such a poor opinion of myself that I could not possibly believe that I had ever made a substantial contribution to the earth.

After reading a few books on the subject, I found my interest intensifying. I continued to dig deeper, and without realizing it, had begun to touch upon ancient feelings of power. Being drawn closer beyond my control, I read every text I could find on Camelot's history. And after I had read enough to feel and to know that I actually had some connection to this time in history, Merlin flashed a blue dot on a page as I read, on the sentence, "I am King Arthur . . ."

"*Oh my God,*" I said to myself, as a part of me began to remember this missing piece. "*My God*"

Walking around my apartment in shock, I stayed up deep into the night considering what this might mean and was left wondering for days afterward. I needed to know more about this. I needed confirmation.

I had recently seen a flyer that advertised an upcoming metaphysical presentation—A woman that allowed a being from the spirit world to use her voice to speak. Although initially hesitant, I knew this was something that I had to experience for myself. Having already been told about witnessing a similar event, Mia's experience had prepared me to seek this out for myself. I was far too interested to let this opportunity pass by and decided to attend their next gathering.

I sat waiting for my turn in a room with many other people that had gathered to hear the woman speak. After answering the questions of several people before me, she finally turned to me,

"And what would you ask?"

Very nervously, I replied, "Did Camelot exist?"

"Yes it did," she answered as I began to feel a rush of energy come over me.

"Was I there?"

"Yes you were," she told me. I took in a deep breath and continued.

"Am I remembering this correctly?" I asked.

"Yes you are," she answered, leaving me speechless. "And you did so much good. But it was a time for the world to step back into darkness and there was nothing you could do to prevent it. You mustn't judge yourself for the errors you made then. It was not your fault. There were others that would not allow you to establish the hope you so desired to bring," she paused. "But in the end your heart longed to leave and you allowed your enemy to fence you in—in a way that you could not escape."

Unable to speak, several people in the room turned around to look at me, and trying to shift their attention away, I nodded to her in thanks.

Spending the next several weeks contemplating her words, I tried to find meaning in what was unfolding before me. Having had such a low opinion of myself, I couldn't imagine how I could possibly have contributed to the earth in this way. Confused, my mind wrestled with the possibility.

I couldn't find all of the answers that I needed, but the path to awakening had already begun. And all I could do now was to participate in God's plan and allow it to influence and change my life. The necessary changes would come about soon enough.

*

Vivianne resisted my interest in the past and aggressively warned me against working directly with the spirit world. I never told her about the memories from my life as Arthur that were returning to me, and I didn't yet know of our connection at Camelot. But she did offer me many gifts that were helping me to grow, although I could not deny the limitations I found within her teaching. Soon realizing that I couldn't allow her fear to stop me, I felt a need to move in a different direction and gain a greater understanding of my own darkness, while allowing the gifts she had given me to continue to expand my awareness. Even though I might lose many benefits by leaving her instruction, I felt it was time for me to begin again on my own, to learn my own vision.

Throughout the following months my vision continued to expand and I became very conscious of myself in the dream world. More past-life memories began to return as my guides brought additional information to me within my dreams as I slept. Beginning to open up, I soon began longing for my power to return.

Having already learned to appreciate the special value in the quartz crystal, I desired to have more of them in and around my house. Knowing their energy can make it easier to see through the veil of earth, I decided to take a trip to a crystal mine where I could dig for them myself and invited Mordred to come along.

After considering our choices of locations, we soon found ourselves alone, in a large and generously producing mine. Several weeks of rain had washed much of the dark red surface dirt away, exposing many crystals that would normally have been hidden. It seemed unreal to us, as we were able to just walk around in the mine and pick them up off the ground as fast as we could go.

With the intense energy of the mine pulling our minds up to a highly spiritual plane, we felt lighthearted, allowing our worries to be washed away. Half joking as I walked down a road beside Mordred, I humorously instructed, "Now this is how you do it."

Reaching down to the earth, I placed the point of my crystal probe into the ground pretending to flick a crystal up to surface.

"Ahhhhh!" I yelled, unearthing the most beautiful crystal I had yet to find. "I was just joking!"

Mordred began to laugh loudly.

With my eyes wide in disbelief, I looked to Mordred and insisted, "I was just joking!"

Then my attention returned to the crystal as I reached down to pick it up. It was clearly the nicest one I had found.

He continued to laugh and began to mock me, as if trying to repeat what I had done.

"How'd you do that?" he asked. "Put a screwdriver in the ground and yell, Ahhhhh?"

Barely aware of his teasing, my mind was still occupied with what I had done. How could this be? How could what I had innocently imagined come true? I was left puzzled.

Later that night, an idea came to me and I began to consider that this might be a special crystal—one that was created just for me. Picking it up, I intuitively placed it in my right hand. There was no longer any question. Its base was perfectly sculpted to fit into my palm.

*

Spending more and more time in silent contemplation, I began to step back further from the outside world. I cut my working hours in half and a shift in my journaling resulted. Finding that I needed fewer words to express my feelings when writing, I began to focus more on the fear that I felt each day during my interactions with others, rather than the specific activities. And I soon realized that additional power came to me more quickly when my sole focus turned toward uncovering unknown fear. Learning to once again feel my feelings through the state of numbness that I most often existed, my progress continued to accelerate.

The day was my thirty third birthday. By now, many forgotten memories had returned and the death of my ego as promised by the spirit world, was soon to begin. Expecting a special gift that day, I believed I would be blessed with more memories from the past, but instead, a gift was about to arrive that my physical eyes could not deny.

Standing on my front porch, I looked into the sky watching the clouds above me curl in what seemed to be a very typical way. Noticing that one cloud directly above me seemed to have an unusual shape, I thought to myself, "That really looks like the head of a horse." My eyes widened and my awareness sharpened as I began to realize what was happening. It not only looked similar to a horse's head, but it was slowly becoming *exactly* identical to one.

Within seconds, I was looking at the perfectly sculpted head of a horse. The vision, a majestic head—its ears pricked forward—broad nose with flared nostrils—was unmistakable.

Wishing that I had my camera with me, I considered running back inside to retrieve it, but instead remained still, wanting only to be witness to the God and Goddess energy. The camera would only have been a distraction.

It took only moments before all evidence of the event had disappeared, with the cloud eventually leaving no trace of its former likeness. I was glad that I had chosen to enjoy the moment, instead of chasing after my camera. Then walking back inside my home, I considered the horse's importance. It was obvious that some force was trying to make me feel very powerful.

*

Although I no longer spent much time with Mia, I occasionally spoke with her and her heart continued to lead my own. I learned that she had recently taken a friend of hers into her home that was dying from Aids, doing her best to make his last days here as pleasant as possible. It was a very courageous thing for her to do as this was during the time when very little was known about the disease. Our world still violently hated its victims, many of them found themselves friendless. But she did not hesitate to help her friend. I just watched, saying very little, but was somehow touched by seeing how badly her friend needed her help. Soon, I would also desire to help others stricken with this horrible disease.

After calling the local resource center for people with Aids, I went through their training and within a couple of months, received my first client. His name was Lawrence, a Native American Indian that was very proud of his heritage. Living a life very close to his culture, he often traveled to pow-wows, where he danced and displayed the beadwork he created. I'm sure he was once very strong and able to take care of himself, but now the disease had already taken his life from him. He barely weighed a hundred pounds.

We first met when I picked him up for an exam with his doctor at the hospital. Having no insurance, he was forced to use the county's health care system because he could not afford to pay for his treatment. Very close to the end of his life, it was now just a matter of trying to make him as comfortable as possible during his last days.

As we pulled up to hospital, he gently asked, "Could you drop me off at the door before you park?"

"Sure," I told him. He was clearly not capable of walking very far and I would have to park quite a distance from the front door.

When I finally returned, I found him sitting in an old and dated wheelchair that the hospital supplied for their elderly walk in patients. I then began to push him into the elevator and up to his doctor's office.

We immediately irritated the nurses when they realized Lawrence's paperwork wasn't in order. They told me that he could not see the doctor until we had filed properly for his treatment, meaning that I would have to wheel him downstairs to the admitting office.

Lawrence was already very sick and the movement was making him sicker. By the time we got to the first office, he was very close to vomiting. Believing we were only minutes from seeing the doctor, they told me he didn't have the necessary information with him to complete his file. Leaving Lawrence in the hall outside the office, I ran upstairs in search of the necessary papers. When I returned, a pool of vomit lay on the floor next to his wheelchair. Having very little control over any of his bodily functions, he urgently needed to relieve himself. I wheeled him into the restroom.

There were people all around us, yet no one could smile at us or offer us any support. Feeling repulsive in their eyes, I focused my mind while growing numb to their stares, only desiring to get Lawrence in to see the doctor.

We finally finished in the first office only to be told that we still had another one to visit before returning to the doctor. By now Lawrence was throwing up almost constantly and I didn't know what I should do. Following their directions, I took him to all of the different offices they requested. Responding to their questions in-between heaves, Lawrence would answer, then we would proceed to the next office. Eventually, I memorized most of the vital information so that I could answer their questions as he threw up. By now I had found him a large cup.

We were finally given the okay to return to the doctor's office and I believed our ordeal was over as we sat waiting for the nurse to call. Lawrence began vomiting again just as the doctor was ready to see him and he asked not to be moved. I froze. The nurse came over to us and forcefully jerked his wheelchair, rolling him into the examination room.

"Please . . ." I began.

"He can't just stay out here vomiting," she angrily snapped.

By now I believed I'd found the most heartless and cruel place in the world. I had never seen people treated so poorly, and it left me feeling sick and powerless.

But now our luck seemed to have changed. A compassionate nurse stepped in and took over Lawrence's treatment—I felt undeserving of the attention.

"*He's too sick!*" she told me.

"What?" my mind screamed in shock, as my mouth visibly dropped open. Thinking to myself, "How can you possibly be too sick to be in a hospital?"

"He'll have to go to the emergency room," she said as she dashed my hopes for immediate treatment. Having been in many emergency rooms over the years, I had seldom seen anyone treated with urgency. I wanted someone to help Lawrence now! And I could only imagine having to wait for hours before receiving any treatment.

"But one of us will go with you," she added, making me feel a little better.

Rolling Lawrence down the hall, she walked by my side until we reached the waiting room, then she left us alone. I took a seat while pulling Lawrence's wheelchair next to me, having already eyed a long row of unoccupied gurneys in the hallway. Hoping that Lawrence would be allowed to use one, I spoke to a passing nurse, "Can he lie down?"

"I'm sorry, he'll have to wait," she told me. I looked at her in disbelief.

"He's very sick and is about to throw up," I insisted.

"There is nothing I can do," she angrily told me.

"Can I at least have something for him to vomit in?" I asked, having left Lawrence's cup in the doctor's office.

"We don't have anything here," she snapped, obviously feeling rushed by other responsibilities.

"He's going to throw up on the floor. Don't you at least have a cup?" I pleaded.

Rolling her eyes, she turned around and reaching over a pass through in the wall, pulled out a small cup from beneath a desk. She handed it to me.

"Thank you," I said, turning back to Lawrence.

Seeing his stomach heaving, I hurried toward him, arriving barely in time to catch in the cup, the liquid already running out of his mouth.

"We shouldn't have to wait long," I lied.

After another twenty minutes had passed, I asked the nurse again, "Can he please lay down now?"

"We don't have the room," she answered as I looked toward the row of gurneys that remained unused, wondering of the source of her hostility. Eventually Lawrence asked too, but she still refused.

The emergency room was terribly understaffed and the nurses under more pressure than they should have to endure. Obviously frantic from a heavy workload, she was doing the best she could. But finally compassion touched her, as she eventually stopped and told me, "He can lay down now, if he would like."

"Thank you."

Five hours had passed since our initial arrival and Lawrence only now had been allowed to rest. Certain that he was moments away from assistance, I told him I would check on him tomorrow to see how things went, then left.

Lawrence phoned me the following afternoon, just after being admitted into the hospital. He had remained in the emergency room overnight without supervision, perhaps forgotten, and had soiled the sheets. The nurses had become angry with him.

"It's not your fault," I assured him. "They shouldn't have left you alone."

But at least now, a doctor had seen him. He was calling me to tell me his prognoses. Told to get his life in order, he was expected to die within the next few weeks.

A few days later, I called the hospital and was surprised to hear that he had checked out! With his condition unexpectedly improving, he had been discharged. Obviously not yet ready to leave the earth, he still wished to impact the lives of the ones nearest to him, while hanging on for several more months.

But the end for him was very beautiful. Unlike many that die from Aids, all of Lawrence's family came to his side in his last hours. Holding on for days, even after his body lost consciousness, he continued to give his family a gift. Having pulled all of their hearts together as one, they kept a constant vigil over him, sitting in the room around the clock with his dying body, as Lawrence slowly let go.

In the end, he returned to the world of light in which he belonged, leaving his earth family's bond to each other, much strengthened.

*

Gifts from the spirit world continued to grow within me and as my heart strengthened, other abilities reached for the surface of my consciousness. Reading a poem while asleep and dreaming, I awoke. It was early morning and with it still fresh in my mind, I got up to write it down. It hadn't occurred to me that I might have been its author. It just seemed as though I had borrowed it. But that moment marked a time when another form of self-expression had come back to me, and words began to flow freely as I began writing poetry and greater works of spiritual self-discovery. I began with short stories, but a book for me lay just beyond my awareness.

*

Sitting directly across from the channeller during a private reading, I waited for my opportunity to speak while listening to her description of my present life.

"This is not who you are," she insisted. "The ones around you taught you to fit in, to not be yourself and your natural exuberance is pushed down," she said, trying to break me out of the pattern that had been so rigidly forced upon me.

"Tall people say many things that are not true. It is their belief that they speak to you, and that is what it must be to you—Just their belief. You must let no one steal your purpose from you."

"Was I really King David?" I asked.

"Of course you were," she answered. "Long before you play harp before the King, you were Shepard. Shepard in the field. And this is where you are today. You are taking the time to get your thoughts together, and then, you will go before the people."

Sitting quietly for a moment, I still felt that I was doing little toward realizing a greater purpose for my life. She responded to my thoughts.

"But you have done many things that you do not even realize. So much work is already complete. You have found the sounds of the Native American, and brought home the crystals from Atlantis," she told me.

Still heavily carrying the aura of failure about me, I asked, "So what happened at Camelot? Why did I fail?"

"Do not think of it as failure. As with all lifetimes, opportunities are presented for growth. It was not your fault as it was a time for change in the earth. But you kept hitting your head and would not stop and take a moment to see through the illusion. You *were* a good King," she paused. "You had many enemies and they would not allow you to establish the hope that was so important to you. You became caught up in castle life and stopped prayer," she answered, referring to the time when I stopped going to the forest to be with God.

"You must not judge yourself for this. Because it is the self-judgment that has the power stop you in this life," she said. "You learned so much then, and it is now time to let the love return to you."

Greatly inspiring me, she touched parts of me that no one else could even have knowledge of, aware of all of my present life actions in the earth. It was as close to speaking with God, as I had known.

"Where is Merlin?" I asked.

"He has visited you once in the dreamstate, but you did not recognize him," she answered.

"Will he come back into my life?" I asked, believing that I needed him to help me.

"He will," she began, as if planting a seed of truth for me to uncover in the future, "But it was when you rose up above him that you found your *true* greatness," she paused. "And you maintained your vision for a time before falling back into the earth. By then you were ready to leave. It was just that Merlin did not agree."

Her spirit beginning to leave the channeller's body, she quickly added,

"You will be in travel when you find the unicorn."

"Through the dimensions?" I asked.

"Yes," she said, placing a finger upon her forehead. "*Take the power from him,*" she told me, then after quickly giving me her blessing, she was gone.

*

While changes within myself continued to manifest, self-betrayal was still a part of my life. My mother called me to tell me that my dog was sick. He had been living with them for the last few months as I traveled seeking a higher vision. Realizing he had a life ending illness, I was faced with the decision to put him to sleep. It was an easy choice. I didn't want him to suffer any further.

We were at the vet's and were given the opportunity to say our good-byes. Sitting on the ground with my father, we stroked his beautiful golden hair. Lying still while we made the most of our last moments with him, he didn't understand what was about to happen.

After a few more minutes, we told the vet that we were ready. She gave him the shot and we watched as his breathing slowed, finally stopping altogether. It was gut wrenching, and the only time I ever saw my father cry.

*

It was now time for me to meet the female that created much of the energy for my murder at Camelot. On a spiritual quest in the South American jungles, Mordred met her and brought her back to the states for a visit.

Morgan was once again very beautiful, and in this life, very reserved. She couldn't remember exactly what had happened at Camelot, but she confessed that she did not feel proud of her contributions there.

Somewhat shy, she was still held to a past that she could not yet forgive herself for. Upon meeting for dinner several days after her arrival, I could still feel a passionate love for her, but could not deny the weakening feeling in my heart. As much as I liked her, I felt powerless around her—the purpose of her visit. It was a necessary part of my healing. I would have to face all of the ones that had taken power from me if I were to ever again receive it.

We had only a few moments together before she left to return to her country the following morning, but we had enough time together to become friends and as we parted, I gave her a gift—a lodestone and the feather of a Blue Jay. I wondered if we would ever meet again.

*

Having faced many of my enemies from the past, I had already worked out much of the remaining karma. Absalom, Titus, Saul, and many others had all come and gone from life. But one still remained. My greatest nemesis had yet to make her appearance.

After many meetings since Camelot, with the edges of my fear worn away, I no longer held the same attraction for Katrina. Part of a metaphysical spiritual group that I had recently joined, when Katrina discovered my interest in the Native American's, she found a way to get to know me better, eventually asking to visit my home.

Telling me she was able to retrieve messages from the spirit world, she wanted to help me in communicating with the world beyond. Immediately sparking my interest, I was very anxious to make clearer contact with the spirit world and found her offer one that I could not refuse.

Completely taken aback during our first meeting, she revealed to me knowledge of my past—information about me that no one else in the earth knew. She told me about many of my past lives and had even discovered some that I had not yet uncovered. With her desire seeming for the moment pure, I believed she truly wished to help me. I was very pleased with our initial meeting and happily agreed to another.

Days later, she called me on the phone.

"Whooo, whoo!" she yelled. "Oh man! You will never believe it!"

I remained silent, unable to understand the extreme change in her personality.

"It's Katrina!" she whooped.

"I thought so," I said, trying to create distance between us, her energy feeling invasive to me.

"You'll never believe it!" she screamed. "I met Merlin last night! He came to me in a dream!"

"Oh?" I said.

"Oh man! He told me everything! How you gave your power away to Mordred during your last vision quest. Shit! He told me all about us and our future together!" she said, raving uncontrollably, unable to slow herself down.

"But he told me I had to wait three days before telling you," she said, before proceeding to finish telling me everything about their meeting.

"We're going to be together, to live in Brazil!"

"Really?" I responded.

"Well, do you want to get together in three days?" she asked, as if bullying me. "Or do you *not* want your power!"

Thinking for a moment, I felt no desire to meet her, yet my mind was still strong. Afraid that I might miss some vital piece of information if I refused, I couldn't pass up the opportunity. I had to at least hear her out.

Walking into my house, days later, her personality now had made a complete metamorphosis. Acting brazen and arrogant, she perhaps believed that she had come to take control. Walking around the room, she sized me up for several minutes after I had already taken a seat.

"*You* are so fucked up," she told me.

With my jaw dropping open, I had no response and continued to focus on the rose quartz ball that I held in my hand.

"Ughhhhh. The energy in here is horrible," she said with disgust as she continued to pace about my apartment, eyeing my belongings, occasionally glancing out the window.

Finally sitting down, she looked across the room toward me, focusing her attention upon me for the first time, "Do you want to know about the dream?"

Mildly shivering, I shrugged my shoulders in disinterest. With her confidence suddenly wavering, she began to recount her meeting with Merlin to me.

"We were sitting on a log in the forest. It was so powerful! And he just began to tell me all of these things. How I needed to speak up more in my relationship with you. That's my problem. I let you screw things up and never say anything about it. I have to take more control," she told me.

My mind was absolutely bending now. Still believing Merlin to be the wise old man that I had read about during *this* life, I could not understand why he had told personal matters to a seemingly dangerous woman.

"He told me about how you gave your power away to Mordred during your last vision quest and how you've been hiding here in this dungeon. Merlin can help you! He's been trying to get closer but Mordred has been keeping the energy around you stirred up, preventing him from reaching you."

There was no question in my mind; she had indeed spoken with Merlin. During my latest vision quest, I had allowed Mordred to influence me beyond my desire. No one could possibly have known this information. Still, I could not understand his reasoning. Why would he tell this to *her*? I was left feeling deeply betrayed. Merlin had left nothing unsaid.

All of his beliefs and desires for me, he had conveyed as if they were unchangeable fact. He told her that she was my partner and life-mate, that she had been half of all the creations that I had been a part of and that it was time for her to step into my life and take control of my future! Inside of my body, I was screaming.

"All these things you've been telling me about spiritual awakening are bullshit! He said awakening can come in a second!"

She continued to relay the same information to me that she had told me over the phone as I quietly listened. Without me perpetuating the conversation, she seemed to be confused, finally stopping, "Well? What do you think?"

"I don't know," I answered as she began to grow angry.

"You just sit there quietly when I bring you all this information! What about the future we could have together!"

"I really don't see that," I told her shyly, my fingers rolling the rose quartz ball within my hand.

"You are pathetic! I can't believe you. We could have everything! And you sit there like this is nothing," she complained, viciously scolding me.

"Maybe I'm wrong, I just don't see it," I answered, my stomach very nervously upset.

"This is it! I can't believe this," she whined, beginning to get up, pretending to leave. Hiding her surprise when I gave her no resistance, she angrily walked out the door, leaving me alone to try to make sense out of this meeting.

Beyond my awareness, I was so infuriated by Merlin's actions, speaking to Katrina, that I emotionally shut myself down. Resisting the possibility that he could betray me, at this point in my awakening I still thought he was here to help. I had not yet realized that it was standing up to his challenges that would set me free. But wavering in self-trust, my hope was destroyed. A part of me knew this to be betrayal and nothing more—but a betrayal that was so bone chilling, that I once again slipped back into darkness, unable to face the truth. My fear took control of my body and within a few weeks, I began to believe that he must be right, that I could not yet see the wisdom in his actions. I became convinced that he was the higher authority that helped to give meaning to my life.

For the next several weeks, thoughts of Katrina continued to dominate my mind, leaving me unable to find any peace. Feeling as if something had been lost to her that day, I could not rest. It seemed I had no other choice than to call her and to try to understand the purpose of her entrance into my life.

"I'm so sorry," she apologized, moments into our conversation. "I was just so excited about the dream."

Again presenting a complete change of personality to me, I was unsure what I needed from her, but relieved that she found remorse for her behavior. Very apologetic, she graciously thanked me for contacting her, and after a lengthy conversation, we eventually agreed upon another meeting.

With still too much karma remaining between us, I could not let her go. I had to face her and give her the chance to make me falter. It was the only way for me to continue to heal and grow in hope.

One day she came over to tell me about some additional information she had retrieved from the spirit world, "Merlin has been trying to reach you so he can help," she insisted. "Mordred has prevented it. He's trying to keep you from finding him."

"Mary has never said anything about that," I told her, referring to the channeled entity that I regularly speak with.

"Maybe she is trying to stop you too," she answered.

Jolted by her words, I considered, "Was I being betrayed by Mary too?" I wasn't sure.

All I knew was that my fear of Katrina was pulling me closer to her, causing me to want to believe everything she told me. While in her presence, she would fill me with doubt. After she would leave, I would be left with hours of journaling, writing about my fear of her as I tried to release my uncertainties. I instinctively knew I must once again find trust within myself.

As my awareness of the spirit world continued to grow, my ability to listen to the internal plane slowly returned. Occasionally catching portions of the sentences that were being spoken, I soon realized that Merlin's desires for me were very different than my own. He seemed to believe that I should live my life as he wished. Extremely intimidating to me at the time, I could not help but be weakened by his challenge.

"You cannot see where you are. Marry Katrina. You need this badly," he demanded, insisting that I couldn't yet understand what I was doing. He believed I should trust him, allowing him to lead me back to my power.

Before long, with Merlin's help, Katrina had taken all of my recently found hope, and my dreams began to slip from my fingers. Merlin and Katrina were greatly influencing my life now and during another visit, she revealed more of Merlin's desires for me.

"Merlin says you should dig up the true story of Camelot, that we should find out what really happened," she told me.

With no interest in remembering, I resisted. But with no true heart of my own, I had little choice but to entertain the idea. Katrina's lust for fame fueled her ambition and was prepared to work with me to retrieve the story. Within a few months, I agreed to begin.

At first, she had been able to bring accurate information to me and I became confidant of her desire to help. But feeling the power she held over me, her motive unconsciously changed. And after a time, almost every piece of information she gave to me became of her own creation. She began unintentionally tying knots in Camelot's truth that I would never be able to untangle—as long as I continued to reach to her for help.

*

Feeling a longing to move to an older and more eclectic part of town, I responded to an ad in the paper about a duplex in an historical part of the city. Ready for a change, I stopped by the property that afternoon.

Tall, age-old trees on the street gave the neighborhood a secure feeling even though it was not far away from a dilapidated area. And the cozy cottage homes, built just after the turn of the century, left me feeling like I had stepped back in time. I immediately liked it. There was something here for me; I could feel it and a few weeks later, I made the move and eased into a new life.

By now, I had really slowed my life down and had begun to live on a very small amount of money, small enough that I only had to work part-time, while leaving me with plenty of time to enjoy my life and to pursue other interests. I was also spending a large amount of my focus toward remembering my past, my ancient past—from Camelot and beyond. It seemed that things were going well now, although Katrina was still in my life.

I loved the new neighborhood, it giving me a very real sense of living in the forest. There was plenty of wildlife around and even the woodpecker was in abundance. Songbirds often sang their melodies and the summer brought hummingbirds to the flowers that had been planted in my back yard by the prior tenant.

But there was a part of me that was unable to release Katrina, and after each meeting with her, I was left feeling more isolated—and hopeless. The false truths she was presenting to me pushed me deeper into depression, leaving me compelled to ask even more questions. She had already convinced me that she was my great love at Camelot and had lived at my side throughout the life. My body was becoming sick, and although I had no conscious awareness of it, the more I reached for her, the more twisted the truth became.

Eventually my body could no longer allow me to walk this walk into darkness, as all of the light had been squeezed from me. Not feeling well, my face had been ashen for several weeks and I could barely eat any food. Then the familiar, deadening pain in my backside returned, a bout with another kidney stone was leaving me momentarily helpless.

Trying to ease the pain by soaking in warm water in the bathtub, I could tell I was about to throw up and leaned over to the toilet. All I could think about was Jasper. And as my gut heaved its contents out of my body, I thought, "I could have never done it without him. Camelot would have never existed without him."

Leaning back, I tried to regain consciousness of my surroundings, feeling the release of energy that had been swallowed as Arthur, the pain that submerged just after Jasper's death. Much of the fear I was faced with when he left had now been released. It was no longer able to poison my life.

*

I was down the street in a neighborhood bookstore, when I noticed an old man that had just walked in the door. Dressed in a deep blue and dated polyester suit, he brought with him the appearance of a doctor. Looking up from the book in my hand, I intuitively realized, "That is Merlin."

Wandering over to where I was standing, he began to look at the books on the opposite wall. Only inches from me, I decided I would remain still and see what this was all about. Certain he had an agenda, and even though I was extremely frightened, I thought it best to face him.

Standing back to back for half an hour, we slowly made our way down the isle together as we each scanned the books on opposing walls. If I were to move along the isle, he would soon follow, usually leaving us no further than a foot apart, sometimes coming as close as a few inches. Sensing that he was finished, I took in a deep breath as he started to leave, but was surprised when his shoulder lightly bumped my own.

"Excuse me," he said, with the slow voice of a confident old man.

He continued into the next room and spoke to the man behind the counter, "Do you have any old medicine books?"

"Did you look on the main isle—over there?" the store attendant asked, as he pointed in my direction.

"I've been through those," he answered.

"Sorry, that's all we have. You might try our other location."

Thanking the clerk, Merlin walked toward the exit. But as I watched him, I noticed that instead of leaving, he stopped inside the front foyer. Standing at the edge of a nook near the magazines, he found a place where he could get out of my line of vision. Then turning backwards, he began to scoot himself into the corner. All I could now see were the tips of his shoes sticking out from beyond the wall.

"He's crazy," I thought to myself.

Closely watching the foyer, I refused to let him step completely beyond my vision. Then as I glanced toward the floor, I realized I could no longer see the tips of his shoes. Even though I had been closely watching the door, I had the feeling he was no longer in the store. My mind asked, "Could he have disappeared?"

It took only a few quick steps to reach where he had been standing seconds earlier. My eyes could not believe, *clearly*, he had disappeared—he was no longer a part of this dimension.

Even though I had already begun to believe that such a thing was possible, I was shocked. My mind just could not agree with my belief system and I began to look around the store for him, even walking outside. He was nowhere to be found.

This really had a strong impact on my mind and I had not understood the effect this would have on my physical body. Becoming severely ungrounded for the next several months, I would remain this way as my body and beliefs began to adjust to allow new possibilities to exist.

The new truths that were being presented to me regularly were in constant challenge of my beliefs in limitation. Having little control over what was happening to me, I just did the best I could to keep myself open. It began to take my fullest concentration.

I could sense that it was time for the logic that had strangled me for so long to release its hold, and I began to focus myself even more internally. By now, I was spending four to five hours a day journaling or in silent contemplation and would often spend the entire day alone. It seemed I had to do this, as it took all of my energy to go into the past, searching for the truth. Remembering traumatic events from past lives, I was unlocking the pain still held within my body.

If I were to purify myself, I would have to begin to throw up the energy that I had swallowed. Sitting in front of the gas stove that heated my house, I would gag up the pain, allowing the flames to transmute my aged fear. Feeling the energy being released moment-by-moment, I remember thinking that I would soon be free. Exhausting work, contemplating my own fear in such a direct manner, after a few weeks I looked horrible. With dark circles beneath my eyes, I looked as though I'd missed sleep for days and my face remained pale.

I had no idea how long this would continue and never realized this would take years to complete. But each time poison was released, I began to feel to greater depths and to believe that greater hope was soon to come.

As I became more aware of myself, I realized that certain foods suppressed more energy that others, and I naturally began to adjust my diet, limiting the consumption of meat, fats and sugars. Still eating the foods I craved, at times I limited my choices, keeping in mind my body's need to purifying itself.

All the while, Merlin continued to visit me when I was away from home and interacting with the world. Other beings also came closer, bringing their calming energy with them to help me feel safe—often doing something to catch my attention—perhaps giving me a wink, then walking away. I had many interesting meetings with the spirit world in this way, but Merlin was by far the most comical.

I had noticed a strange woman watching me as I ate my lunch at a nearby restaurant and realized that I had already seen her on more than one occasion. I still didn't pay much attention when I saw a similar looking woman at another restaurant, on the opposite side of town. But when she sat down next to me as I watched a movie in a public theater, I knew that this was no coincidence.

"*Hmmmm,*" she moaned, arriving several minutes after the movie began.

"*Hmmmmmm,*" she continued, tossing in her chair, trying to get comfortable.

Looking in her direction, the thought occurred to me, "Could this be Merlin?"

"*HMMMMMMMM,*" she moaned again, even louder this time.

Glancing toward her, I felt a butterfly in my stomach, knowing that I was sitting next to him. I thought to myself, "What now?"

Shaking my head, I returned my attention to the movie, trying very hard to maintain my focus as *she* continued to toss back and forth in her chair. But after a few minutes, she decided to leave. Being very overweight, she had trouble just walking and the steps in the isle seemed to be difficult for her to navigate as she made her way up, hanging tightly to the rail. Then Merlin began his game. She began to pass wind!

Thoroughly amused, I laughed quietly to myself as she noisily continued along passing wind, as if scripted with each step she took.

Although it was confusing at the time, Merlin was showing me another side of himself. Vicious in one moment and comical the next, I never knew what to expect from him. But the job before him, although *unknown* to him, remained the same—to help me release my fear him. And there would be many more similar episodes along the way in the attempt to bring us closer together.

*

Having wrestled with Merlin and Katrina for too long, the earth had no choice but to show me of my error. On my way to work, I walked out of my house and onto the street where I had left my truck parked the night before. Stopping a few feet short of where it should have been, I realized—my truck had been stolen.

I had seen the theft over and over in the dreamstate, but I had never understood the depth to which I had lost my power. With my vibration dropping low enough to magnetize a desperate event, the earth could only comply. Showing me the loss, I was forced too see that a problem existed.

Arriving at my favorite restaurant in a rent car a few days later, I noticed a familiar energy in the vehicle parked next to me. Merlin, always prepared to lend a hand, stumbled out of his Talisman Caddy. Appearing now as an old man, he smiled at me as I noticed the jacket that he was wearing—a jacket identical to the one left inside of my truck, only the color was different.

Leaving the engine running and the window rolled down, he walked around the corner and inside the restaurant. Knowing that I was certain to be entertained, I said nothing. He got in line just ahead of me, ordered his food and sat down at a table to eat. Taking a table not far away, I occasionally glanced toward him, unable to stop thinking about his car being left in what seemed to be a very vulnerable state.

I finished my meal, headed for the door and was not surprised when I turned the corner to see that his car remained unharmed, untouched, with the motor still running. I would be left considering this for weeks. Why was his vehicle safe when left alone and unsecured, when mine had been taken forcefully while locked?

Spending the last couple of years in a chaotic relationship with Katrina, trying to appease her, while slowly regaining control over my life had been very difficult. It was very hard to balance her in my life, and her dissatisfaction in our relationship grew. Finally reaching the point where I was no longer willing to keep her entertained, I refused to continue providing her with the excitement that she craved.

In a typical conversation with her on the phone, she tried to start a fight. I simply told her I had to go. I hung up and never called her back, the greatest portion of that challenge seemingly complete.

*

The absence of my resolve was becoming more obvious to me, even though I had nothing from this life to base that assumption. Although I had powerfully expressed myself at times, the truth was that I was still living the desires of others. I had not yet found the courage to see deep enough into my own soul and find my own unique expression.

In the year's prior, Katrina had convinced me of the importance of being able to reach Merlin. Having already come to me in many situations in the physical world, I had refused to speak or directly acknowledge him. And when I began to realize how he was betraying me, with his demands for more control of my life, I tried even harder to create distance between us—making him try even *harder* to reach me.

Beginning by making noises inside of my house, he tried his best to intimidate me. Every time I had a thought that he did not like or agree with, he would make a loud noise, "*Crack*!"

Completely unnerving at first, he continued to wrestle me around the clock, sometimes even preventing me from sleeping. Once after keeping me awake late into the night, I became enraged.

"Shut your God damned mouth!" I yelled, lying in bed while trying to sleep.

"I'm warning you!" he demanded, hearing his voice on the internal plane.

"What are you going to do about it?" I asked. "Not a God damned thing! You're dead! You can't do shit to me!"

"God damn it!" he yelled.

Feeling tremendously threatened, I lost all control of my mouth, proceeding to call him every name that I could imagine, cursing him like I had never cursed anyone before. Shocked to see how frightened and angry

I could become, it took me several minutes to calm down, but eventually I began to drift off to sleep. At the precise second that my consciousness drifted into slumber, Merlin countered.

"*Wow, Wow, Wow, Wow, Wow,*" an alarm screamed.

Realizing that he had set off my neighbor's car alarm, my frustration peaked, even though it wasn't such a bad thing to happen in itself. It was just that my neighbor was not home, and that he was not going to return *all* night. Forced to lie in bed, pillows covering my head, I spent an entire night without sleep only able to consider my dilemma. I was convinced that no one could be more cursed.

Wrestling with our aggressions over the next several months, Merlin continued to harass me with a myriad of noises. Keeping me in a very angry and irritable state, I was left unable to cope with the stresses in my life. There seemed to be no end to his taunting and I often entertained very dark thoughts of taking my own life. One day as he began to make noise, I lost control. Grabbing a knife, I held it to my throat.

"You make one more noise!" I demanded. "It's over. Come on you son-of-a-bitch."

Reaching a moment of breakdown, I had taken all I was going to take from him. Prepared to leave the earth—I wanted to leave the earth.

"Come on, you bastard."

The room was completely silent.

All the noises that sounded around the clock—instantly stopped. Until this moment of quiet, I had not fully realized how much he was torturing me, how much energy he was expending in trying to get my attention.

Sitting there with the knife to my throat waiting, I hoped for a noise that would push me over the edge. Wanting him to give me an excuse to leave, I waited—but it would not come. All remained quiet and after a lengthy period of silence, still very distraught, I dropped the knife and crawled into bed. After an additional hour of restlessness, I finally began to drift off to sleep hearing Merlin's voice as I lost consciousness, "*You owe me.*"

The state of depression I existed in would continue for many months as all of my anger, my deep hatred of Merlin was forced to the surface. And the wrestling with him did not stop. It even got worse. It was just that now I was becoming more determined to win, desiring to beat him at his game of hate and to somehow find protection from him. *I wanted to learn how to trust myself enough, that his beliefs could not alter my confidence.* Then, he could have no power over me.

Digging deeper, searching my consciousness for hidden fears, I worked even harder to understand them. Every time he tried to steal something from me, I searched to expose my fear, strengthening my own resolve. Soon, I began to see *his* weaknesses and understand some of his behavior. And as I became more certain about my own feelings and desires, my need for his agreement and approval began to weaken. My willingness to feel all of my feelings would soon overpower his ability to control my life.

But I was still living a very lonely life and couldn't seem to reach out to anyone. Having secretly adored a girl at the grocery store for the last few years, I was too shy to talk to her. In allowing myself to feel all of the feelings that were within me, I had brought my deepest self-hatred to the surface. And now, my belief about myself was so poor that it was impossible for me to find the necessary confidence to bring anyone else into my life. As badly as I might want to be loved, I just couldn't receive it.

Merlin continued his challenges. Waking up from a dream in which he stood before me with all the confidence of a God, his image had already faded, but his voice rang through from the inner plane, "I want you to go to church every Sunday." Very convincing, it sounded like a cure for my problems, leaving me to believe that it was something that I needed to do.

Regularly giving me direction in this way, he sent me to many different places, greatly exhausting my energy. Although some were positive experiences, his adventures were often in complete disregard of what my soul might be seeking. Somehow, he was still able to coerce me into following his advice, later leaving me questioning myself, "Why am I doing this?" My intuition had not led me to these places; it had been Merlin.

Continuing to push me to the point of exhaustion, I could no longer take Merlin's constant pressure and trying to get him to release me had failed. But something was happening within and I was becoming less serious about his aggressions. I began to tease him, as he had so often done to me, finding joy in making fun of him.

"Merlin, I have your power name for you," I teased. "It's, *Butt.* And this is where your power lies, in knowing that you butt in to other people's business. I will give you another name later when have come to understand this one."

He did not think this to be funny.

*

Hating my same sex interests into submission, its suppression had now put a stop to my spiritual growth. Taking years for the spirit world to help me release my judgment of these feelings, they often spoke with me about them in the dreamstates.

"But this is who you are," a higher being told me, trying to encourage me to accept all of the feelings that I had.

Early in the morning, while still sleepy and close to the spirit world, I could accept my feelings. But when walking back out into the physical world and feeling the hate that existed there, I would freeze, my feelings slowly slipping below the surface again. The suppression strangled me, preventing me from reaching the high vision of God I had so often seen before Merlin's challenge.

Believing this acceptance to be an important factor in the recovery of my heart, I knew I must find a way to get beyond the resulting fear, guilt and self-judgment. The world, or the world I lived in, hated this part of me. People withdrew their love from ones with such thoughts, and more than anything—I needed love. It seemed I was being held prisoner and there was little I could do to change the world's vision, so I began by looking at my own beliefs.

My involvement with aids hospice work had brought me closer to others with varying sexualities and I often went to functions getting to know these people that much of the world had condemned. Finding them to be of little difference than the others that had an acceptable sexuality, my beliefs about myself began to change. I began to more clearly see that there was *nothing* wrong with sexual desire.

Once afraid to let anyone know of my secret feelings, I had now become somewhat open about them. The black cloak of self-hatred began to lift as I found more freedom and Merlin's hold over me began to weaken. It was not as though he had given up. It was quite the contrary. He still regularly tested me, but now, my greater self-acceptance made it harder for him to get under my skin.

Waking from a dream, I had been speaking to a female seated at a potter's wheel. She told me of the power that she had gained after breaking a piece of pottery that she owned. Opening my eyes, I got out of bed and walked over to a clay statue of Merlin standing in my bookcase. Taking it out, I threw it to the floor, picked it up and threw it down once again to make sure that it had been broken into small pieces.

After spending my life worshipping Merlin, making him into someone far greater than he was, I emptied my frustrations. From now on, I was determined to live my life without his influence.

Still beyond my awareness, a small part of the statue had survived unharmed—the crystal ball that had been held in his hand rolled to a stop beneath a chair. Days later, remembering when placing the broken bits of pottery into the trash that I had never found it, I looked beneath the chair. Seeing it resting against a leg, I reached for it. *Now*—its vision was my own.

*

A year earlier, a unique private high school had been created for the purpose of freeing a student body from facing many unnecessary prejudices. Their policies gave the children unusual spiritual freedoms that included tolerance and acceptance, for *all* sexualities. No one would be discriminated against within its doors.

Naturally drawn to the school as a volunteer, I attended their first graduation, immensely enjoying the powerful ceremony that the students had created. Beginning in darkness, the students walked into the room holding candles, stopping in front of the stage. The overhead lights were turned on and the opening address began. Leaning back in my chair, I casually glanced upward to the ceiling, focusing my eyes in disbelief.

Stuck on the ceiling, two stories above, was a playing card. I looked in amazement, wondering how it could have been placed there as my mind began to wander further into my past. Remembering the sixth grade, when my teacher had taken a card from me, my eyes began to widen. Paying closer attention—*I saw it to be the ace of spades.* Awestruck, my mouth dropped open as I marveled at the coincidence. But magnetized by the ceremony, I slowly allowed my mind to taken back into the present.

This event was one far ahead of its time, created by ones with a vision of the future. These courageous people were living their lives as an expression of God's most purest thought, to freely express their feelings as innocently as they come. I was grateful to bear witness.

*

Unable to visit Mary as often as I would have preferred, I felt an especially strong need to speak with her and called to schedule a meeting. With arrangements often difficult to make, I was surprised to hear of an immediate opening and we were soon once again engaged in conversation.

"We believe it is time for you to go into the mountains and be near the great healing lake," she said. "It is a place where you go to pray when you are not of the earth."

"In-between lifetimes?" I asked.

"Yes. It is where you will find your power. When in spirit, you often spend time there, by the water in prayer. Many go to this lake for healing, but now it is for you to go and drink of your own energy. And there will be many things that come from this journey."

"Do I need to go soon?"

"Yes, when you have the time. We feel it is important. This is a place that is *yours*, not even Merlin will be able to get in your way there," she added.

"He *is* making me crazy."

"Well—he believes that he created you, that you owe him for what you have become. But he had only been with you as a teacher during one lifetime. And much of what he told you then was worthless," she mused. "What you are is the result of hundreds of lives. Ones in the Native American tradition have a name for such a teacher."

"Heyoka?"

"Yes, the fool."

"Why does he insist that he is so wise? Do greater beings ever speak with him?"

"They try, but he is very arrogant. He will not listen," pretending to be Merlin, she flipped her hand away as if dismissing another's help.

With many questions to ask in a brief period, I proceeded quickly.

"Will I find the sword?"

"It will be found, but not in this life. You thought it had been lost, but it was not. It was taken by others and placed back into its sanctuary."

Instantly intrigued, I asked, "Will I come back to get it later?"

"Oh no, you will be off and doing other things. It will be found by others, perhaps in a few hundred years. By then, the world will know of your book, and they will finally believe. They will then know that this magic was truth."

Already overwhelmed, I pushed on with my questions, "I hear someone apologizing to me, everyday, over and over. *I am sorry. I am sorry,*" I told her. "It's overwhelming. What is this about?"

"It is the one that was grandfather to you," she explained. "Long ago, he betray you."

"Before Arthur?" I asked.

"Oh yes, long before," she answered. "You were a teacher in an ancient mystery school and he betray you to the church. It was in a time when the church did not wish for truths to be spoken. But he did not know what they would do and he believed your punishment harsh. You were forced to drink poison. And he is here to ask for forgiveness."

"Jasper?" I asked.

"Yes, Jasper. He did not know they would do this to you. He just wanted you stopped."

Feeling the tension within my body ease, my lungs seemed to expel a poisonous breath. Speechless for a moment, my mind wandered. It was almost something that I had been expecting to find out, that Jasper was not always my friend. Very painful to know, I could see that much contemplation about this lay ahead of me.

Slipping from the channeller's body, she finished, "We must go, but know you are doing it correctly. *Write*. Put your mind and your soul into this. Let yourself remember. Remember the passion. Remember the joy. Remember your vision. And follow the sword to your completion. Walk in great love and light. *We* believe in you. Join us for that."

In the weeks to come, I realized that it had actually been Merlin, as an authority of the church, to petition for my death during my life as a spiritual teacher. With Jasper's testimony, I had been found guilty of teaching false truths and misleading youth. Refusing to believe that greater possibilities existed, Merlin pressed for the most severe penalty. It was the easiest way for him to deal with his own darkness—to send me back into the spirit world where I could no longer confront his reality.

It would take me several weeks to come to the greater understanding my conversation with Mary created, but I would soon begin to think about making the trip to the mountain. Still feeling the hope that she had inspired me with, I heard Merlin from the internal plane.

"God damn it—" he cursed.

Confused, I wondered, "Why is he cursing my plans for a quest?"

Furious with me because I was going to make the trip, he began to try to steal my confidence. I had believed that he might support me and my thoughts were torn, "Perhaps I just need to wait before going. Maybe it's not the proper time." Having become very ungrounded from my deliberations, I decided I needed to first go to the forest, to gain a clearer direction.

Sitting quietly on a bench just off the trail, I relaxed after a brief hike and began to consider the trip. Again, I heard Merlin's voice, "God damn it—"

Unconsciously, I refused to hear anything more from him and having already stolen my confidence, I was left senselessly frustrated. Standing up, I turned to face the bench and knocked my head against its wood surface, as if he were inside of me and I was trying to force him out.

Often criticizing me and hatefully reprimanding me for all of the errors that he believed I was making, I had heard all that I could accept. With all the suffering he has caused me, I wondered how could he still believe that he could help me.

Feeling isolated and lost, I slipped into a soulless void, and back within his control. My own doubt still disabling me, I was too afraid to trust myself and reasoned that it was best that I not yet go to the mountains; that a better moment would exist in the future. It would be necessary for me to spend additional time following his lead, proving by revealing his vision for me, that he truly lacked wisdom.

Weeks later, a surprising revelation came. Realizing the challenges my mother faced had also been extreme, I was no longer able to find fault in her role as my parent. Actually giving me a better life than she had received, I could see that she had done her job. And becoming thankful for her challenges, I saw that she had actually prepared me for my future. I would never have been able to face Merlin had I not received the challenges she presented. By standing up to her, I passed the test that helped me to develop the confidence needed to face Katrina, Merlin and the others.

*

Waking with unexpected resolve, I stepped from my bed and reaching for the phone book, looked up the number for a travel agent. Already a year had passed since Mary had first told me of the quest and if I waited just a few more weeks, the snows would come and months would pass before another opportunity arrived.

Dialing the phone, I could hear Merlin, "God damn it!" Pushing forward, I shut him out and firmly committed to the quest—with or without his approval.

Days later, the plane touched down and after retrieving my bags, I stood in the line to get my rental car. I was informed that even though I had made reservations, I would have to wait. They didn't presently have a car for me. Then, another problem. They wouldn't take cash as they had promised over the phone and my credit card was almost at its limit, preventing me from being able to charge the full cost of the rental.

"I asked specifically if this would be okay before I made the trip," I explained to the attendant.

"There's nothing we can do for you. We do not take cash here," she coldly explained expecting me to leave.

Finding resolve, "*You* need to call your regional manager. I *have* to have a car," I demanded.

Reluctantly, she picked up the phone and began dialing. After speaking briefly, she handed the receiver to me and I spoke with the manager. Quite surprised, the manager agreed to rent the car to me. No more obstacles existed.

Gaining altitude as I followed the winding road, my eyes sparkled as the mountain parted for the first time, allowing the pristine waters of the ancient lake to come into view. Having never seen inland water so magnificent, I was captive to the pull of its creative energy. The clarity of its deep blue waters equaled that of an ocean and its healing energy secretly began to transform me. Stopping at a park, I walked toward a lookout perched high upon a cliff. Looking across the waters surface, I marveled at its beauty as my eyes occasionally glanced higher up, at the deep crevasses in the walls of the surrounding mountain.

Feeling as though I had reached a pinnacle, it seemed like I had entered into an ethereal world, a world ruled by laws different than our own. After breathing in the mountain's cleansing air, I felt a strong need to find a place to spend the night, and getting back into the rental car, drove to a nearby motel.

I had believed that I was here to go into the mountains, to do a traditional vision quest, but I received additional direction that night in the dreamstate. Listening to a guide speak, he told me that it was time for me to be closer to people. The vision quests of solitude and deprivation that had become a part of my life were, for the time, to be replaced by interaction with others. It was time for me to be *of* this world.

After breakfast the following morning, I returned to be the near the water, and finding an empty beach, I sat down at the water's edge. Still early in the morning, cool air gently breezed across the turquoise lake, its transparent waters revealing all of the life it contained. Several small fish swam nearby. Digging my bare feet into the sand, just below the waterline, I let the cool liquid embrace them as I considered my future.

I could see that I wasn't yet ready for everything that lay ahead of me, but I could feel that beneath the surface, deep within my unconscious, healing had began. Taking in a breath, a deep breath, I felt the hope of life moving closer to me.

Spending time near the lake for the next few days, I allowed the water's healing energy to work upon my spiritual heart and aura. Very subtle, the work of healing can easily go unnoticed. And while my mind was given no dramatic event to mark this passage of time, transformation would continue with or without my conscious acknowledgement. Leaving the lake, my vibration edged upward, as wholeness, moved one step closer.

* * *

Compassion for my mother continued to grow as I looked at her life with new eyes, seeing the tremendous amount of pain and suffering that she had endured. Surviving a traumatic childhood, she did not have the energy to live her dreams. And as a child, I had asked her to live beyond the belief that she had in herself, encouraging her to take more control of her life. But her level of confidence could not allow it and she handled me the only way she knew how, just as Merlin had done ages ago—she silenced me. By injuring my confidence, she kept me quiet. It was the only way she could find peace.

But with any injury, always comes a great gift. Teaching me to respect another person's life, to allow others the room to live as they are able, regardless of what level that might be, she had given me what I most desired. This wonderful gift, of *self-protection,* is what I had sought during so many lifetimes.

And with my world now expanding, I felt more comfortable allowing others closer to me and I began *living* my spiritual expression. And for the first time in many years, I felt blessed.

As I awoke one morning, I realized that I had been speaking to Mary in the dreamstate and that we were still speaking, as I lay motionless in bed.

"Where is she?" I asked in thought, referring to the female love I had so longed to meet.

"In deepest waters . . ." she began, "When you have found the greatest depth of your soul, you will know *exactly* how to find her."

Find myself, and I will find her. Then my mind continued further, seeing the great distance I had walked in this life. Interacting with many different types of people, with many different belief systems, I had learned much. And seeing *their* desires, I realized what *I* most desired—acceptance. Not all the truth, at least not yet. But my need for acceptance was so great that I could not overlook it. I needed to know that I was okay, that I was good and that no matter how much I might fear other people or the future, I would be okay.

All these years, I had really been fighting no one other than myself. It had been my own fear that had caused me to strike out against another in the name of truth. And it had been my own darkness to cause my failure, as the hand of hatred only desires guidance. I had so often pushed frightened ones away from me when more than anything, they needed my reassurance, and that, I had often been unable to offer. When I lost certainty in my own belief and pushed them away, they were left with no choice other than to try to strike against me.

I then saw that no one had ever betrayed me before I had first betrayed myself. And the gift of freedom was now returning to me—I was finally setting myself free. Forgiving myself, I forgave all of the ones around me that had caused me grief. We had all made mistakes together.

And then—a great, great dream. Standing before Merlin, I saw him as never before. In his fullness, he seemed twenty feet tall, but in this meeting, I was not beneath him. Standing together, we seemingly held respect for each other.

I could see that he was in fact very powerful, although I could not feel an understanding for the source of his power.

"I am wanting to move on now, to do other things," he told me.

Although I didn't dismiss his words, as if it were another one of his tricks, I remained uncertain of its meaning.

"You will do as you wish," I said, with no malice toward him.

"It has been a long time. I only wish to be free," he replied, referring to the war that had existed between us, binding us together for ages.

I had only moments with him before I would awake from sleep, but the energy from the meeting had made its impact upon my body. *I was going to remember this.*

Lying awake in bed, I had not yet realized the greatness of what had happened. But Merlin had freed me, not by his words in that moment, but by his challenges, by forcing me to trust in my own belief and to know that I had the strength to follow my dreams. His job all along had been to stop me from acting in fear, to hold me back when he could, cause me to face my doubt, and to force me to once again accept power. I was now free to go— his debt to me had been paid.

And then I took a breath and looked inside of myself. Seeing all of the steps I had taken back to my heart, I could finally feel the self-acceptance that I had been seeking throughout so many lifetimes. Feeling a sense of calm emanating from within, I then realized, God had once again brought my power back to me. And this time—I found peace with it.

And Merlin whispered, "*The future is waiting.*"

In Our World Today

When we are able to see beyond our anger and forgive ourselves for the errors we have made during our lives, a new perception enters into our awareness. Looking out into our world, we no longer see acts of desperation as solitary acts of vengeance, but instead, action with a recognizable source.

All suffering, even if unknown, add to the collective negative emotion in the world, helping to create future acts of violence. These acts give voice to the fact that desperation is still allowed to exist in our world, for it is not possible for a person to act desperately without feeling a deep sense of hopelessness and despair at some level in their consciousness. And in the effort to express this, to tell the world of their suffering, injured beings act out their frustration upon others, completely beyond their control.

But we do have the power in this immediate moment, to eliminate many acts of desperation that are presently within our future.

When every individual is guaranteed the right to live in safety, to exist without fear of starvation or physical suffering, the greatest acts of desperation—*will be eliminated.* By ensuring each person's right to survival, we remove the energy source for the creation of violence, as its existence is dependent upon human suffering.

When we are able to put our grievances aside, we will find the power to heal our planet, and when we make certain that each individual is protected, we empower ourselves. When survival is guaranteed—when each soul is cherished, assured a home, food, and a hopeful future—the darkest actions in the world will no longer be able to manifest.

For information on classes in lucid dreaming and vision questing, or to contact the author, write John Stone, at dreamclasses@yahoo.com

Printed in the United States
17909LVS00004B/214-225